Lord of WORTH

LADIES *of* WORTH

PHILIPPA JANE KEYWORTH

ISBN (eBook): 978-1-7397076-0-6

ISBN (Print): 978-1-7397076-1-3

ALSO BY
PHILIPPA JANE KEYWORTH

LADIES OF WORTH SERIES

Fool Me Twice

A Dangerous Deal

Lord of Worth

Duke of Disguise

REGENCY ROMANCES

The Widow's Redeemer

The Unexpected Earl

MULTI-AUTHOR SERIES

Finding Miss Giles

FANTASY

The Edict

CHAPTER ONE

London, England 1776

"Maisy, for heaven's sake, to be slow at a time like this! It is unforgivable."

A terrible cacophony rent the air as Rebecca's maid sent an empty milk pail clattering down the corridor.

"Honestly! We have visited this house through the servants' entrance countless times and yet you still look like a scared lamb. Come! Quickly! There is a baby to be born, of which I will be the honorary aunt, and I shall not allow it to happen without me present in the house."

Lady Rebecca Fairing, a tall, dark-haired and commanding young woman, had an unusual habit of invading the Feltons' home from below stairs. She had found out long ago that it allowed one much faster access to the house, and seeing as Caro Felton, her closest friend, was regularly drinking tea in the kitchen with her housekeeper Libby, it was often the most efficient route.

Today, however, she was using it because Caro was about to deliver her first baby and Rebecca had no intention of being left on the street while the servants were preoccupied with the house's happenings.

"Quickly now!" Rebecca urged again over her shoulder, the wooden heels of her silk mules clipping on the stone flags of the floor. The housekeeper's parlour and kitchen were deserted. Rebecca headed straight for the stairs to the ground floor, and just as her foot hit the first step, there was a loud cry from somewhere far above them.

"We are not too late!" Rebecca cried with glee.

She skipped up the stairs, two at a time, Maisy following hurriedly behind. As they came out into the hall of the Town house, Rebecca spotted Tobias Felton, the father to be, pacing across the first-floor landing. She drew back, unwilling to be seen.

"I should like to attend her, but I do not think Felton will let me pass," Rebecca whispered back to her maid. "According to Aunt Etheridge, he has hired one of the best doctors, no expense spared. We shall wait in here, I think." She pointed to the morning room door with her embroidered muff still on one hand.

Maisy obligingly opened it and her mistress swept into the room before she realised it was already occupied.

She halted two steps in, her dark brown eyes taking in the figure of James Worth, Caro's brother, standing before the fireplace. She froze, staring at him as he looked up and his eyes focused on her face. Some unreadable emotion flickered across his countenance.

"I apologise," Rebecca offered, her voice transformed from loud and authoritative to a half-whisper. "I didn't realise anyone was…" She trailed off, loathing herself for sounding so lame.

This was extraordinarily awkward. In her haste to ensure

she was present at Caro's first birthing, she had been silly enough to forget James would likely be there as well. James, the man who had proposed to her three months ago and whom she had unequivocally refused.

"Good morning, Lady Rebecca." He bowed politely.

It was too late to retreat.

"Good morning, my Lord."

She curtseyed automatically, and left the spot where she had been mired in indecision. Maisy followed suit, and took a chair a discreet distance from the couple. Rebecca crossed the room, taking a seat beside the window, as far from James as she could get. What a dreadful situation.

There was an uncomfortable silence punctuated by far-off conversations in the birthing room.

"You are well, I trust?" James asked, turning towards her, his hands clasped behind his back. Every part of his frame was rigid, even his face, the well-formed features and blue eyes a mask of civility.

"Yes, thank you."

She racked her brains to think of some way to extend her reply, but none came. Goodness, she wished she was anywhere but here. They may be stuck like this for some hours. According to her aunt, many women took a long time to birth.

It had not been that there was anything particularly wrong with James. No glaring character faults, or debt, or debauchery. Those were not the reasons Rebecca had refused his proposal. No. It was that the man had never actually courted her.

A woman expected it, at least a little, before they were being proposed to. But he had not played the game as her other flirts had done. There was no word-sparring and love-making so that she might know where she stood and be certain of her own feelings. He had done the courting in his head without the rigmarole of bothering Rebecca, and had simply come to her at the end of it to ask for her hand.

It was true they had gone through a great deal together. Rebecca had been acquainted with his sister, Caro, first. Their friendship had been forged in the fires of potential scandal. It was during this coil that James had arrived back from his self-imposed exile in the West Indies. He had offered his aid, after reconciling with Caro, and that is what had brought him into Rebecca's orbit. There was no denying that from the first revolution of that orbit he had caught her eye.

But catching her eye was a far cry from a marriage proposal, and James had done none of the flirting, the love-making, the witty repartee and charming conversation that Rebecca had expected from an amour. In fact, he had barely spoken at all, he had been so reserved in her presence.

Despite her rejection of his hand, James had offered his help when another coil had enveloped her sister Rachel in her recent marriage to Lord Arleigh. James had been a true gentleman in that case, but though it had concluded happily, Rebecca had not seen or heard from him since.

"And your sister and brother-in-law, they are well?" James asked, his question so in line with her thoughts she felt her cheeks heat immediately.

It wasn't as though he could read them—her thoughts, that is—but sometimes she was not so sure when he looked at her with those clear blue eyes of his.

"Yes, very well, thank you. Rachel is still a little way off her confinement." Rebecca paused, considering what to say next.

She risked a look in his direction and saw he remained as rigid as he had appeared on her entering the room.

"I never did thank you for helping me to make sure my sister was well."

James bowed in acknowledgment. "Think nothing of it."

They lapsed into silence once more and Rebecca resorted

to counting the tassels on a cushion next to her. Anything to avoid the feeling of wishing to be swallowed up by the ground.

This was the problem with James. He was so very... quiet. When he had sprung the proposal on her without warning, and in such a public place as the Pump Room, she had allowed her immediate reaction to rule her and refused him. Afterwards she had been shocked, she had cried even, and that reaction had surprised her. Did that mean she had been wrong? Was it wrong for a woman to expect to be flirted with, to be courted and complimented?

"I am sure Caro will be upset that she did not make it to the Feltons' country house for her confinement," Rebecca said airily, looking out the window to escape James' gaze. "The babe was impatient, it seems."

She could still feel his eyes on her. His gaze had always caused her breath to catch. She felt a burning need to explain herself. To be the cause of another's pain was never something she wanted.

"James, I—"

A cry from above cut her off.

All three occupants' eyes went to the ceiling.

"Maisy, you must find out what's happening," commanded Rebecca, turning to where Maisy had been sitting quietly.

The maid, eyes wide with anxiety, rose reluctantly and hurried to the door. She slipped out, leaving it ajar.

A few seconds later, there was a great crashing down the stairs and then shouting. Maisy reappeared, slamming the door shut again and collapsing against it.

"I—I apologise, my Lady, but it's Bed... Bedlam out there! It's Miss Libby," Maisy carried on breathlessly. "She just threw a chamberpot at the doctor for trying to bleed her mistress again, shouting about birthing half the babies in her village before he was more than ten."

There were incoherent voices from outside the door. Maisy's eyes grew wider still. Then footsteps sounded, thundering as if a cavalcade were descending upon them. Maisy leapt away just as Felton burst in, face shining.

"I have a daughter!"

It had been three weeks since Rebecca's visit to the Feltons'. Three weeks since her honorary niece's birth, three weeks since she had last seen Caro, and three weeks since her interview with James.

"I had hoped for something a little brighter for the summer," said Rebecca, her hands lightly tracing over the squares of fabric in the book she had been given to peruse. "I saw Lady Mires in a rather fetching botanical silk a few days ago."

"You mean the dress she was wearing at Ranelagh Gardens?" asked Rachel.

Rebecca's elder sister was on a chaise longue, leant back on its cushions like Dionysus, her pregnant stomach accentuated at this angle, so she looked ready to give birth right there and then.

"Yes, that's it," Rebecca replied, thankful she had persuaded her sister to attend the modiste with her. Anything to fill her mind rather than mulling over her meeting with James. "Cream silk with the most beautiful birds and flowers."

They had been left alone, the French mantua maker, famous for both her clothing confections and her artistic temperament, had disappeared in a flourish of silk to order tea for her clients and find another swatch book for Rebecca.

"The print was a little large for my taste," said Rachel, shifting.

Rebecca's sister was now six months with child, and it was

causing her a little discomfort. She wore a *robe à l'anglaise* that had been let out at the back, but from the way she rubbed at the waistline, Rebecca deduced it was not enough.

"How do you feel?"

The question caused the most stunning smile to overtake Rachel's face. The rubbing at her waist became more of a gentle caress.

"I shall not complain one moment when I have waited so many years for a baby." Rachel's brown eyes grew wistful.

It was special to see her sister and brother-in-law's relationship blooming after a less than auspicious start. They were so well matched in their opposite characters, tempering each other's excesses.

"Now, ladies," Madame Depardieu said, whirling into the room like a windstorm, silks flaring, arms raised and carrying a book in her hands so high she might have been offering it to the gods. "I have found my very special catalogue of fabrics here for you, mais oui!" She lay the book reverently in Rebecca's hands and took away the other.

"Bah! No good!" she said, tossing it with a clatter onto a side table. "Numéro sept - what do you think of that?"

Rebecca opened the book and flipped past the first few pages, halting on silk square number seven, a pale cream, almost white, with the heads of exotic flowers she could not name and little birds with long beaks and sharp wings pointed backwards.

"Oh yes, that's beautiful," she said, her fingers tracing the embroidery.

"Of course it is," said the dressmaker with a regal wave of the hand. "Now to style—ah—the tea."

A very old maid, one who Rebecca thought may even lay claim to great grandchildren, came into the room exceedingly slowly. She held a Chinese tray, beautiful porcelain cups and a steaming silver pot placed carefully on it. She might have been old, but the ancient maid had a steady hand and deposited the tray with certainty on a matching Chinese table.

Madame Depardieu poured, talking to Rebecca as she did so. She ran through various dress styles, vetoing an English gown and recommending a *robe à la française* if she wanted something different. Then there was an Italian gown of a new construction that might show the fabric to advantage. The dressmaker spoke so quickly and without any break that Rebecca had no choice but to be carried along on the current of her recommendations. In the end she opted for an open-fronted gown and said she was sure her father would be far happier with a pleated back. He was forever complaining about the cost of his daughter's dresses and a pleated back meant it might be altered to suit changing fashions at a later date.

"Take it from a growing woman," said Rachel, a curve on her wide mouth, "Alterable clothes are a godsend."

At that moment the bell of the shop sounded.

"Sacre bleu!" exclaimed the modiste, arms in the air and offering profuse apologies before whirling out of the room. A conversation was struck up in the front of the shop, soft murmurings humming through the open sitting room door.

"Have you heard how Caro goes on?" asked Rachel, taking another sip of tea.

"She sent me a note two days ago to say her and the babe are doing very well. She admits she is quite happy the baby arrived early now, as it's much cosier in their London home than it would have been at Lord and Lady Felton's estate."

"There is nothing worse than being from home." Rachel paused a few moments and then said in an undertone, "And James?"

"He is well as far as I know," Rebecca replied with forced indifference.

Rachel quirked a brow at her sister, her hand stilling on her stomach.

"Don't look at me like that!" Rebecca whispered peevishly. "I do not know what you expect me to say. You know very well how it was left, for I told you the minute I got home. Though now I wish I hadn't."

"Oh Becky, do stop fussing." Rachel reached out a hand to take one of Rebecca's wildly gesturing ones and squeezed it firmly. "I am asking how you think it stands between you now? How do you feel?"

The answer to both questions eluded Rebecca. James had been unreadable and quiet. Rebecca had not had the chance to say... what? She had no idea what she had intended to say, unless it was sorry, and the desire to explain why she had refused him. Perhaps it had been for the best that she had the opportunity to do neither. She felt the same awkward tension she had felt for days, and beneath the surface of it, a little ache in her chest. She pushed back that feeling furiously, not willing to allow any emotions to rise up and overwhelm her.

"It hardly matters," she said briskly. "I do not believe he can have any more romantic intentions towards me. It is settled."

"Settled?" Rachel looked less than convinced. "All right, how do you feel about that then? You harboured a tendre for him before he proposed, even though you refused—are you telling me you feel nothing for him now? Perhaps it was just the wrong time."

Rachel was needling her, and if it had been anyone else but her sister, Rebecca would have given them her curtest set-down and finished the conversation there and then.

As it was, she did not need to finish anything, for in the next moment they were interrupted by someone in the doorway to the front of the shop.

"Oh, Lady Arleigh, Lady Rebecca," came a syrupy sweet voice. "I thought I heard voices I knew."

Both women turned to see Lady Goring standing in the doorway. The woman was posed as if she had walked in on them by accident, but her eyes held a keenness, and Rebecca wondered just how long she'd been standing there

Rachel spoke first, no welcoming tones in her voice. "Lady Goring, we did not know you were there."

The words bordered on impolite, but Rachel was known for her blunt speech and Lady Goring was impervious to social cues.

"Oh, only for a moment, ladies." She was smiling at them condescendingly. "I've been speaking to our redoubtable Madame Depardieu, but when I heard you talking, I could not resist." There was a smug look in her hawklike eyes. "But I think I have interrupted a little sisterly tête-à-tête."

Lady Goring was a woman whose looks had been entirely enhanced by fortune rather than by any goodness of character. Today she was dressed in a gaudy aquamarine silk far too young for her years, her face was heavily powdered, and there was a questionable application of rouge on her lined cheeks. Those with sharper tongues in Society declared her a middle-aged mallard masquerading as a youthful swan.

"Ah! I told you already, my Lady," Madame Depardieu cried from behind her. "You are too early!"

"I am sorry to have interrupted such a *private* conversation," said Lady Goring, ignoring the protestations of the dressmaker.

She was not sorry. That Rebecca knew. The woman was absolutely thrilled to have overheard whatever she had. That's why she had said 'private' in that manner. She wanted them to know she had overheard something.

It was not so much the vulgarity of Lady Goring's dress, nor her overt social climbing, that was unappealing to the ton in whose circle she was a firm member. No, it was her propensity for gossip.

The Countess of Goring was a woman who made it her business to know everything that happened to anyone of importance in Society. More than that, she had no scruples in sharing anything she learned with anyone to whom it might prove to her advantage. Despite a communal dislike for the woman, she had not been cut from Society thanks to the plethora of secrets she held on almost every member. Secrets that she might at any point spill onto the public stage.

"Oui! Oui! You are interrupting, voyon. Madame Goring, please to leave!" Madame Depardieu ordered. Rebecca caught a flourish of her laced cuffs flashing over the interrupter's head as she gesticulated wildly.

"But of course," said Lady Goring, "I must go and fetch my daughter from the Pot and Pineapple anyway. She is enjoying an ice with Lord Mire's eldest daughter."

"How lovely," Rachel said, the expression on her face not attempting to match her words.

Rebecca said nothing. No easy quip came to mind. No sharp set-down. All she could think about was that the vile woman had just overheard one of the most private matters of Rebecca's life.

After Lady Goring retreated from the sitting room, there was a stream of French and English in equal measure until the bell went again and the shop door shut behind the uninvited guest.

Her sister turned immediately towards her, but before she could say anything to Rebecca, Madam Depardieu came rushing back in.

"I apologise again for that—that woman's entrance." The dressmaker threw her hands up in the air, her green eyes rolling. "She tries to—how do you say?—talk to me like the honey. I have a dress made up for her daughter and now she does not want it! And here she is, always interrupting my guests whenever she feels she would like. Bah!"

"Do not worry, Madame, she has a habit of turning up where she is least wanted," Rachel said caustically.

"Ha!" the dressmaker cried, a light in her eyes.

"But to turn down one of your creations," Rachel carried on. "There truly is no accounting for taste."

Rebecca listened to the rapid conversation with only half an ear. Lady Goring, the woman with the worst tongue for gossip, had heard that James had not only proposed to her, but that she had refused. How long would it be before half of London was ringing with the story?

"Précisément!" Madame Depardieu broke into Rebecca's thoughts. "But non, it is not taste on this occasion, but a crying-off as you English say—ah!" The dressmaker threw a dramatic hand over her mouth. "I should not have said that."

"But now you must tell us everything," Rachel said firmly, sitting forward and grabbing her sister's arm with a little shake.

Rebecca was hardly in the mood for finding out gossip of her own about Lady Goring. She didn't care a jot for the woman. What she cared about was that she might tell others of what had happened between her and James, and that James would find out. Rebecca might have refused him, but she certainly bore him no ill will. Quite the opposite. She still cared for him, at least a little. That feeling of care had just been magnified with the possibility he might be hurt by this gossip.

"Non!" Madame Depardieu dropped her hands to her sides and lowered her eyes in surrender. "I must keep my client's confidentiality. I can say no more. Now, where were we?"

Suddenly botanical silk number seven and the discussion over an open-fronted gown no longer appealed. All Rebecca could think about was how long it would be before the whole of Society rang with the news of her refusal.

***

"It's put me in mind of what is due to the Worth name," James said to his solicitor.

He was sitting in the morning room of his Town house. The room, much like the rest of the home, was plainly furnished and was more in keeping with the residence of a merchant than a nobleman. James' tastes were modest, and besides, he was always travelling. He had no time to think of decor. At least that was until recently. His return to Society, forced by his estranged sister's scandal last year, had brought with it the knowledge that he needed to take his place in it. No longer was it appropriate for the son of old Lord Worth to shun Society and all that it entailed. His reconciliation with his sister and the subsequent prolonged stay in England had thrown up a great deal of things for him to contend with.

"Of course, sir, that is to say, my Lord," said Mr Lewis. He was a surprisingly young man, plain-faced, and wearing a smart wool suit and neat queue wig.

James had appointed him last year, but hitherto, he had put off any real sorting of the family affairs.

"I suppose I shall have to get used to that," James said.

He had refused to use the title until now. His father's ignominious death at the hands of drink and debts, and the falling out between James and his sister Caro, all on a regretful misunderstanding, had instilled in him a wish to part with anything associated with his heritage.

But that was before. He and Caro were bonded once again and suddenly all the things he had thought he never wanted to contend with had grown in importance. The birth of a child could do that.

"If I am to restore glory to the old name for the sake of my sister's child and the next generation, it's high time I looked to the estate."

"An honourable intention, my Lord. I have taken the liberty of sending for the accounts and all pertinent papers from your estate," said the solicitor, conjuring up images of the Worths' Sussex seat in James' mind.

He had not been back since he had left for the Indies four years ago. He remembered the Jacobean house where he and Caro had grown up. It had been happy for a time, when their mother had been alive. She was always a kind and joy-filled mother, who had made up for the deficiencies of their profligate father, until her death had brought them into the unforgiving light.

After that the house had not felt like home. It had instead become the haunt of old Lord Worth's gaming companions who had formed salacious house parties that had been the gossip of the county. The house staff mismanaged, their former home had sunk into ruin and disrepair. The rooms and decor which had served two generations were left to age and moulder.

What money James and his sister might have spent on the house's upkeep was lost to those disreputable friends of their father, who saw in him a good time and a loose purse. Whatever time their father had spent without his companions at Worth Manor had been under the cloud of his belligerent moods. The salve of their mother's presence had been sorely missed in those years.

The last time James had seen Worth Manor he had been leaving in anger. Old Lord Worth had died, and James had thought his sister as profligate as their father. Escaping to foreign shores where people did not know the Worth name, James had sought out his own kind of peace. That was until he realised that reconciling with Caro was the peace he sought.

"It is in some state of disrepair," said Mr Lewis, bringing James to the surface of the pool of memories he had been diving into. "I understand from the steward that the roof of the chapel is leaking, and there are several rooms suffering from damp and blown plaster. If you have a look here, if I may."

He spread several papers on the desk before James and used two heavy candlesticks to hold them down. "And here are the estate accounts." An ancient, cracked leather book was put on the other end of the table with a thump.

The solicitor, warming to his work, licked his fingers, flipped back the leather cover with a dry crack, and leafed through the pages.

"You'll see from the plan that the chapel, well, I expect you will remember, my Lord, it backs onto the long gallery, and it is there the plaster is blown and some of the panelling is rotted."

"The paintings?" asked James, suddenly aware of just how much he had neglected over the last few years. It had compounded the disrepair his father had let the place fall into.

"Some were damaged, but your steward did move several to storage once the damage became apparent."

James allowed a fleeting memory of the family's steward, Godrich, and wondered how he had enjoyed the absence of a master for so long.

"The rest of the house?"

"In a reasonable state of repair, as I understand it from Mr Godrich, though I am sure you may wish to make alterations."

"Hmm," was all James offered in response to the assumption.

"The gardens have been allowed to grow wild unfortunately."

"For what reason?" asked James.

"The gardener and undergardener both left your employ, I

am led to understand, some nine months since. Your steward did not inform you?"

"He did not. Nor was I aware of the chapel roof."

"Ah," said Mr Lewis, unable to think of a more suitable response.

"What of the tenants on the estate?" asked James, giving the embarrassed solicitor a way out.

"Ah, yes." He pulled another book out and began scanning the pages. "One of the farms is still inhabited and run by the same family—the Olivers. The other two have been left vacant, one for six months, the other a year. As to the labourers' cottages, many are standing empty as there is less farm work to employ the inhabitants."

James passed a hand over his brow and rubbed his eyes, a sigh escaping.

"You were not informed?"

James dropped his hand and directed his calm blue eyes to the solicitor, responding levelly. "I was not. It appears there is much to do."

He did not allow himself to say more. The thoughts in his mind were not appropriate to be heard by a solicitor or the servants. As James lived alone, they would likely be heard by no one at all.

"Indeed, my Lord."

The look of pity on the solicitor's face, however kindly meant, chafed James, and pierced his attempt at calm. It should be the steward delivering this information to him, but Godrich had cried off travelling to London due to some vague ailment, and thus James had asked Mr Lewis to gather an overview for him.

"Perhaps you can leave these with me for now," James said, gesturing to the papers and books.

"Yes, of course, my Lord. Send for me should you need anything."

"Thank you, Lewis. Good day."

"Good day, my Lord."

The solicitor bowed and left, the same look of pity on his face.

After he had gone, James stood still for several minutes surveying the piles of papers and books. He cast a glance at the shelves which housed his own business accounts from the trading he undertook. They were neatly arranged in clean journals in date order, the antithesis of the work laid before him. Yet he hated to acknowledge that some of the workload was caused by his own choice to stay overseas for so long and the time it had taken for him to reconcile with his sister. What a mess.

Restoring the estate and continuing his business alongside would be demanding. At least, he thought ruefully, it might distract him from the ever-present memory of his rejection by Lady Rebecca Fairing. The thought brought her face to his mind's eye, and he wondered briefly what she might have said that day in the Feltons' drawing room while they awaited the babe's birth. But then he remembered that the look in her eyes had been similar to the pity in the solicitor's, and he was thankful she had been cut off.

James knew now that he had reached above his station in asking for Rebecca's hand, even though he had thought she returned his affection. Why would she take on his sullied name? The question caused his chest to contract, and the deep, dull ache that had haunted his every moment since the rejection hit him afresh. He clenched his jaw, recognising once again that he must deal with the aftermath, however uncomfortable. He had no choice. She had said no and that was that. Yes, this work on the Worth estate was the perfect distraction. Now was the time to focus on restoring his family estates for the sake of his sister's children and the next generation.

What was clear, as he thought on it, was that he could not

run his business and restore his estate alone. Most nobles might be scandalised at the thought of personal involvement in trade, but it had given James a living after his father died penniless, and he had excelled at it. He had amassed a fortune that exceeded the one his father had inherited and squandered so carelessly. James had the means to restore Worth Manor, but he did not have the capacity to oversee the restoration of the estate and his business. He needed help, and he knew the man for the job. Clearing a space at the desk in the piles of paper, he took a clean sheet and a pen with a freshly cut nib, and began a letter.

Dusting and blotting the finished sheet sometime later, he folded it precisely, sealed it and wrote the direction on its front before ringing the bell for a servant to take it by the first mail. After that was done he looked again at the papers and tried to decide where to start. At length, his mind a jumble of thoughts, he left the study untouched and headed out. He needed physical activity to clear his mind.

Since returning to London he had found the best place for exertion was the tennis courts on James Street and he headed there now. Hitting something incredibly hard and working up a sweat seemed the ideal response to the mess he had been landed in. All frustration could be released, and then common sense would prevail.

CHAPTER TWO

"F elton." James hailed his brother-in-law on one of the wide promenades that ran the length of the south side of Hyde Park.

As they drew closer, James grasped Felton's arm warmly, noting the shadows beneath his brother-in-law's green eyes.

"How goes fatherhood?"

The weariness on Felton's face broke away in a grin.

"She's an angel."

They turned together to walk west.

"An angel that cries," Felton corrected, his cane striking out on the gravel.

James chuckled.

"And you? What have you been doing of late?"

"A friend of mine was up from the West Country. I dined with him the past few evenings."

James laid claim to few whom he would call friend. His father's scandals had made many shun James in his youth, and those who did not had found their loyalty tested on the death of old Lord Worth and James' loss of fortune. He had never been the carefree man-about-Town that many of his peers were and when he had left for the Indies, it was not only Caro he had left in his wake, but all acquaintances too.

"Ah." Felton brought his cane handle to the brim of his hat and tapping it as if to make memories appear. "You told me you had a friend coming to Town—the travelling Cornishman?"

"That's right."

"Ah! So my mind has not been completely lost to fatherhood. Caro insists on rising with the babe at night even though we have hired a wet nurse. When she rises I, like the dutiful husband I am, rise also."

Felton's self-deprecating words revealed a closeness to his wife that gave James pause. Did that mean they shared the same bed every night? If he had been the kind of man who showed emotions freely in his expression he might have looked surprised. Then again, James reasoned, he should perhaps not be so surprised as he knew just how very much Felton and his sister loved each other.

"Has he been in Town long?" Felton asked.

"No, only a few days. He had some business here, but he'll soon be sailing again."

"A shame, I should like to have met him."

"Perhaps you shall in the future, though he is not one for Town."

"Like someone else I know," Felton said, winking at him.

James' relationship with his brother-in-law had been slow to start. In fact, when they had first met, Felton had had much to say on James' abandonment of his sister Caro. James knew now, as he looked back on it, that Felton had been right. Upon James' reconciliation with Caro, Felton—much to his credit—had treated James with grace, and they had begun to grow closer despite their opposite characters. Felton might appear a scoundrel and a scapegrace, but in truth, James had seen him act with more gentlemanly honour than most in Society.

"I asked you to meet today to speak about Worth Manor," said James, his face growing hard as he said the name.

"Oh? You did not wish to see me for my sparkling conversation?" Felton gave him a half-smile.

"I always look forward to that," James replied, having grown used to his brother-in-law's propensity for funning. In fact, he found it rather amusing these days, and he might have laughed, had his mind not been on other things. "But I did have an ulterior motive. I am not ready... not ready yet to speak of it to Caro. The house, you see, is in some disrepair. I am recalling my man from the north to oversee the works. I had never expected to return to that place," he added as an afterthought.

Felton remained silent this time, offering no rejoinder.

"But my niece's birth—it made me think that it is not for myself that I should look to the estate—but for Caro and her children."

"You are a thoughtful brother," Felton replied, no amusement in his voice.

James did not answer the statement. If he had been a thoughtful brother, he would never have left his sister to fend for herself two and a half years ago. The stab of guilt that still haunted him struck again.

"Surely it is for you too, though?"

Both their eyes stayed on the path ahead. It was half past eleven now, and a smattering of the ton were appearing to promenade on the wide pathway, either on horseback, in carriages, or walking like Felton and James.

"I am not sure I shall return there."

"But when you marry and have children yourself—"

"That is not certain," James said, cutting him off, his voice sounding flat. He rolled his shoulders back and exhaled. "I do not know if that shall happen—and even so, I intend on giving the house over to Caro and yourself. It is the least I can do."

They carried on for a few minutes in silence. When Felton did not argue with him, James felt the tension begin to roll off his shoulders. He had said what he came to say.

"I do not wish Caro to see the estate as it is. It will not be the place she remembers from her youth, and I have no wish to pain her further with my neglect. We have hardly spoken of Worth Manor since I've been back, and if you can refrain from mentioning it to her until it's ready, I should appreciate it."

"You realise she will not hear of you handing it over to her when it is *your* birthright? As much as I appreciate the thought, we do not need charity, or recompense for what happened. Worth Manor is yours." Felton's voice was firm at first, but turned to funning as he finished. "And I do not think Caro has written you off as a confirmed bachelor yet. Nor have I. What happened after—"

Whatever it was that Felton had been about to ask James, they were interrupted.

"Hallo! Is that Felton I spy?" The hail came from a passing landau.

The open-topped carriage slowed, and James turned in time to see Lord Avers springing down from the vehicle in which two ladies also resided. Avers called back to the driver and the carriage moved off again with the women still aboard. The gentleman swaggered towards them in his finely embroidered green suit, without a care to those he had abandoned.

"Well met," Felton said, clasping Avers' hand.

"Indeed, I had thought you lost, my friend, since the birth of that daughter of yours." Avers' slow smile spread across his face, his eyes merry beneath the rakishly set tricorne atop his head. "And Worth, my good man."

They shook hands just as warmly, though James was not nearly so well acquainted with Lord Avers as his brother-in-law.

"John!" came a cry from the carriage. "John! Where have you gone?"

Avers rolled his eyes, a smile still hovering over his lips.

"Alas, I do not so easily escape my shackles, Felton."

The landau was taking a wide arc across the path towards them, cutting across several riders and nearly causing an accident.

"Brace yourselves," Avers murmured.

"Who are you speaking to now, John?" came the same high voice, and as the carriage turned James saw it was Lady Goring and her daughter sat within. "You know you have stopped us three times now—one would think you know all of London and we really must be—" She broke off, a look of surprise and then delight passing over her powdered face. "Driver, stop! Stop!" she snapped.

The landau had made a full turnabout and come alongside the gentlemen.

"Aunt," Avers said, a forced smile upon his easy countenance, "I apologise for my endless acquaintances. I am a man of many friends."

"Shush!" she said, her gloved hand resting on the side of the carriage as she looked reprovingly at her nephew. "He is always funning, and mostly at my expense," she said, smiling at Felton and James. "But he is one of the most well-connected men in London and you do so love to tell me of the latest *on dits*, do you not John?"

"I am not sure, aunt," he carried on in his characteristic drawl, "whether interrogation can be so easily exchanged with the words 'love to tell'."

Lady Goring laughed, the sound well-practised, and then leant back a little to reveal her daughter.

"John, you will not be so uncivil as to exclude us from your little tête-à-tête?"

"Incivility is not one of my sins, aunt, much as I try. Lady

Goring and my sweet cousin Lady Sophia, I'm sure you remember Mr Felton and Lord Worth?"

The gentlemen both murmured appropriate pleasantries. James had heard enough about Lady Goring from his sister to feel the hairs on the back of his neck rise, and his brother-in-law did not seem any more pleased to be caught in conversation.

"My cousin, Lady Sophia, is recently returned to Town," said Avers, a genuine smile lighting his face as he looked upon the young lady beneath the bergère hat.

Lady Sophia revealed a shy smile at that, and James thought her quite pretty. He remembered being introduced to her at some ball or rout. She had been quiet and reserved.

"Yes, indeed. We have both been in Bath for an extended time. But the company grew insipid, and I desired to be back in London," Lady Goring said. "I hear you have been delivered of a healthy girl, Mr Felton." Before he could respond she added, "Do not fret, I am sure you will have a boy next time. And Lord Worth, how are you?"

The power of the conversation seemed to have been taken over entirely by Lady Goring. James felt the keenness of her eyes upon him and shifted uncomfortably.

"Well, I thank you, my Lady."

"And your business? I have heard great things from John on that front—you are quite successful, are you not?"

James shifted again. "I am blessed thus far, my Lady."

"Modest too." She smiled, but the expression looked misplaced upon her powdered and rouged face. "Is that not so, Sophia?"

Lady Sophia gave a small nod.

"We must be away," Avers interjected, no doubt realising that the conversation would only be monopolised by his aunt if they stayed. "For my dear little cousin wishes to see the zebra they have at the Royal Menagerie. I don't suppose seeing the little striped horse appeals to either of you gentlemen?"

Felton and James shook their heads in unison.

"I am afraid my wife is expecting me back," said Felton.

Avers gave an exaggerated bow. "But of course."

"And I have business to attend to," said James.

"Nonsense," Lady Goring chimed in. "It will take but an hour of your time and I am sure my daughter would be most appreciative of your company, Lord Worth."

"But not mine," Felton muttered under his breath.

James did not allow any reaction onto his countenance.

"While I am more inclined to let you go," Avers said languidly, sounding far more like he did not care either way, "my aunt will not be refused."

James looked between the party and Felton, feeling an increasing pressure to accept the invitation.

"You will come then. It is settled," said Lady Goring, not waiting for an answer.

She was already turning, calling to the driver to let down the steps. James had hesitated too long. He could not easily refuse now.

"Did I not warn you that my aunt would not be gainsaid?" Avers said, turning to the waiting landau.

"It appears you have been snagged," Felton said, when Avers climbed into the carriage.

"It appears I have," said James uncomfortably.

"Avers will look after you—it's good to see him in such high spirits. He recently had his heart broken, you know. He is yet to tell me the details, but I believe it involved a serious case of fortune hunting on the side of his lady love. His fortune was found lacking and another's more desirable." Felton's gaze, which had been on the ground between them and the Goring party, refocused on James. "Anyway, me thinks that now you have taken on your rightful title and news of your fortune is spreading, you are becoming an eligible bachelor, dear brother."

James emitted a sound close to a growl.

"So I might ask you not to do anything about handing the estate over to Caro just yet. I have high hopes you shall not be a bachelor for long." Felton winked at him, James giving him an answering eye roll. "But for now, go and enjoy your new role as a sought after single gentleman and prepare be interrogated by that mama."

"You will not come with me to fend off the attack?"

"Such sharp words from you, brother, not like you at all." Felton was grinning.

The darn man was enjoying this.

"No, I think *I* shall return to your sister, and *you* should revel in the attention. A little distraction never hurt anyone, especially distraction from a... well, anyway, enjoy yourself."

James watched Felton walking away, leaving him to his fate, and was very sure he would *not* enjoy this next episode. Not one bit.

CHAPTER THREE

"Lord Worth is handsome, is he not, Sophia?" Lady Goring asked while they stood at the side of the cage in which the exotic zebra stood.

The animal was taking exception to the crowds and every few minutes was making the most extraordinary sounds. It set the crowds to hollering which only put the animal further on tenterhooks and now it was hoofing the cage. The second swipe it took at the bars drew blood from its foreleg.

"If you like the angelic sort," Avers answered for his cousin, shooting a lazy grin at James who felt even more uncomfortable than he had in the landau on the way here.

Avers tapped his silver-topped cane against the bars. The zebra struck out again and he leapt back laughing.

"Poor creature," James murmured, two lines appearing either side of his mouth as he pursed his lips in disapproval. The look went unnoticed.

"You are a tease, John, and that is why you shall never marry and present a respectable image to Society."

"Perhaps my definition of a *respectable image* differs from yours, my dear Aunt Goring," Avers replied, unperturbed by the censure.

"I am sure he will, Mother," said Lady Sophia, her voice gentle and light. "But you must be kind to John after…"

Avers cast a warning glance at his cousin and her words trailed off.

James watched the interchange but was distracted when the animal in the cage struck out again, sending a metallic bang around the enclosure and startling Lady Sophia. She fell back a little, bumping into James, and he instinctively raised his hands to steady her elbows.

"Sweet cousin," said Avers, his eyes dropping on the space where James' hands connected with Lady Sophia's arms, and then taking his cousin's arm and drawing her to his side. "Always seeing the best in me."

James had the distinct impression that there were two conversations going on here, and he was only privy to one.

"There is no hope for you." Lady Goring huffed a little, a look of aggravation marring her countenance. "With your father at death's door and with no large inheritance to look forward to, you would be far better exerting your efforts to please the ladies of your acquaintance rather than teasing them."

"Mama," Lady Sophia chided softly.

"Have no fear, my sweet little cousin." Avers patted her hand. "Father's illness has forced me to become head of the family before I intended—a distasteful amount of responsibility, it's true—but the power makes me far less terrified of my big bad Aunt Goring."

"As I said, a lost cause," Lady Goring cut in sharply. "I had high hopes for you when you showed interest in the Curshaw girl several months ago, but you let her slip through your fingers, and now she is engaged to another."

James saw something move in the depths of Avers' eyes, but the man's face remained an impassive mask.

"Mama," Sophia begged, too softly for her mother to take any notice.

"We will waste no more conversation on you, John, though I am sure we are obliged to you for escorting us on another of my daughter's wild fancies." She turned to James purposefully. "Tell me, Lord Worth, was there much society in the Indies?"

"Some," James replied, still feeling he was missing half the conversation that was going on between the family members.

"But not, I'm sure, full of comely young ladies like my Sophia, I should think? Far too hot there for delicate beauties from what I've heard."

James admired the conversational manoeuvring of Lady Goring, but at the same time felt resentful of the corner she had pushed him into.

"Lady Sophia is indeed a beauty," he said with a bow, his expression giving nothing more away than a polite smile.

"You are very kind. Of course, many have said so, have they not Sophia?"

Her daughter blushed.

"She is humble, you see, Lord Worth—a great quality."

"Not an inherited one," Avers murmured.

Lady Goring either missed it or chose to ignore it. She sucked in a gust of air and was about to launch into another series of comments when Avers spoke.

"Look how the stripes go all the way up its haunches," he said with exaggerated volume. "Have you ever seen one of these creatures before, Worth?"

It was a deft manoeuvre to a new subject.

"No, I haven't."

James' reply was swallowed up by another stream of noises from the animal.

"Oh, will it just desist! Honestly, Sophia, I am at a loss as to what you find interesting about such things." Lady Goring huffed at her daughter. "I am now regretting my agreement to attend you."

"What you are forgetting, dear aunt, is that you chose to attend. I was happy to bring my sweet cousin after she read about the zebra in the Society sheets. As I said, Worth, my aunt is not a woman to be refused."

Whatever sharp reply had been about to come out of Lady Goring's mouth, she appeared to think better of it. Her expression changed as something new came into her mind.

"Now that you are back in Town, Lord Worth, you must be looking forward to enjoying the company of such estimable young ladies as my daughter. There are, of course, many ladies in Society at present, but some are older than others. It is my opinion that if you cannot secure a match in your first two Seasons, there is something at fault."

None of the party responded to this statement and Lady Goring carried on.

"Take Lady Rebecca Fairing for instance," she said.

James stiffened.

"One of Society's celebrated beauties, and still unwed. But then, I have never seen the appeal myself.

"I shouldn't think you would, aunt, being a female," Avers countered.

"Oh, you are silly, John," Lady Goring said, batting at his arm playfully, all viciousness from earlier dissipated.

It was as though she were two different people, James thought, and he noted that Avers was now watching his aunt with a certain degree of wariness. James sighed inwardly, wishing himself at his accounts, or with his solicitor. Anywhere but here.

"Women who are the toast of the Season often have a sense

of their own entitlement," Lady Goring continued. "No doubt, Lady Rebecca has that, and it is not an appealing quality. Would you not agree, Sophia? Of course, you are nothing like that, are you child?"

"Lady Rebecca," Avers said before his cousin could reply, "is one of the few women of Society that I should be happy to call wife. Though I am not the marrying kind."

If the casually spoken statement had not hit so close to home, James might have admired the way Avers once again took the penetrating heat of his aunt's focus off his cousin. There was a brotherly mentality there that James could see. As it was though, he bristled at the words.

"Moving on so soon from the Curshaw girl?" asked his aunt, her words as sharp as the look in her eyes.

James saw Lady Sophia glance worriedly at her cousin, but the mask of affability did not alter on Avers' face, and he merely returned his aunt's look. There was a hardening in the man's eyes.

"She is so tall," Lady Goring said, turning back to the subject of Rebecca. "A man can hardly think her a pretty sort of lady. As for that sister of hers—"

"I have always thought," Lady Sophia said, finally finding the courage to speak up, "that Lady Rebecca is very—"

"But does that mean," Lady Goring said, cutting across her daughter, a new gleam in her eye, "that you have designs on Lady Rebecca?"

James saw those small eyes move between Avers and himself and the discomfort he had been feeling magnified. He needed to leave. Now. Mamas and their machinations were not something he wished to be in the middle of. This is what Felton meant by saying James was now an eligible bachelor, and James had no time for it. He had an estate to restore and a recent past to forget. Besides, whatever matrimonial games

Lady Goring was playing would be fruitless. His heart was not free. He should not raise Lady Sophia's hopes. That, coupled with the fact that he did not wish to hear of another's intentions to court Rebecca, gave him resolve to depart.

"I should go," he said a little more bluntly than he intended.

"So soon?" asked Lady Goring, turning her penetrating gaze from Avers to James.

"I'm afraid so. I have business to attend to, and as much as this has been a pleasant diversion, I must return."

Lady Goring tried a few more times to persuade him to stay but James would not be moved.

"Lady Goring." He bowed to the Countess. "Avers," he said, with a brief nod. "Lady Sophia, a pleasure." To her he gave a deeper bow. And with that, he left, only breathing easily again once he was out of Lady Goring's presence.

Avers raised a challenging brow at his aunt after Worth left. "All this talk of tendres, I would be surprised if you did not tell me you have one for Lord Worth, aunt."

"Don't be so silly," she snapped. All pleasantness from her face had left with Lord Worth.

In general, Avers had more patience for his aunt than the majority of people. It was not that he had a particular partiality for her. It was that, if her machinations only affected others and not himself, he did not get involved, except perhaps to offer an amusing censure here and there. Over the many Seasons he had spent in Society, Avers had found that it was best to leave small people to their small ways.

That being said, his aunt was in a particularly cruel mood today. Not only had she mentioned Miss Curshaw—a wound that had not healed—but she was brazen in her designs for Worth and his cousin. Sophia was a good woman. They had grown up and borne Lady Goring's interfering ways together. There was a sibling-like connection there and he could not allow his cousin to be ridden over rough-shod.

"Is it not a little premature—to set my cousin's sights on Lord Worth?" he said, moving to stand a little closer to Sophia. "The last time we met I thought my cousin was harbouring a tendre for someone else." Avers looked down at Sophia. "A Mr Malvon, wasn't it?"

Lady Goring rolled her eyes, hissing in displeasure.

Lady Sophia, who had relaxed momentarily when Lord Worth had left, looked uneasy once again.

"We will not be discussing that mishap," Lady Goring snapped, a look of distaste descending on her face.

Lady Sophia flushed a furious red.

"Mishap? I may be jaded, but that is rather too hard of you, aunt. Young love," Avers sighed melodramatically, gazing upward. "It is a precious thing, no? Did you not feel the throes of it with my uncle when you were a young belle yourself?"

Lady Goring bridled. Avers was the only member of the ton willing to mock her. He knew if she were to throw mud on his reputation, it would only damage her own. Being related had its benefits.

"Don't be ridiculous, John. Mr Malvon is less than eligible for Sophia's hand and so she told him when I talked sense into her. Sophia was not born so pretty to be thrown away on a nobody."

"I understood him to be a respectable gentleman." Avers kept his voice soft and drawling. There was no sense poking the snake if one could tiptoe around it.

"No title! No fortune!" Lady Goring cried, eyes flashing with agitation.

Out of sight of the Countess, Avers covered his cousin's hand and pressed it gently. It was hard to imagine how Sophia bore her mother's moods.

"At the very least, the Worth name can be traced back to the Wars of the Roses, even if it is not to the conquest like the earldom of Goring," Lady Goring carried on, oblivious of the looks passing between her younger relatives. "And a fortune not to be sniffed at, even if he is personally involved in trade."

"Such rancour! Surely you, with all your wit, have seen that even the most blue-blooded of us are not averse to a little mercenary profit where we might get it? Why even I have an investment in shipping."

Lady Goring eyed him with displeasure. "That you might, but you have an agent acting on your behalf. You are hardly among the merchants yourself, John. One has servants for that. Lord Worth will no doubt remove himself from contact with trade now that he is back in Society. It is the only proper thing to do. Besides," she said, a look of evil glee in her eyes, "I have it on good authority that Lord Worth has recently been rejected by a lady to whom he proposed. He is no doubt in need of soothing company."

"Do you mean to say he really proposed?" Avers asked, unable to hide his surprise.

It had been clear to him for some time that Worth was in love with Lady Rebecca.

"To Lady Rebecca, yes he did."

"You needn't have said the name," Avers murmured.

So that was why his aunt had turned the conversation to talk down Lady Rebecca.

Lady Goring shrugged, looking smug as she did so. "I heard the lady in question telling the tale herself. Clearly anonymity is not something she worries over. Lord Worth is most probably ready to put that refusal behind him and find another more eligible lady."

Avers followed his aunt's gaze to his cousin who was looking more and more uncomfortable.

There had been definite sorrow in her eyes at the mention of Mr Malvon. Avers wished he might wash away that sorrow. He hated to see it, and he knew that pain all too well from his own recent liaison. But this situation was different. There was no third party involved, only a disapproving mother. At the very least, Avers might remove some of the focus from his cousin.

"Now, now, aunt. Perhaps we should wait a little before being so overt. There is time enough for Lord Worth and dear Sophia to fall in love if that is the will of the Almighty. Perhaps let the natural course of things unfold?"

Lady Goring's powdered brow puckered. "Love—oh!" She wrinkled her nose as the animal lifted its tail and deposited an obscene amount of manure at the side of its cage.

"It appears the animal is just as unimpressed with our aunt as she is with the beast," Avers muttered in his cousin's ear. "Is that our cue, aunt?" he called to Lady Goring, straightening and pointing his cane towards the door.

"Filthy creature!" the Countess hissed as they exited. "Hardly worth the shilling."

Lord Avers allowed another sleepy smile onto his face. "Then let us be thankful that it was not *your* shilling that was wasted."

"Impertinent cad."

They made it onto the main thoroughfare, the London streets busy around them with men and women from across society. There were hawkers sounding their cries, artisans at work with shop-fronts open to the elements, tradesmen running to and fro from places of business, and here and there a bright spot of fine silk or cotton that denoted someone of the upper classes.

Lady Goring noticed nothing of it except those brighter

spots whom she called out to her daughter and nephew as acquaintances or those of the ton beneath her notice.

"Tell me, do you require my attendance at the Mires' card party, aunt? I had hoped to join some friends for a card game."

"Oh yes, we shall," Lady Goring said, not allowing him any recourse. "Do you think Lord Worth will be there?"

"I can only hope, for his sake, that he is not, for I see he has become the focus of your insatiable interest, aunt."

Lady Goring huffed as she was handed back up into the landau.

"Someone must think of Sophia's future, and this being her second Season, I wish to see her matched by the end of it."

As Avers settled opposite his cousin, his hooded eyes flicked to her face, studying it for a moment before answering.

"I bow before you, aunt, knowing that nothing can stand in your way when you have your mind on a goal. I shall attend with you." At least if he was there, he might aid his cousin in tempering his aunt's behaviour.

"Good," said Lady Goring, turning then and looking at London's passing streets, her mind on her machinations.

No longer at Lady Goring's conversational beck and call, the other two lapsed into silence. Avers closed his eyes, appearing to nap, whilst his cousin gazed at the people on the streets, a look of sadness on her pretty face.

Mamadou Safi had arrived on English shores several weeks ago and been on Lord Worth's business in the north of England. Hearing of the success of Arkwright's spinning mill at Cromford in Derbyshire, James had sent his man to investigate the opportunities. That had been before James had met with the family solicitor and discovered the true extent of the Worth estate's disrepair. The exploration of new business ventures would have to wait until the estate could be resurrected and for that task he needed his most trusted servant.

"It's good to see you, Safi." James grasped his hand warmly, the shake was firm, denoting the sinewy muscle beneath the layers of shirt and coat.

The African was tall and broad-shouldered, but slight in weight, his light frame belying the strength that lay within. James had seen that strength in action when Safi had hauled on ropes and sails alongside a ship's crew during a particularly hairy Atlantic crossing.

A free black man, Safi had met James in the West Indies. He had the unusual accomplishment of being literate, and James had quickly learned after hiring him as a clerk, that he had a strong mind for numbers and business. He'd been promoted accordingly, looking after James' business affairs in his absence, and since Lord Worth's winding down of his investments in the Indies, he had followed his Lordship to England.

"How was Derbyshire?" James asked, his familiar welcome more in keeping with that of an old friend than a servant.

"Cold and wet, my Lord," replied Safi, his face expressionless.

In spite of the mood James had been in for the last few days, he laughed. He walked over to the sideboard and poured two glasses of port. As much as Safi had been happy to follow his employer from the Indies to England, he had thus far been appalled by the weather. In fact, as James turned to pass Safi a full glass, he noticed the man still wore a greatcoat and muffler in spite of being indoors.

"And Arkwright's water frame?"

"Cold and wet also," Safi said, his mouth a straight line and his dark eyes showing only the veriest hint of humour.

"But a clever invention. His mill produces far higher tonnage a year than his competitors and the cotton yarn is stronger." Safi did not touch his port, holding the glass against his stomach. "Arkwright has yet to adopt Newcomen's engine, though I believe it will not be long before he does."

"If I had my way I'd send you straight down to Cornwall to see my friend Axton's mining operation. He had the engine installed last year to improve his ore production while he was overseas. Claims it saves in labour what it costs in coal. I'm yet to be convinced." James was musing, the edge of his glass pressed against his lips, the drink within forgotten.

Despite the familiarity with which James spoke to Safi, the freeman never returned it, maintaining the boundary between master and servant at all times. Where other servants he had known for years took liberties, Safi refused, always standing in James' presence, never drinking what was offered.

"Would you recommend the investment?"

Safi bowed. "Whatever you should decide, my Lord. I have written up my findings and the figures Arkwright's foreman was willing to share." He dug a hand in the deep pockets of his greatcoat and pulled out a leather-bound journal, worn and stained, and tied round with string. He placed it carefully on the desk.

"Excellent." In truth, James was amazed that the foreman had shared anything with Safi. A black man travelling alone came with its challenges in spite of the letter and Worth seal that James had sent him with.

"As to why I recalled you," said James, leaning back in the chair he had taken and crossing his legs at the ankles, "you'll remember I have an estate in Sussex I have not seen to in some time. I've been informed that it needs attention, and I would like you to oversee the work."

"I am honoured, my Lord." Safi bowed deeply.

The man had excelled in overseeing the closure of James'

West Indies operations. The so-called patriots in the colonies had gone so far as to declare their independence and it appeared Britain's hold over the Americas had been dealt a death blow. After several years of problems due to the conflict, James had come to the end of his willingness to battle on in the Indies.

If he were being honest, it was not only the trouble in the colonies that had convinced him to broaden his concerns outside of the realms of cloth. It was also the growing friendship he had enjoyed with Safi over the last several years. The longer he had been in the man's company, the less he could justify his profiting from enslaved Africans on the plantations. It may not have been his main reason for finishing his trade in cloth, but it was certainly something that had weighed in the decision. James had seen first-hand the origins of the fine cottons that the women wore in London and farther afield. The beauty of the gown hid well the darkness from which it came.

The moral dilemma he had found himself in, as well as the unrest, had meant his West Indian concerns were not worth the continued risk when there were opportunities on home soil. While investing in the latest innovations in industry here might prove profitable, there was also the estate to consider. At its height it had provided the Worth family with a handsome income. That was the way to look at it, he had decided—as an investment for his sister and her children.

"Rest here a day or two," said James, a more caring master than most, "and then go to the estate."

"As you will."

"While you're here, you can look over the papers my solicitor sent to get an idea of the project."

"Yes, my Lord."

"And don't bother with Worth Manor to start with. Aside from making it water tight, I am keen to focus on the estate's farms and their production. The sooner we get those running well, the faster we might expect a harvest.

"I have written to the incumbent steward, Mr Godrich, to let him know of your coming. I believe he may be in for a shock now the master of the estate has returned."

"That will not be his only shock with my arrival," said Safi, the slightest curve on his lips.

"I don't doubt it. But for now, go and rest."

Safi understood the dismissal, placing the glass of untouched port on a small gap of paper-free desk, and with a bow, he left.

Now that the resurrection of the estate was in hand, and James' business ventures were on hold, he felt at least a little of the weight lift from his shoulders. But with the most pressing concerns removed from his mind, thoughts of Rebecca rose to the surface. That was why he liked to be busy. Being occupied pushed those thoughts down and the dull ache that came with them.

He exchanged his seat in the centre of the room for a chair by the window overlooking the street below. He watched as various persons came and went on business or pleasure, and then spotted a couple exchanging a whisper and a laugh. He saw the look of delight on their faces, the stolen glances, the closeness of their figures.

Rubbing his chin as he watched, he felt the firm line his mouth had formed while watching and sighed. The couple stopped their secret conversation, and the gentleman took the lady on his arm so they could continue down the street. Whatever words had passed between them remained theirs and theirs alone—a private partnership, a private understanding, a private love.

Feeling aggravated with himself for the melancholy thoughts that were consuming his mind, he rose, shaking his limbs, and went back over to the desk. But even as he arrived in front of it and picked up his quill, meaning to sit and continue going over the estate accounts, he was frozen in thought again. Thoughts of Rebecca and a potential future that had lain before him. Thoughts of how she had refused him and how he had felt so wholly exposed. He had offered her himself and she had not wanted him.

The memory caused tension to run through his frame, that same sick feeling in the pit of his stomach, that same disgust at his own vulnerability. He raked a hand savagely through his hair, forcing it half-free of the ribbon. When he and Rebecca had met at his sister's house three weeks ago, she had spoken to him as nothing more than an acquaintance. That was all he was to her. But that had never been all Rebecca was to James.

In his early twenties, the thought of marrying had always seemed so far off, so unattainable in light of his father's shame. Yet Rebecca had seeped through the cracks of James' walls of logic. That logic had driven him forward through the trials of his youth. It had kept his feelings at bay and protected him from scorn and derision all these years.

Until Rebecca.

Until she had drawn out emotions that had long been off limits. For the briefest of moments she had given James hope. Hope that he might have a future to eclipse his unworthy past. Hope that she might accept him as he was. Hope that he might finally allow himself to feel and be safe to do so. But he had been a fool.

Without realising, he pressed the nib of the quill so hard on the sheet of paper before him that it shattered. He observed its pieces, scattered across the sheet. It did not matter what had happened or what he had hoped and desired. Rebecca had made her decision and he did not see a future with another. He would not have a family of his own. His purpose was to restore the one he had abandoned—the family he already had with Caro. His purpose was to provide for and care for her and her children no matter what Felton said.

And so he pushed those feelings of regret and rejection back below the surface. As they sank deeper, their sharpness was obscured beneath thoughts of the estate and the work that lay before him.

CHAPTER FOUR

11 March 1776

D*ear Aunt E,*

London is lost without you. There is no card party or ball the same. I have been asked by half of Society where my amusing aunt is. I was quite close to taking offence, for you know I consider myself rather amusing, but I must bow to your superior place within the ton's heart.

Now to me, I am well, enjoying my stay with the Arleighs. Julius is proving a fine brother-in-law, though not exactly a loquacious man. One cannot, for instance, attend the dressmakers or go for ices at the Pot and Pineapple with him, for he offers little in the way of conversation, and so when Rachel is resting for the good of the babe, I am left very much to my own devices. These 'rests' are becoming more frequent, and I fear it will not be long until Rachel's confinement. She would rebuke me for saying so, but she is growing incredibly large, aunt. I believe they will go to the Arleighs' Somerset estate for her confinement soon, and I must consider where I am to stay once they have gone. I wonder, with Mother and Father still abroad, whether I shall have to return to Bath. Do not be offended by the words 'have to', for you know I love your company. It is just that I tired of Bath after the incident and am much preferring being elsewhere.

I can feel your piercing eyes on me as you read this letter as though, even while I write, you are here looking at me. I would like to say that the incident in the Bath Pump Room is a thing of the past and I no longer much think of it. But rather than growing dimmer in my memory, I find myself continually dwelling on it and wondering of all the other outcomes that may have been. Yet I do not think it could have turned out any other way. For though I felt for him, I cannot... bah! As my dressmaker would say. I have no way to describe my thoughts in words. Words are not adequate.

I so wish, in the most dreadfully selfish way, that Caro had not just had a baby. For I have lost her first to marriage, and now to motherhood. I have never made friends lightly, as you know, and to lose any, even to so noble a calling as motherhood, is a challenge.

Though even if Caro were here I could not speak to my dearest friend of the uncertainty in my mind because it is her own brother who causes it. There are times when I do not think I am uncertain. On the contrary, in my sounder moments I feel that I must simply move on and forget the unfortunate episode. My feelings are often hard for me to understand, or allow, and so instead it is best to put them away somewhere they cannot cause mischief. As to that though, I fear I may not be able to do so easily, for I did quite a silly thing. That woman, you know of whom I speak, the one whom you cannot abide, she was in the dressmakers when Rachel and I were the other day. I am tremendously anxious that she overheard something I was saying about Lord Worth... I shall find out what my lack of awareness has cost me soon enough.

How maudlin I sound!

I shall talk of other things, though related to that woman. It may have reached Bath already, by way of that voracious Societal menace 'gossip', that I am not the only one who has recently rejected a suitor. Mr Malvon, a little-known gentleman who had been paying court to Lady Sophia, has received the cut from her. Though she showed an initial partiality, Society now rings with the news of her actions due to his lack of title and fortune. I had not thought it of the nymph-like creature. She has always seemed a gentle girl and the antithesis of her mother, so her behaviour seems odd in its coldness.

Lady Goring, usually so garrulous, has not mentioned a word of it, though I am sure she will not be so stoic when it comes to speaking of my unfortunate incident. Time will tell.

Now I have been a sufficiently bad niece, and cost you a pretty penny for this long letter, I shall ask how you are? Do the waters do their job or continue to vex you? How is Society there now that I am gone? I am at the edge of this sheet, and I know how you hate me to cross it so I will finish here.

Your ever-loving niece,
Rebecca

Rebecca put the quill in its holder and leant back in the chair, happy to allow the ink to dry in its own time without sanding and blotting. She had time to spare with her sister resting above and her brother-in-law out.

While Arleigh was still not a lover of Society, thanks to his extrovert wife he had made a handful of friends in Town. To the surprise of many, he was often seen with the redeemed reprobate Tobias Felton—an odd pairing to those looking on. Aside from that, it was those of the ton whose interest lay in estate management and agricultural innovation. Arleigh had given Rebecca unrestricted use of his library for her correspondence when he was out. So it was here she had taken up residence.

She inhaled. The scent of old smoke lingered in the air, ghosts of a fire long-since out, rich, woody and comforting. Dark tapestried chairs, opulent wooden panelling and heavy furniture came together to form a wholly masculine domain. It was a practical room, like its owner, laid out for work not idle pleasure. Rebecca lay back in her chair, eyes drifting aimlessly over the busy shelves and desk.

She had spent many an afternoon like this recently and it gave her entirely too much time to think. She did not want to be left alone to think on things. To feel things. She wanted distraction from all quarters. Was that not why she enjoyed others' dramas and Society's *on dits*? If she could just be absorbed in what 'Lady this' had said or what 'Lord that' had done, it saved her from... herself.

It was uncomfortable to *feel* things. It was outside of her control. She had learned long ago that it was far easier to occupy one's mind with the feelings of others. Caro had accused her of obsessing over other people's dramas. But it was easier. It was far easier to be logical about another's circumstances, another's feelings, than it was about one's own. And hadn't that interest in other's lives helped Caro out of the coil she had found herself in with that malicious Marquis? Hadn't it helped Rachel come to the realisation that she really was in love with Julius?

Besides, distraction not only kept her feelings at bay, but it also kept reality away too. For if she stopped for too long, she might notice that she was five-and-twenty now and unmarried. She might remember all the proposals and courting she had turned down because she had not loved the man who had offered it.

A long time ago she had told Caro that she could not

marry unless she felt compelled to do so by a deep love. Living with her sister and brother-in-law had only raised the standard, for theirs was a true love-match even if it had not started as one. She could see in them an equal pairing, where one's faults were offset by the other's strengths, and all was encompassed within a deep, abiding affection. That's what she wanted in order to marry, but none of the witty, dashing and handsome men of her acquaintance had shown that depth.

And while James had the depth he was... not witty, or dashing, though he was handsome. He had not fit her expectations at all. Even flirting with the notion that she might have been wrong to refuse him—that perhaps her expectations had not been correct—filled her with a sense of dread. So she did not think upon it. She did not think about the lost future or the stark contrast between that and her reality. No, she found distraction.

The Boulle clock on the mantelpiece struck one and Rebecca decided she had spent enough time with her feelings. She sat up, shaking her head briefly, and then folded and sealed the letter for her aunt. She took it into the hall and exchanged it for half a dozen invitations laying on the silver tray. There must be something in this pile that would be the diversion she so desperately required.

The Mires' card party was a moderate affair without the suffocating atmosphere of a great crush. The windows of their first-floor apartments had been thrown open to the night air and, thanks to most of the everyday furniture having been exchanged for extra chairs and card tables, it was a comfortable gathering of the ton.

Lady Mires, a woman of middling age who had never been a beauty, was nonetheless a great favourite of Society, and living proof that generosity and humour occasionally counted for more than looks. Those were not just qualities belonging to Lady Mires, but also to her husband. Their characters made them genial to everyone they met, and no one in Society had a cross word to say about them. Thanks to a handsome fortune, they threw some of the best gatherings of the Season, and should one be fortunate enough to receive an invitation, declining never came to one's mind.

That was the first reason James was at this evening's soiree. The second was that he needed to take his place in Society if he wished to redeem his family's good name, and as much as he would rather be conducting business elsewhere, he would make these sacrifices for the sake of Caro's child.

"You come alone this evening?" asked Lord Mires, clapping James on the back and grasping his hand as he entered.

"I do," James replied.

"No matter," said Lady Mires, her cheeks rounding as she smiled. "There are many fair ladies you may wish to make the acquaintance of this evening. Or who may wish to make *your* acquaintance," she added, her pale blue eyes twinkling as her smile broadened.

James responded with a forced smile of his own.

"You are so often a man of business," Lady Mires carried on, unaware of James' discomfort, "it is a treat for us to see you as a man of Society tonight."

James bowed and this time smiled genuinely. "You are too kind, my Lady."

He moved from the entrance soon after to allow the Mires to welcome more of their guests. The antechamber gave way to a large room brilliantly lit by two chandeliers and decorated in the French style. Green flocked papers adorned the walls along with large portraits in heavy gilt frames. Mirrors along the left-hand wall echoed the windows on the right and doubled the chandeliers making the room glow in a magical fashion.

James passed chairs set in small clusters—wooden Chippendales in threes and fours, and larger tapestried chairs for reclining in more intimate pairs. Many were taken up as perches by the ladies present, with gentleman flocking around them, smiling, laughing and showering them with compliments.

Through a set of double-doors located in the centre of the wall of mirrors was a room set aside for gaming. No games of hazard or deep play here, just friendly rounds of loo and piquet, for those with a gaming bent. James paused in his perambulation and scanned the room, looking for anyone he knew, and realised to his discomfort that many eyes were watching his progress. He noted several Societal matriarchs he recognised—mothers of eligible young ladies recently out, observing him keenly over their fans and whispering to their charges.

"Well met," came a low drawl from across the way.

James turned to see Avers approaching from the card room.

"Good evening." James bowed stiffly.

"You are much admired," Avers observed, picking up the quizzing glass he had dangling on a ribbon, and putting it to his eye.

"I hardly think so." James shifted uncomfortably, feeling his cheeks warmed and not by the full room.

"They do not look for me," Avers carried on, clearly not needing a partner in this conversation. "As my aunt said at the menagerie, I am a lost cause. Too many mamas have wasted time thrusting their daughters beneath my disinterested nose. You, on the other hand, are a man of significant fortune, the knowledge of which—I hazard a guess—has finally reached the Marriage Mart. No doubt thanks to my aunt. It can only mean one thing—the stares are for you, Lord Worth."

"I..." But James could think of no response. He could not counter it, for Avers was right. They *were* staring at him. And he did not wish to own it, for he was hardly used to anyone looking his way who was not commenting on the disgrace of his deceased father.

"Don't be shy, dear man. Revel in it. I certainly did, until I felt the bite of the snare around my ankle and the bait already gone. I still carry the scars and have since avoided such risks. Tell me, do you carry similar scars?"

James disliked the line of conversation.

"I'm unsure as to your meaning, but I have no intention of making a game of courtship with any ladies in Society."

"And here again is the stoic gentleman that is Lord Worth." Avers inclined his head to James. "I am sure that many a mama would be relieved to hear you have no intention of breaking their daughter's heart. But as I said, you'll have your pick of the eligible ladies of the Season. Being keen for marriage as you are, I'm sure one lady will be fortunate by its end."

Keen for marriage? First asking James about carrying scars from previous romantic entanglements and now a comment on his keenness to wed.

"Oh?" James rose one brow.

Avers' gaze retracted from the matriarchs. He shifted to his other foot. Was that sheepishness James saw in the man's hooded eyes?

"Am I wrong? Are you not?" There was something feigned about the question, but Avers carried on confidently, "I, as I say, am not keen for the holy office and instead content myself with admiring from a distance. Speaking of which, here is Lady Rachel, sister to the *incomparable*!"

Avers flourished a hand at Lord and Lady Arleigh just

entering the room. James' frown cleared at the sight of them, and he smiled. The tall couple had a great deal of presence as they walked side by side. Arleigh's broad shoulders in a plain red silk suit matched his Amazonian wife swathed in a complementary *robe à la française*. The pleats of the dress had been let out and the stomacher pinned cunningly to allow the dress to fit around her growing bump. They were quite the pair.

"Worth!" Rachel called, her brown eyes alight with pleasure, no thought to the unconventionality of addressing James just as her husband would.

She made ready to bound towards him, but her husband's protective hand found her elbow. At Arleigh's touch, Rachel slowed her pace, but still made her way towards James.

"I'm delighted to see you here. I hadn't thought it of you —to come willingly to a party without the need to escort your sister." She came to a stop before the gentlemen, her height putting her at eye level with James. Her brown eyes were twinkling at him. "We are honoured indeed, are we not Julius?"

Lord Arleigh, his hand now resting gently on her lower back, offered an incline of his head but said nothing.

"You wound me, my Lady," Avers said without the least sincerity. "If only my presence conjured as much gratitude as my friend Worth's."

"Nonsense," Rachel replied cheerfully. "You couldn't be wounded if someone pinked you, Lord Avers. I believe immunity to others' opinions is a family trait. Speaking of which, is your ghastly aunt in attendance?"

Arleigh cleared his throat and James saw a look of meekness pass briefly over Rachel's face.

"Of course, I meant your *gracious* aunt, Lady Goring," she corrected, flashing a mischievous smile at her husband.

"A deft manoeuvre," Avers replied, a half-smile curving his lips and his green eyes flashing at Rachel from beneath their heavy lids. "Yes, I escorted my aunt and cousin here, though I have seen little of them since arriving. I've been in the card room for the most part."

"Oh, there is gaming? Julius, may I?"

Arleigh looked at his wife, his face expressionless. When she broke out into the most devilishly persuasive smile, his lips twitched almost imperceptibly.

"If you wish, my dear. Anything that keeps you seated."

"Oh stuff and nonsense! I'm perfectly capable of standing. I have half a mind to stay here now."

"If you'll excuse me, I shall go in search of drinks and a chair for my wife."

"Nonsense—I'm fine," Rachel replied with asperity.

"I know that," he replied, his tone never varying, "but I shall be getting one anyway, and you shall sit on it."

And he left, Rachel looking amusedly after him.

"And your most delightful sister?" asked Avers.

James turned away, taking a sudden interest in the rest of the room.

"She is here. I believe she was caught speaking to Mr Went when we arrived."

"Ah! At last, I'll have a gaming companion in Went—and you, Worth, will you join me? We need only find one more and we shall have a fine game of loo."

"I shall decline," James said, any softness in his expression dissipating. "Thank you."

The age-old feeling of shame, heavy and suffocating, rested on him, and he did his best to rise above it, thrusting memories of lost fortunes and a ruined name back into the recesses of his mind.

"Oh come!" Avers declared, an amused smile hovering over his mouth and a provoking look in his half-closed eyes, "I swear on my *gracious* aunt's life, I shall not fleece you."

Avers was an avid player. James knew it from Caro's years of living two lives and gaming in London's most notorious hells in order to make enough to sustain herself. Another wave of disdain for himself rolled over him. A muscle at his jaw twitched and his mouth became a thin line.

"I thank you, but no." His tone was steady, but harder now, and to those who knew him, all openness in his eyes was gone and in its place a shuttered look.

"Ah, at last, Went and the *incomparable* Lady Rebecca!" Avers saluted.

James turned to see Mr Went, a small wiry man of thirty, and on his arm was Rebecca. James' shoulders rose a fraction.

"*Incomparable*, you are looking as beautiful as ever." Avers bowed, hovering over Rebecca's hand so close he might have kissed her glove.

"You rogue," Lady Rebecca chided, pulling her hand away.

"Always. Now, Went, be so good as to persuade Lord Worth to join us for a game. He is being a positive bore."

"What are we playing?" asked Mr Went, his voice eager.

"Only the most proper games," Avers replied, going into a description of what was on offer.

James felt every muscle in his body tense as he drank in the sight of Rebecca. She wore a green *robe à la française*, the fine silk following the line of her small waist and then flaring wide at her hips in the fashionable style. Her brown hair was up and powdered showing off her slender neck where a braided loop lay. His gaze followed the green ribbons in her hair wondering what it felt like to weave his fingers into those places. In her hand, she held her customary fan, painted with trains of ivy and gold. She was wafting it over herself, her expression half hidden from the company, oblivious to the affect she had on him.

"Loo! A dreadful bore!" said Mr Went. "But it is easier than piquet, I own, so I'll put up with it for a while,"

"How gracious," replied Avers sardonically.

"Come now, Worth, you must play," said Mr Went.

"I will have to decline," James said, sensing Rebecca's gaze on him, but refusing to return it. "I do not play."

A small silence descended on the circle and for the briefest of moments, James' eyes met Rebecca's. He saw pity in hers which forced his old feelings of shame to the surface.

"Of course, of course," Mr Went said, suddenly going very red. "Wouldn't want to play, would you? All that business with your father."

"Such tact," Avers drawled after another awkward silence. "Children do not always follow in the footsteps of their parents. Speaking of which, I see my dear cousin approaching —ah, and my aunt."

CHAPTER FIVE

At the same time Lady Goring and her daughter arrived at the gathering, Julius also arrived to whisk his wife away to a seat he had procured for her, leaving Rebecca without allies. She watched with trepidation as Lady Goring approached, hating that she allowed herself to feel like that. The Countess was dressed in bright yellow silk with large ostrich plumes in her hair that bobbed as she walked. The older woman surveyed the group, her eyes pausing on Rebecca with a look akin to that which a cat might give when seeing a bird in its path.

"Good evening," the Countess said, offering a slight incline of the head, but nothing more, and waiting for the party to bow and curtsey.

There were murmurs of greeting and then Lady Goring inhaled gustily as if preparing to give a rousing speech to the troops.

"Well, I for one have been enjoying a delightful evening. The Mires are always the most gracious of hosts." A syrupy smile unfurled across her lips, revealing a set of yellowing teeth. "There are plenty of notables here, though I am a little put out that more were not invited. Lord Carey and his sister, for instance, though no doubt they are at some gathering or other with the Devonshires. They are dear friends, you know, dear friends." She sighed wistfully. "Never mind, though, for I am sure the company is agreeable enough with you here, Lord Worth. It is a pleasure to see you again so soon after our last meeting, is it not, Sophia?"

"A pleasure to see you again, Lady Sophia," said James, bowing to her.

"Ah, such a gentleman!"

"Not an accolade my aunt bestows freely," Avers murmured. "I have yet to gain the title."

Rebecca would have smiled at the joke had she not been in fear of every word that came out of Lady Goring's mouth. How she loathed this woman for being the busybody that she was. Perhaps Rebecca should excuse herself. She might attend her sister and then maybe Lady Goring might not feel the need to repeat anything she had overheard at the dressmakers.

"Oh shush, John, you are too much," Lady Goring said, patting Avers' arm affectionately. "But Lord Worth, it is so good to see you this evening."

"The rest of us are not here," Avers muttered in Rebecca's ear.

"And to see you two together—it is the mark of a gentleman, don't you think?"

The pleasant smile on Rebecca's face cracked, breath catching in her throat. Lady Goring was looking between her and James meaningfully. The rest of the party, not quite following the line of conversation, looked on expectantly. Rebecca had thought she might have more time, but the Countess was not waiting to loose the missile at her disposal.

"Oh! You look shocked, Lady Rebecca—have I said something amiss?" Lady Goring put a hand up to her mouth, her face assuming an expression of regret, but her eyes as sharp and knowing as ever. "I just thought, as you were speaking of it at the modiste's so freely the other day, that it was common knowledge you had rejected Lord Worth's proposal of marriage."

And there it was, laid bare. Rebecca felt her stomach turn. In the face of Lady Goring's relentless smile, her own broke completely. She couldn't speak, no matter how much she wished to deliver a stinging rebuke. As her smile fell away, so did all coherent thought. The only thing remaining in her mind was James.

Her dark eyes darted towards him, and she felt the sickening in her stomach worsen at the sight of the deep red staining his cheeks. If he noticed Rebecca look towards him, he chose not to return her gaze.

"Aunt—always one for capturing a conversation," Avers said, his drawl and expression unchanged by the revelation.

James shot Avers an indecipherable look.

"But it is all over and done with now, is it not?" Lady Goring asked cheerily. "I am sure it will not be long before another catches your eye, my Lord. There are many eligible *young* ladies in Society."

The emphasis on young was not lost on Rebecca, though James seemed not to hear the Countess, and refused to follow the accompanying look towards Lady Sophia.

"If you will excuse me," James said abruptly, bowing to the members of the group.

"What a fuss I've caused," said Lady Goring, sighing and offering more protestations of innocence to James and the others. "I had thought it a thing of the past. Especially as you were speaking of it in public."

Rebecca ignored the woman whose words were aimed at the whole group and in no way formed an apology. She stared at James who was rising from his final bow and about to turn away.

She reached out a hand towards him, but snatched it back when she realised what she was doing. Next she opened her mouth to say something to stop him leaving. Nothing came. She opened it once more to say she was sorry. Still nothing. Now he had turned on his heel, step never faltering, and he retreated from the group.

His figure was soon obscured by the crowd. Rebecca felt the vestiges of her muteness evaporate in the heat of sudden anger. She faced Lady Goring, eyes alight, and sucked in a gust of breath making ready to attack.

"Cards!" Avers interrupted, his drawling voice louder than usual. "You promised me a game, Lady Rebecca—you will play with me?"

In truth, Rebecca was unsure whether a stinging rebuke or tears would come out if she gave vent to her feelings towards Lady Goring. For a brief moment, all the emotions she had carefully put away flooded upwards, the look of hurt on James' face the key to their unlocking.

Lord Avers did not wait to offer his arm. Rather, he took Rebecca's hand, and turned her from her warpath before she could charge.

⁂

"Do I detect a little melancholy?" Avers asked.

Rebecca, Avers and Went had found a gaming table and were in the midst of play. Though it was hard to tell from Avers' attitude. He was lounging back in his chair, a set of cards in one hand, a glass of claret in the other, looking as though he did not care whether he won or lost.

"I can hardly own such a feeling at a gathering of Lord and Lady Mire's. They are the most exquisite hosts, as always." She pasted a false smile on her face and ignored the rising irritation at such an inane question.

"Is it melancholy caused by regret that you allowed the gentlemanly Lord Worth to slip through your fingers, or by my aunt's announcing it to the room?" He took a long draught of wine and then smiled sleepily at Rebecca.

She pushed down the sick feeling that was threatening her equanimity again. Shooting a quick look at Mr Went, who was too intent on working out his play to pay attention to them, she then levelled a glare at Avers.

"Whatever has happened to you, Lord Avers? I remember you being a gentleman. Now you are positively—" She broke off, nothing ladylike coming to mind. "You had best take a leaf from Lord Worth's book, and remember how to behave as the gentleman you are. These are hardly proper questions."

"You're right," he said, straightening in his chair and playing a card. "Forgive me, *incomparable*. Perhaps it was jealousy to hear you have another admirer besides me."

"Nonsense," she scolded, using her non-card-holding hand to wrap a fan on his arm. "Now let us focus on play."

Rebecca hoped he would heed her warning to desist in this line of conversation. She could not bear it, not when her mind was already whirring, wondering where James had gone and what he thought of her now. She cursed herself inwardly for the tenth time for not having the courage to explain herself there and then when James had been leaving the group. He must despise her now.

"But still, I cannot put the look of pain that was haunting your eyes just now from my mind."

"Are you so well-versed in heartbreak that you can discern it in others without fault?" she asked peevishly. She dearly loved to exchange a witty word with his Lordship, but now was not the time for his funning.

The smile on Avers' face flickered out for a second before returning. "So you admit it?"

"I admit nothing except that you are a provoking cad."

"True," Avers replied affably. "Be that as it may, perhaps I wish to commiserate with another ailing from the painful effects of romance."

"So, what I heard rumoured was correct—you were smitten with the Curshaw girl?"

"*Was*," Avers said, emphasising the word. "I understand better than most how painful it is when heartbreak is brought up by others."

Rebecca huffed, relenting at his admission. "Your aunt can be most trying at times."

"I could not agree more."

How Lord Avers and Lady Goring could be related, Rebecca would never know. He might be a provoking cad, but he had none of the malicious spite of his aunt. But then, Lady Goring's daughter was nothing like her either. The poor child had looked as shocked as Rebecca at her mother's outburst and had tried to mumble something conciliatory as Avers had escorted Rebecca away to the gaming room.

"Still, I am sorry for your heartbreak with Lord Worth. I am not surprised at your refusal for he is hardly in your usual line of suitors, but still, he is a good man."

"He is," Rebecca answered. "But I can assure you, there is no heartbreak between us. It was a misunderstanding."

"I have heard a proposal of marriage called many things, but not that. I hardly think Worth a man to propose to the wrong woman."

"Gracious, you drive me to lunacy, Lord Avers!" Rebecca cried, a sudden desire to scream overtaking her.

"Love does that to individuals."

"Oh do shut up!" she snapped in an unladylike fashion.

"Yes do!" Mr Went barked, eyes intent on his cards.

"But Mr Went, do you not think Rebecca looks a little broken-hearted?"

"Dashed if I know!" Mr Went scoffed, refusing to be

drawn into the conversation. Rebecca expected he was not taking in a word that was said.

"There, you see," she carried on with authority, wishing to quell Lord Avers' sudden interest in her romances once and for all. "You are speaking of nought."

She laid a card and allowed her expression to relax, not wanting any trace of emotion to show.

"I must have misread your beautiful face," Avers replied, laying a card.

"I should be wary of reading me at all, Lord Avers. Many men have tried, and I have eluded the understanding of all of them."

"Ouch!" Avers said. "I had almost forgotten what a sharp tongue you have, Lady Rebecca. I find it amuses me somewhat."

"As long as my suffering amuses you," Rebecca said with a trace of bitterness.

"But I thought you weren't suffering from a broken heart?" Avers quizzed, his brows rising and a gleam in his hooded eyes.

Rebecca could not stop a small huff from escaping.

"More and more intriguing," Avers murmured.

"Come now, we're here to play!" said Went, having missed the import of this conversation and grown testy at the lack of input from his gaming companions.

"My apologies, Went. I had forgotten you were a serious gamer."

"And you have forgotten that I have told you already my heart is not broken," said Rebecca, laying her final card. "And your focus on entirely the wrong thing has lost you this trick."

Mr Went groaned as Rebecca won, but Avers just smiled at her in that sleepy way of his, before saying, "I concede it willingly."

After finishing the game of cards, Rebecca cried off joining the gentlemen for another, and went in search of the ladies' withdrawing room to gain a few moments alone. She needed to regain her composure.

As she came back through the double doors into the room with the wall of mirrors, Rebecca noticed Lady Goring speaking to one of the dowagers present, gesturing and shaking her head in the direction of her daughter who sat nearby, quiet and unassuming. Rebecca's eyes were so focused on others that she collided with someone as she turned into the antechamber. "Lord Worth," she gasped, looking up at him.

When she realised they were the only two people in the antechamber her chest grew tight. Her surprise was mirrored in his eyes and that sent a cold embarrassment flooding through her.

He bowed stiffly, his mouth pursing, not saying a word to her. He made to step past her.

"I..." She halted, wanting so very much for him to stop, for her to explain, but feeling so wholly unprepared, so wholly wretched as she looked at him. "I'm so sorry, James. I did not mean for Lady Goring to find out and—oh!" A gloved hand flew to her mouth. "I should not call you that. Oh—dash it all!" She wrung her hands. "You must understand—"

He held up a hand. "I do understand."

"It was not intentional," she added quickly, looking in his eyes to see the truth of how he felt, but they were shuttered to her now. "I hope you do not think it of me, that I would be capable of betraying your trust in that way." Concern and a hint of indignation fractured her face.

"Let us not dwell on it. I have borne worse speculation in Society than the rejection of a lady—especially a lady of quality. Our engagement would have caused a stir in Society due to my past. Your rejection will be accepted far more easily."

"But I—"

"I shall not embarrass you again by repeating my offer. You have nothing to fear on that count."

The statement, which was calculated to bring relief, hit Rebecca in the chest with more power than she thought possible. It knocked the breath from her. She blinked.

"Oh, Lord Worth," came the irritating voice of Lady Goring from the main room, "we had thought you gone."

It arrived in Rebecca's ears as if through water, all gurgled and faint, and all she could do was stare at the unreadable face of James.

"Come, you will rejoin us, I hope? It is so good to be able to see more of you now that you are returned from the Indies." The Countess was stepping back and encouraging James to join her circle.

He hesitated, looking briefly to Rebecca and then back to the antechamber door. She saw the muscle in the side of his jaw flex.

"Of course," he called back. "Will you join us?" he asked, offering Rebecca his arm.

Rebecca wished, for the second time that evening, that the floor might swallow her whole. It did not oblige, so she took James' arm mechanically, and accompanied him back to the group, all the while his last words repeating in her mind.

Should she be happy he had said it? Now they might go back to what they were before. They might forget this unfortunate episode. But what had they been before? Was that really where she wanted to go back to?

As they arrived in the circle, Rebecca saw Lady Goring's eyes resting on their connected arms. She removed her hand from James' arm, and he did not look at her as she did so.

"Surely your sister will be wanting your company, Lady

Rebecca?" Lady Goring said, a polite smile on her thin lips. "You have been at play some time. My daughter is not a fan of cards, Lord Worth. You will rarely find her at the tables unlike the more seasoned Lady Rebecca."

There it was, that obvious throwing of attention onto her daughter. This time coupled with a slight to Rebecca. The latter action revealed the Countess' game, and Rebecca scolded herself for not seeing it before. Lady Goring was attempting to pave the way for her daughter to take centre stage in Lord Worth's affections. No wonder she had been so quick and taken much delight in telling James that Rebecca had broken his confidence.

Ordinarily Rebecca would not give in to such manipulative tactics, even if doing so caused her discomfort. But this time it was not her discomfort which was the concern, but rather James'. She considered leaving before Lady Goring's tongue could drip anymore poison, but then Avers rejoined them.

"I see this is where the *incomparable* escaped to after our last game," Avers said, his admiring gaze on Rebecca before it drifted over the rest of the company—a dowager and her young daughter just out in Society, his aunt and cousin and the others. "If you will not play cards with me, Worth, is there another sport I may find you at? Do you drive?"

"Not as sport," James replied. "I play tennis."

Tennis? Rebecca had not known that.

"We must come and see you play," said Lady Goring. "John, you will play with Lord Worth."

"I will? That sounds rather energetic." Avers covered a yawn.

"Yes, John," said Lady Goring, an edge to her voice, "for Sophia has expressed a desire to see a game played before, have you not Sophia?" Before her daughter could reply to the contrary, the Countess carried on. "She should very much like to see *you* play, Lord Worth."

The young woman in question made no audible sound in agreement with her mother. In fact, she looked highly harassed by the Countess' forwardness. Rebecca looked on with increasing sympathy.

"I'm sure Sophia would rather do anything rather than watch myself and Lord Worth play tennis," said Avers.

Rebecca resisted the urge to echo Avers' sentiments and save the girl from a forced engagement she clearly held no desire for. But Rebecca would not be able to do so without drawing the wrong conclusions from Lady Goring who clearly already saw her as a threat.

"You will play, John," Lady Goring commanded again, her tone as sharp as the look in her eyes.

Lady Sophia's expression of mortification worsened. Rebecca saw a softness in Lord Avers' eyes as they rested on his cousin.

Avers gave in. "Very well, aunt." His sleepy eyes took on a sudden gleam, flicking between James and Rebecca. "But only if Lady Rebecca consents to be one of the audience. I will stand in need of her wit to get me through. Not to mention the encouragement of her pretty face."

Rebecca could have struck him for the look of amusement in his eyes. He was doing it on purpose. He was deriving amusement from her suffering, and the more unbearably uncomfortable he made it for her, the more he was amused.

"Well, Lady Rebecca?" Lady Goring asked, her tone peevish. "If my nephew insists you must attend, will you not agree?"

"I suppose I might," Rebecca replied in a voice that was not her own, unable to think of an excuse, "though I should not wish to intrude on the party."

She glanced at James whose face was as unreadable as ever.

"Then it's settled," Avers said, bowing handsomely to Rebecca and taking her hand before she could stop him.

He hovered inches above it, glancing sideways at James before laying a kiss on the back of her gloved hand.

"What a merry party we shall be," he said, standing upright again.

As Rebecca looked around the group she decided she had never heard a statement more untrue than the one Avers had just uttered.

CHAPTER SIX

25 March 1776

D*ear child,*
The tone of your last letter was despondent and that disturbs me greatly. It is not in your character to despair, and I forbid you to accept the loss of your friendship with Caro so readily. You know in my experience as a childless wife I had many such friends called to motherhood. There is no spell that may be cast to keep things as they were. I am afraid it is much like marriage, and you must meet them on their ground as they can no longer come to yours. I have enclosed notes I like to call 'motherhood talking points'—things of grave concern to young mothers which you can use to learn of the condition and show your love to your friend in a way, until now, alien to you. Have faith, my dear niece. True friendships withstand life's seasons and are the richer for them.

As for the waters, they are as wretched as ever, and the company has grown insipid with most of Society returning to London. If it weren't for my aching limbs I should be back directly. Lord Fortnum does a tolerable job of entertaining me.

The other day he sat with me for several hours playing cribbage which I know he dislikes. He is a good man, his kind nature often overriding his attempts at being witty as the young bucks are. I forgive him for it. Kindness, I think, is undervalued.

Now, on the incident three months since that you spoke of, I believe, though you deny it, that you are wounded by it. The nature of the wound may still be a mystery to you, though it is not to me, and I shall not explain it for I believe you must come to the realisation yourself. What I will say, is that it can be hard when a woman such as yourself—beautiful and confident—is injured, because those attributes do much to hide it from those around us. Sometimes even from ourselves.

The story you imparted regarding Lady Goring's daughter and her flirtation with Mr Malvon is indeed news to me. It appears Lady Goring has done well in not repeating the tale, much as she will repeat others, so I am interested by it. I always thought the Goring girl a sweet creature. No doubt Lady Goring is on the hunt for an Earldom or the like for her. Poor child. To marry without love at all must be a lonely thing indeed. I have no doubt her mother is behind the cut.

Should my nemesis Lady Goring have overheard your words at the dressmakers, be on your guard. With her precious daughter on the stage of Society's attention, thanks to her broken flirtation, she will be looking for any other such scandal to take its place. I speak from experience when I say you must brace yourself for that inevitability. While it is not in your nature— or mine, I confess—to remain silent, I tell you, in this circumstance silence is likely to be your safest ally. Any speech will only be fuel to the fire, causing it to burn hotter and longer.

Consider it, dear niece, though silence is the antithesis of your character, and do not immediately roll your eyes and sigh in exasperation when you read this advice. I shall hear you from Bath if you do.

. . .

Keep safe and well dear niece.
  All my love,

Aunt E

⁂

"She looks very well in your arms," Caro said, her face soft with emotion as she watched her brother holding her newborn daughter.

"For now," said James ruefully. He had a gift for making his baby niece cry within a few minutes of holding her. "Have you settled on a name yet? It is too long to be calling her *niece.*"

"Yes." Caro's smile widened. "And you shall be the first to hear it. We have settled on Anne."

James' mouth curved a fraction more. "After mother." His blue eyes were full of unspoken emotion, his face looking boyish as he smiled.

Caro came to stand beside him, resting a small hand on his arm. She smiled up at him, raised herself onto tiptoe and kissed his cheek and then kissed her daughter on the forehead.

"Anne," James whispered, raising the baby in his arms and putting his lips to her forehead.

There was a blissful moment when Anne opened her dark blue eyes wide. Her tiny cherub mouth was open in surprise, her cheeks dewy and plump, soft creases on her small forehead. Then, deciding that, no, she did not like being kissed by this strange man who did not smell of her mother, she took a gusty breath and let out a cry. It took seconds for her face to screw up like creased cotton and the beautifully milky skin turn red with dissatisfaction.

"And now, my darling Anne, I think I shall return you to your mother."

James returned her with relief to Caro who began crooning over her immediately. A nurse, who had evidently been waiting in the hall, came quietly in and took the child, though Caro released her reluctantly.

"Make sure she has the yellow blanket, and do not put her down until she has been soothed." Caro's hand stretched out as though an invisible string pulled, connecting her to her daughter, and she could not let it go."

"Yes, madam. Don't worry. Little Anne will be happy as soon as she's fed." The nurse smiled at the baby in her arms and whisked her from the room before Caro could protest anymore.

"And where is your husband this morning?" asked James, changing the focus for her benefit.

"He and Lord Arleigh are breakfasting at the club."

"Oh yes?"

"I know—an odd pairing," said Caro ruefully, her eyes finally retracting from the door and resting on her brother again. "I have come to the conclusion that opposites can attract in friendship as well as love." She took a seat on a chaise longue.

James didn't wait to be asked to take a chair across from her. Their relationship had grown familiar since reuniting. There were times when their time apart was noticeable, but for the most part their sibling relationship was recovering, and they now boasted a closeness many could not.

"I think Lord Arleigh is one of those men who has a few distinguished friends rather than many," Caro remarked.

"I sympathise with that mentality," said James, thinking of Axton and their close friendship.

"And how goes it with the estate? Tobias mentioned there

is much to do. I am only glad you may finally claim your birthright."

James pursed his lips. There was no keeping secrets between his sister and brother-in-law. He should have known Felton would tell Caro about the estate.

"Yes, though it's hard to view it as such. Father still comes to mind when I'm called by my title."

"Yes," said Caro softly.

They remained silent a moment, each remembering their version of a childhood that had a communal sadness. Some wounds, even healed, caused residual pain.

"We could have lost it, if it was not for you paying the mortgage when you were in the Indies. I have not thanked you for that," said Caro, drawing them both back to the present.

"Thanked me?" James frowned. "You have no need to do so."

"But I am thankful," said Caro, leaning forward and stretching her hand out to James. He clasped it, feeling her squeeze. "Do you remember the orchard? I used to love playing there in the autumn with Mother. The sun seemed to collect within the walls, and we used to sit in the afternoon eating all the apples we had collected."

"I remember the stomach-ache you had." James took his hand back and rubbed his chin. "That's likely been left to overgrow."

"Really? What about the gardeners? Surely they have been keeping the place up."

James explained what the solicitor had said to him.

"My man Safi is trustworthy and hardworking. He will see to everything in my stead, and it will be restored to the state it was in before father managed to ruin it."

"You will not go back?"

"No." James exhaled and leant back in the chair, bringing his fingertips together. "I hold no desire to."

"Oh, but I had hoped you might hold a house party there once the house is repaired."

"You may hold whatever parties you wish, sister."

"But it is your home."

"It is *our* home. *Yours.* It's the least I can do after deserting you."

Caro's brow puckered and she looked searchingly at her brother.

"James, we both know now that it was a misunderstanding. I have long since forgiven you."

James listened, but the feeling of guilt did not abate.

"You know that, don't you?" she asked, her large blue eyes like pools. It was in moments like this, when she was gentle, that she reminded him most of their mother.

"What I did was unforgivable. I should never have left you alone when our father died. You are too kind to me."

Caro's face gave up its inquisitive look for one of softness.

"If I had not been so proud, the estate would not have gone to complete ruin. Each day Safi sends me updates and each day brings a new issue."

"Oh James,"—Caro sighed—"that sounds like a lot of stress."

He rolled his shoulders back. "I can bear it. It's important I see to its restoration for the sake of little Anne."

Caro's eyes were now on the floor, studying the carpet, a look of thoughtfulness on her pretty face.

"There is something I wanted to speak to you about," she said.

"Yes?"

"Tobias and I have spoken, and we wish for you to be Anne's godfather and…"

That was all James heard. Caro continued but he did not follow. Godfather? He had known it was a possibility, but he and Caro had spent so many years apart, he had thought it likely he would be passed over for another.

Caro was still talking. "I hope you are not too upset—I had thought not to ask her." James scrambled to pick up the thread of conversation again. "I considered it for a long time and though I am so sad about what happened between you, she really is my dearest friend."

Sad? What was she talking about?

"Oh James, don't stare at me like that. Are you really so angry that Rebecca will be the godmother?"

James blinked. "Not at all," he said evenly. "I understand. You have taken me aback by asking me to be the godfather, that is all."

"Well of course I've asked you. You are my brother." She came to kneel before him and take his hands in her own.

"Will you?"

"Of course," he said, smiling.

"Oh, you are very good to me!" Delight at his acceptance was evident on her face.

"You look so very like mother when you smile at me like that," he said gently.

"I miss her."

"So do I."

They stayed looking at each other and then the moment was gone, and with an inhale of breath they broke apart, Caro going back to her chaise longue.

"You should know something," he said, disliking the memories of the Mires' party that were surfacing in his mind. "What happened between Lady Rebecca and me is no longer a private matter. Lady Goring is taking great pleasure in spreading it abroad."

"What!" Caro gasped. "How does she know?"

"It hardly signifies. I only mention it to prepare you. Your choice of godparents might set Society talking when baby Anne's christening comes around."

"Stuff and nonsense!" Caro said with sudden asperity. "Society can go hang!"

James could not help himself from chuckling.

"I am sorry," she said, anger suddenly dissipating. "It must be dreadful for you. But—" She broke off, uncertain. "I hope the wound is healing?"

James could not hold her gaze. His eyes moved to the middle distance. He wanted to say yes, the confirmation she no doubt wished to hear, but he could not lie.

When the silence stretched too long, Caro spoke again, her words a little hurried. "Tobias was saying you were much admired at the card party. I believe you are quite the eligible bachelor, brother. Who knows what woman might take your fancy?"

"I have no desire to meet another," he replied, quietly and without malice.

"I wish you to be happy," Caro said, speaking quieter still.

The corner of James' mouth pulled up in a half-smile, his eyes soft as he looked at her again. He rubbed the back of his neck, sighing, and then spoke again in a far brighter tone. "Now let's speak of other things. I have a task I believe you will rather enjoy, sister."

James felt the tension seeping away from his frame as he moved the conversation further from the subject of Rebecca. "As we have lost several paintings to the leaking roof of the chapel, I wondered if you wished to attend the Royal Academy with me. It is their Annual Exhibition, and I believe it is high time the Worth family was seen abroad. You may select paintings you think Anne will like. And you, of course."

"Oh! That would be lovely," said Caro, clapping her hands.

The sound of a baby's cry sounded somewhere above them. Caro glanced up at the stuccoed ceiling.

"I will leave you to your babe," said James, rising and smoothing down his breeches and waistcoat.

"Thank you, brother," she said, her voice thick with emotion.

James responded by wrapping his arms about her and resting his chin on top of her golden head.

"You have nothing to thank me for."

"On the contrary, you are a good brother to me," she replied, muffled by his wool coat.

He grunted something incomprehensible, squeezed her tight and then pulled away.

"Go to your daughter," he chided.

She did not wait for a second bidding, skipping to the door and leaving him to see himself out.

CHAPTER SEVEN

Bright sun shone in through the high windows of the tennis court in James Street. Recently arrived, Rebecca was being escorted, along with her maid Maisy, to the viewing gallery. On the outside the court was a plain brick-built building and inside all decor was equally reserved. At least, that was what Rebecca was thinking until she caught sight of the court through the gallery.

The floor beyond the low partition was a savage red, burning brighter in the sun. She saw numbers emblazoned on the walls and lines along the floor. There were two men on the court already, sending the hard ball back and forth with resounding thwacks.

There must have been another game arranged before that of Avers and James. She took a seat on one of the wooden chairs placed in a row before the gallery partition, her maid, Maisy, sitting just behind. The man that had shown them in bowed away and Rebecca was left to wait for the rest of the viewing party.

Having no brothers, she had rarely been the spectator at sporting activities other than those appropriate for ladies such as archery and bowls. While there were female tennis players, it was not a common sport for women. At least, not outside the informal circumstances of a picnic at some estate or other.

Her eyes fell once again to the players, focusing on the nearest. A shot came flying across the court at speed, but the player was ready. Darting right, he planted his feet and stretched out his arm so the far end of his racquet caught the ball and returned it. It was only when the player straightened that Rebecca realised it was James.

She emitted a small gasp of surprise. He was stripped to breeches, linen shirt and waistcoat, his fair hair unpowdered. She barely recognised this informal version of the man she had only ever seen as staid and correct. His blue eyes, usually steady and calm, were alight with concentration. She caught the glisten of sweat at his temples, and was that a half-smile on his mouth?

Then James stopped, straightening, his body relaxing, and she realised the other player must have stopped as well. A practice game maybe? Without warning, James looked at the gallery and straight into her eyes. His brow raised slightly, and she was horrified to realise her mouth was hanging half open. She snapped it shut and returned a hurried bob of her head to his formal bow.

"Good morning, Worth," came a friendly drawl as Lord Avers appeared on the court. "I see I am late. It does not bode well for our game, does it? Ah, the *incomparable* is the first here. You were excited to see me play?"

Rebecca looked between the gentlemen and saw that unreadable look on James' face again.

"I am sure it will be an excellent match," Rebecca replied, keeping her voice steady. "Lord Worth appears well-versed in the game."

James' blue eyes lingered on her.

"Then I shall have to take this seriously, shall I not?" Avers smiled, grasping James' arm in a comradely shake. "You will excuse me while I take off my jacket."

Avers wandered to the far side of the court and James turned to the wall opposite the gallery, his fingers plucking at the strings of his racquet. Rebecca determined that Lord Worth would rather stare at a brick wall than her. She was right, then. He despised her for letting Lady Goring find out about the proposal.

"Lady Rebecca, you are here, I see," said that particular woman, recently arrived with her daughter and a servant in tow. She waved a hand to dismiss the man who had previously shown Rebecca her seat.

"I am." There was plenty Rebecca wished to say to this woman, but the worst thing to do with a wolf in sheep's clothing was to show any blood. If the ghastly woman knew just how much she had upset Rebecca at the Mires' party, she would no doubt revel in the injury. She must do as her aunt suggested and stay silent.

"Lady Sophia," Rebecca said, smiling at the fair-haired woman approaching behind her mother, "will you sit with me?"

Anything to keep Lady Goring from sitting near her.

"Thank you."

"Yes, I can see Lady Rebecca has chosen the seat with the best view of Lord Worth's play. You should sit there too, Sophia. After all, it was *he* who invited *you*."

That was not the way Rebecca remembered it.

Lady Goring hailed the gentlemen on the court who were speaking by the net.

"How goes your Season, Lady Sophia?" asked Rebecca, using the opportunity for a little conversation.

"Mama says it is going very well. She has been pleased by all the invitations we have received."

"I am not surprised. You are quite a beauty," Rebecca said simply, always an advocate of direct talk.

"You are very kind, Lady Rebecca."

"Rebecca, please," she said, smiling. Lady Sophia was like a scared lamb. Who would ever have thought her Lady Goring's daughter?

"Are you excited for the match?"

"Yes," said Lady Sophia, though her face did not reflect the sentiment. In fact, she looked as if she would rather be a million miles away. As if realising, and thinking she may appear rude, she added, "Mama very much wished to see Lord Worth play, and I came for my cousin John."

Rebecca's brow quirked upward. Not for Lord Worth? It had been obvious what Lady Goring was doing at the Mires' party. She had been driving a wedge between Rebecca and James to make space for her own daughter. James was an eligible bachelor now he was returned permanently from the West Indies with a fortune and a title. He may not have a gift for witty repartee, but today, Rebecca had to own he was handsome. Very handsome.

"I am sure Lord Worth is pleased you came," said Rebecca, testing the waters.

Lady Sophia did not answer, giving a small nod instead, her eyes on the partition before them. Rebecca's gaze drifted away as well.

The young woman was not an objectionable match for James. From a good family, presumably with a handsome dowry, and the antithesis of her mother. Rebecca felt a growing discomfort within, but pushed it away. It did not matter what she felt or thought. It only mattered what James wanted.

Rebecca felt Lady Sophia's hand lightly press her arm, drawing her back to the present.

"My Lady?"

She turned, a little surprised by the covert gesture.

"I wished to say... to say I am sorry for... for my mother—well, for what she... what she said," she whispered hurriedly, glancing over at the large posterior of her mother, who was flailing a handkerchief over the gallery at the gentlemen as if at some medieval joust.

Rebecca felt a sudden tenderness towards the young lady. She put a hand over Lady Sophia's that was still on her arm.

"You are very kind," Rebecca said quietly, "but you needn't worry on my account." Her brown eyes were wide and open as she looked on the other woman's anxious countenance. There was such earnestness and gentleness there. Perhaps Lady Sophia would be a good match for James. Rebecca's breath caught in her throat.

"Lord Worth is a fine gentleman," Rebecca said honestly. "I have no doubts he will make a wonderful husband to a deserving lady."

There was a catch in her throat again and Rebecca cleared it decidedly. What was wrong with her? Hadn't she made her decision regarding James? And he had told her he would not offer for her again. Whatever feelings she still had for him would die away soon enough and in the meantime she would continue to bury them. She must not get in the way of his happiness with another.

"They are to start," said Lady Goring, swinging round and eyeing the two women.

Rebecca retracted her hand and Lady Sophia took her own back under the unhappy eye of the Countess.

"Sophia, come and wish Lord Worth luck."

The young woman rose obediently and went to her mother's side to wait for James who was coming over.

"And me?" called Avers, walking to the partition from his side of the court. "Lady Rebecca, will you wish me luck?"

She rolled her eyes and exhaled.

"You are the picture of support," he chuckled as she rose and came over to him.

"And you, my Lord, are determined to cause mischief."

"Me?" He put his free hand to his chest, proclaiming his innocence. "I hardly know what you mean." His eyes twinkled as he flashed her a wicked smile. "Can you blame me for amusing myself—"

"At the expense of others," Rebecca cut in. "I shall not wish you luck," she said ungenerously.

"You mean to say you wish your Lord Worth to win."

"He is not *my* Lord Worth."

"Not if my aunt has anything to do with it," he said, nodding his head towards the little trio a small distance away. Lady Goring appeared to be orchestrating the conversation, her daughter speaking shyly and James murmuring polite replies.

"Your cousin is a sweet creature—perhaps it would not be the worst thing," Rebecca replied, forcing any emotion out of her voice.

"Yes, maybe not," said Lord Avers, a glimpse of a smile on his mouth. "But perhaps it is not only Lord Worth whose heart... would lose."

Then he stepped away, leaving his words hanging in the air. What was his game?

"Shall we play for the honour of the ladies present?" Avers called, holding his racquet casually, looking as if he had never played a game of tennis in his life.

"As you wish," James replied.

Rebecca saw a hardness on James' face that had not been there earlier.

"You can play for my cousin Lady Sophia, and I for Lady Rebecca," said Avers.

Rebecca rolled her eyes again and if she had not been frightened of being overheard she would have huffed as well.

Lord Avers knew exactly what he was doing. He was enjoying this. Whatever he hoped to gain was a mystery to Rebecca.

In a few more moments the game began. Play was hard from the off. Lord Avers, who had appeared half asleep just moments ago, showed more energy in the next half hour than Rebecca had ever seen in the noble. But if Avers was showing previously unknown athletic prowess, James was displaying far more. He returned Avers' hits, shot for shot, and moved with lightning speed across the court.

Soon, Rebecca was no longer sitting back in her chair waiting out the tension of this gathering, but on the edge of it, her gloved hands pressed to the partition.

"They play very well," Lady Sophia breathed, a hand hovering by her chin, ready to cover her mouth should a surprising point be scored.

"They do indeed," said Rebecca, watching the skill of James as he kept the ball going to Avers' weaker backhand.

The ball came spinning back over the net. It landed on James' side of the court and span off unexpectedly to the right. He had not anticipated the strange bounce and lunged. His left knee scraped along the floor and his racquet clattered against the wall. The recoil rippled up his arm and sent him over backwards.

Rebecca and Lady Sophia rose at the same time, each emitting a gasp.

"Worth? Are you all right, man?" Avers called.

James grunted, rolled over and rose. He pushed his shoulders back.

"Fine."

Rebecca noticed that the stocking over his left knee was ripped, and a bright spot of blood had appeared against the white.

She wanted so much to call out in that moment. To ask if

James really was all right. But her aunt's recent advice surfaced in her mind again, and she opted for silence. All calling out would do would be to cause unnecessary attention to fall on her relationship with James. Attention which had already been on them and caused him considerable discomfort. She bit her lip, watching James pick up the ball and go to the service line.

Lady Sophia retook her seat and Rebecca followed suit, both women holding their breath as James raised his racquet again.

"He plays very well, does he not, Sophia?" Lady Goring said, at the moment of James' serve. The distraction was enough that he hit the net.

"Mother," Lady Sophia pleaded.

"But he does, doesn't he?" It seemed as if Lady Goring had tired of the attention being on the game and not herself. "A fine man. I hardly know why a lady would refuse him."

"Mother!"

Rebecca's chest tightened, but her eyes did not move from James. If he had heard he showed no sign of it. It had not been meant for him. It had been meant for her, to push her further out of the way. She could feel Lady Goring's eyes still on her, but she refused to turn her head, biting her lip again, the taste of blood entering her mouth.

"Are you ready to keep fighting for the honour of my cousin? For I am ready to continue fighting for that of Lady Rebecca."

Avers' words seemed to dispel any wavering in James and he nodded his agreement. Fixing his eyes on the other side of the court, James became the epitome of focus. With careful deliberation, he raised his racquet and served again, this time perfectly into Avers' half. A rally was struck up, and Rebecca noticed James was slower now. Perhaps he really was hurt. Play continued at this more sedate pace for a few minutes, and then it began to pick up speed, James' eyes sharper than ever. His half-smile reappeared.

Had he been feinting the extent of his injury? How clever. Legs tensed beneath the breeches he wore, his white shirt wet with sweat, and his broad shoulders straight and strong, he delivered blow after blow back to Avers who was tiring. James did not let up, and before long the game went to him.

"Well played, Lord Worth!" Lady Goring clapped her hands. "Sophia, congratulate Lord Worth. He won the match for you."

Lady Sophia rose, and did as she was bid. James came hesitatingly over to the gallery and bowed formally to the mother and daughter.

"Perhaps you might show Sophia more of the game, Lord Worth. She understands only a little. May she join you on the court while you explain it?"

"It would be a pleasure," said James. He waited for Lady Sophia and then walked to the centre of the court with her and Lady Goring in tow.

Rebecca was left alone. On the other side of the court, Avers was enjoying a drink brought by a servant. She listened to the conversation between the Gorings and James. Lady Goring was all effusive compliments and chatter, James all formal politeness and Lady Sophia responding in kind. Then Avers was asking the servant something about a tennis champion who trained here early in the mornings. Her eyes moved back to James, studying his face, wondering if it was more than polite interest in his expression when he engaged with Lady Sophia. The chatter went on and Rebecca allowed it to wash over her.

"Letters—her Ladyship is most strict about them, I can hardly breathe when I am carrying one tucked into my stays, for it's the only way to get it passed her Ladyship's maid, Miss Dent, cruel woman that she is. But the gentleman is so insistent about it when he catches me on errands, that I cannot say no. The shilling is no harm either."

Rebecca recognised Maisy's voice when her maid replied in vague agreement. Turning her head to the side, Rebecca saw the Gorings' maid out of the corner of her eye. It had been her who had been speaking.

"Aye, but the time her Ladyship caught one of the letters, she burned it before my mistress and told her, 'No more!' with such a screech I thought one of them exotic birds my mistress likes to see pictures of had got in the house. Of course, that was before I was bringing the letters myself, back when he sent them direct to the house."

Maisy whispered something in return too low for Rebecca to hear.

"I swear, 'tis the truth, and the blunt I need, for my pay's not what it was. Not now. That's Miss Dent's doing, I'm certain, for though she says it's the same with her, I don't believe her. Mind I happen to know that she's been filching her ladyship's kerchiefs, fine lace that they are, and selling them, so mayhap—"

Rebecca straightened in her seat and the movement caused the two servants to fall silent. She cursed herself inwardly.

"Lady Rebecca," the Countess called over. "We may be some time. Please do not feel you have to stay. You may go now."

Rebecca bridled at the summary dismissal. She looked to Avers who was still busy speaking with the tennis court servant, to James standing beside Lady Sophia—his eyes avoiding Rebecca's—and finally to Lady Goring who was scowling over at her. She rose.

"Come, Maisy," she said, turning to walk down the aisle of seating and leave the gallery. She received polite farewells from both the gentlemen and a sweet smile from Lady Sophia. Once she was out of the building, the warm sunshine hit her cheeks, and she could breathe again.

"Now, Maisy," she said, when they were inside the Arleighs' carriage. "I think you know I overheard you speaking to the Gorings' maid."

Maisy looked nervous.

"Yes, my Lady."

If Rebecca wished to forget the confusing feelings this morning had stirred up, she needed a distraction.

"I command you to tell me all."

James towelled his hair, the fair locks falling across his face and shoulders. The bath he had ordered on arriving home from the tennis court had done an excellent job of relaxing his aching muscles. It had been a good match. Avers had proven a proficient opponent, but James had won. A little crease appeared at the corner of his mouth as he thought of it.

But the curve soon straightened. Whatever game Lord Avers was playing off the court, James did not appreciate it. He threw the towel over the chair beside the copper bath. Choosing not to call his valet, he shrugged himself into his shirt, stockings and breeches. Pushing the towel out of the way, he slumped into the seat, tiredness washing over him. He stared into the middle distance, thinking.

Avers had been provoking him on purpose today. He had initially liked the man whom he'd come to know through his brother-in-law, but his behaviour recently was... vexing. Perhaps the man was more like his aunt than James had realised. Avers knew of the rejected proposal between him and Rebecca and had no problem in mentioning it. Not only that, but he was openly flirting with Rebecca in front of him.

Playing for the ladies' honour! It was that kind of flirting that James had never been adept at. Then again, he wasn't sure he wished to be. He had found out the emptiness of people's verbal sentiments when his father had died. No previous professions of friendship or affection for the Worth family seemed to carry through scandal and debt. James had learned words were meaningless where actions did not follow.

His mind drew from memory the face of Rebecca. Had she been flattered by Lord Avers' words? She had always been a wit herself. They were well matched in that regard. He had seen them talking freely at the game. Far more freely than she had ever spoken to James. He sighed, rubbing a hand around the back of his neck and feeling the heat there.

He rose from his chair and went over to the dressing room window, throwing it up and letting the cool air blast through his shirt. He took a deep breath, as if he hadn't been breathing this whole time.

He had to let her go. She wasn't his.

Lady Goring's attempts to throw her daughter before James were as transparent as window glass. He would not be rude to the girl, no matter the irritation her mother caused. But Avers seemed to take James' politeness to Lady Sophia as licence to flirt with Rebecca. Then again, what was James expecting—for no man to do so ever again? He had no right to be possessive.

James took another deep breath, his fingers digging into the wood of the window frame. He clamped his mouth shut again and ground his teeth, making the muscle at the side of his jaw bulge. He could not remove Rebecca's face from his mind. He had not played for Lady Sophia. No, not for her...

Rebecca's deep brown eyes stared back at him from his memories. Full rose lips, curving up in a smile. The line of her neck, and her fair skin. The kindness in those eyes. That's what cut him to the quick. Not Rebecca's beauty, but herself. He had not only seen her speak to Avers at the match, but also to the shy Lady Sophia, speaking gently and coaxing the woman from her shell. He had seen her do that before. It was that part of Rebecca that made him...

"My Lord."

Had that been knocking at the door? James hadn't noticed. He turned, and was surprised by the figure on the threshold.

"Safi—what are you doing here?"

"My Lord." Safi bowed. "Forgive my intrusion, but I thought you would want the news immediately on my return."

"What's wrong with your eye?"

Safi looked as though he were perpetually winking. As James took in the swelling, he also noticed a tear to the seam of his servant's coat. James stepped forward.

"Tell me."

"Godrich, my Lord," Safi said, his face an emotionless mask. "He threw me from Worth Manor when I found discrepancies in the estate accounts. I have travelled without ceasing for the past two days so that I could deliver the news. I expect he will have sent a letter to discredit me."

"Two days—what happened to the horse I sent you with?"

"He would not let me take it. He had me barred from the stables."

James sucked in a breath, letting it hiss back through his teeth on the exhale. He pushed thoughts of Rebecca from his mind.

"I have not gone through my correspondence today. I've been otherwise engaged. Come with me and we'll get that eye seen to."

"I am well, my Lord."

"Good. That means you can walk yourself down to my study where I will have that eye seen to," said James sternly, walking towards Safi who moved aside for him to pass.

James strode through his house, Safi following behind, and rang the bell as soon as they entered the study.

"A raw steak," he ordered from the servant who appeared and then turned back to Safi. The man still stood to attention and James couldn't help but sigh at the sight of him.

"I'm sorry, Safi, I should not have let you go alone."

"Do not apologise for another man's actions. However ignorant the man," Safi added, his usual restraint temporarily suspended.

James nodded unconvinced. "Sit down," he commanded. "Now," he added when Safi looked ready to refuse.

James poured two brandies and handed one to Safi.

"Let me see it." Again, he spoke it as a command, knowing that Safi would refuse if he asked.

The man tilted his head back. James could see the swelling had nearly shut Safi's right eye. There was a split in the skin across his cheekbone.

"Can you still see?"

"When I hold the eyelid open, yes."

"That is a good thing. Are you hurt elsewhere?"

Safi hesitated and then gestured to his abdomen, wincing as he did so.

"Likely broken ribs. At least your lungs weren't punctured or you'd not have made it back."

"I am a blessed man."

The expressionless tone Safi used made it impossible for James to know whether he was in earnest.

The servant who had been dispatched to fetch the steak reappeared and James took the meat from him, dismissing him again.

"Swallow your drink—doctor's orders."

He waited for Safi to down the brandy, a puckered expression taking over his face before it relaxed again. Then James took the steak and placed it carefully over Safi's eye.

"My sister says it is the best cure for bruises."

"I look forward to meeting her and thanking her for her expertise," Safi replied.

"Now let's see what Godrich has sent to explain himself."

James turned to his desk and picked up the day's post, flicking through the invitations that had been delivered until he came across several letters. Eventually he opened one from Godrich and read it in silence.

"Well," he said, when he came to its end. "According to Godrich you have stolen my silver, Safi, and been drinking all of my fine wines."

"Yes, my Lord, and rather than using common sense and running with my stolen goods, I have chosen to return to you."

"Hmm." James' brows rose as a wry grin spread across his countenance. "I'd have more chance believing Godrich if he hadn't mentioned the silver. That was sold long before father died. Not that I would believe it anyway."

"I appreciate your faith in me, my Lord."

"I appreciate your loyalty, despite such treatment." James rubbed the back of his neck, the letter crumpling between his fingers. "What to do."

"I have a suggestion."

"Oh?"

"If you will permit me to travel with a sealed letter from yourself with Mr Godrich's dismissal by your hand, I might dislodge him from Worth Manor. We were making good progress until I went through the accounts."

James considered the suggestion.

"Very well, but I won't send you back until I've engaged some men to return with you. And you shall return not as my servant, but as the new steward of Worth Manor."

"I'm honoured."

"It is deserved. In the meantime, you might go to the

Royal Academy's Exhibition with myself and my sister to find new paintings for the Manor."

"As you wish, my Lord."

"Another?" James tipped his glass towards Safi.

"No, thank you, my Lord."

"Tell me, how does the place look?" James asked, settling into a chair opposite.

"Now that much of the house has been opened up, aired and mended, it is looking very fine. It would make an excellent family home."

James ran through his memories, back to his childhood, trying to remember the place as he had grown up. It had not felt like a home at the end.

"My sister will be pleased."

The conversation lapsed into silence.

"Tell me, Safi, how would you deal with a competitor... in business?"

"Competitor?" Safi's one good eye filled with curiosity, resting on his Lordship. "If I remember rightly when we were competing with Everett, you chose to show that the value of our product was superior to his, and eventually he agreed to back us instead of continuing to compete."

"Hmm," James murmured, eyes on the desk littered with ledgers and papers.

"Time always tells," Safi added.

"Wise words," James replied. "Go and rest now. I'll order you a bath."

Safi rose and bowed, leaving the study.

Alone once again, James mused on his new steward's words. *Time always tells.* But what would time tell for Rebecca, for Avers and for James?

CHAPTER EIGHT

It had been five days since the tennis match in James Street and the event had not left Rebecca's mind for a moment. Lord Avers' mysterious words at the match about losing hearts, and what Maisy had learned from the Gorings' maid, had set Rebecca's inquisitive mind whirring.

According to Maisy, Mr Malvon—Lady Sophia's previous suitor—had been sending secret letters to the young woman for several weeks now. Lady Sophia might have given the public appearance of cutting him in accordance with her mother's wishes, but her acceptance of his letters, even though she did not reply to them—what did that mean? That question had not left Rebecca alone.

The recent meetings with Lady Sophia went through Rebecca's mind. On every occasion it had been clear that Lady Goring was pursuing Lord Worth for her daughter. The enthusiasm for the pursuit, however, had not been shown by the daughter in question. Lady Sophia had been embarrassed by her mother's obviousness at the Mires' party. She had apologised on Lady Goring's behalf for her cruelty in revealing the proposal between Rebecca and James. She had even said she was at the tennis match five days ago for her cousin's sake, not to see the eligible Lord Worth play.

Rebecca knew it was not her place to get involved, but the idea Lady Sophia was not happy played on her mind. Besides, if Lady Sophia was supposed to be a good match for James, then Rebecca needed to be sure she was not in love with someone else.

From her acquaintances, Rebecca had gathered that Mr Malvon was from a respectable family in Essex. He had no title, but he did own a small estate specialising in apple growing and providing a modest income. He was therefore not from the echelon of Society that Lady Goring might aspire to for her daughter, but he was hardly the ineligible match Rebecca and the rest of the ton had been led to believe by rumours. Rumours that he was a poor tradesman's son with no fortune. Rumours, Rebecca had no doubt in her mind, that started and ended with Lady Goring.

Yes, Rebecca would have to listen to her heart and help the girl. And wasn't it the least she could do for James, to ensure that Lady Sophia was not attached to another? Yes, those were the only reasons she was getting involved—for James and Lady Sophia's sake.

It had been fortunate, then, that Rebecca should find out that Lady Sophia was due to attend the Royal Academy's Exhibition. It was the ideal place to try and catch her alone and offer aid. That was what had brought Rebecca here with a companion she had managed to secure at short notice.

"You walk apace, Lady Rebecca," Avers remarked as she tugged at his arm.

Rebecca checked herself. "I am just eager to see the paintings," she replied, bestowing a disarming smile on her escort.

Rebecca had tried to persuade her sister to go with her, but Rachel was feeling increasingly tired and had cried off in favour of a luxurious nap. It seemed providence was on Rebecca's side, or perhaps playing some sort of joke on her. For Lord Avers had paid a morning call to the Arleighs to discuss a horse he was thinking of buying, and he had offered to escort her.

"And my aunt and cousin?"

Rebecca had been needling Avers for information on their way here. Apparently she had not been as inconspicuous as she had thought. She never was good at dissembling. Her skill laying far more in directness.

"I so enjoyed speaking with your cousin at the match, I confess I am rather keen to see her again."

"She's a good girl," Avers replied, an authenticity in his tone at other times lacking. "And your eagerness has nothing to do," he said, his amused tone returning, "with the attendance of a certain Lord, does it?"

Rebecca narrowed her eyes at him, but he was nodding towards the crowd that swelled the entrance to the auctioneers in Pall Mall. She followed his line of sight and saw ahead the familiar set of broad shoulders, the fair hair tied back at the nape, and a glimpse of the strong profile. James. In spite of herself, she felt the breath catch in her throat a little. Memories of James on the tennis court, powerful and fierce, came back to her. As she looked at him now, she had to acknowledge her view of him was altered through the lens of that memory.

She cleared her throat. "Why are you so intent on provoking me?"

"The honest answer?" Avers asked, turning his gaze towards her.

She saw a glint of challenge in their depths. She nodded as they both stepped forward again in the swell.

"I wish to know," Avers said, leaning in close so that no one else might overhear, "what feelings lie between yourself and Lord Worth."

Rebecca was too stunned by the blunt statement that she could not answer immediately. What Avers had said was not a proper thing to say to a lady. She had expected candour, yes, but not such a direct question! Usually a fan of frankness, Rebecca found the breath squeezed from her chest, and when she tried to speak, it came out in stutters.

"Well... I... it's not—oh!" She threw her free hand up in the air in exasperation. "What business is it of yours?"

Avers shrugged, the action belying the look of seriousness on his usually amused face, "I have a cousin whom I care for very much, whose heart is tender, and I do not wish for her affections to become engaged to one who loves another." He grimaced. "That is not a pleasant position to be in."

"Is that why you wished to escort me here—to interrogate me?" Rebecca replied, her dark brow arching accusingly at him.

"Yes," he said simply. "But I am equally as sure that you wished for me to escort you for your own purposes. Didn't you? To see a certain Lord?"

"Absolutely not." To that question Rebecca could reply earnestly and with asperity.

She only hoped he would not ask about her feelings again. She had absolutely no desire to face them. Since the night that Lady Goring had spread the story of James' proposal, Rebecca had found them far too overwhelming to face. They were locked away and she had no intention of using the key.

"I cannot speak of Lord Worth's feelings," she said, "but I refused his offer of marriage and time cannot be turned back. He has told me himself he will not offer for me again."

She said it with curt pragmatism, but beneath the exterior was a feeling of discomfort. Or was it pain?

"Well, in that case I am at your service." Avers halted in the crowd, causing several protestations from those behind them. He bowed reverently towards her. "In my weaker moments, *incomparable*, I would most certainly offer for you."

Rebecca huffed. "Oh, do stop talking nonsense, Lord Avers. All of Society knows you shall never marry."

"And all of Society is right," he murmured. "So how shall I be of assistance to you then, my Lady. Are you intending on purchasing work today?"

"I *intend*," said Rebecca with feeling, "to see your cousin —if we can find her in this swell."

Their conversation came to an end as they approached the door to the main rooms and had to concentrate on negotiating the crowds.

Once inside, the throng dispersed to gaze up at the myriad of paintings that hung from near floor to ceiling. It allowed Rebecca to see more clearly who was there, and up ahead, she spied Lady Goring and her daughter.

"Caro, do stop fussing and try to enjoy this—I need your help in selecting the paintings and you're the only one who knows Worth Manor," said James sternly. A moment later he squeezed the hand she had placed on his arm and whispered, "Little Anne will be quite all right without you for a few hours."

He straightened and turned to address Safi who was following just behind them. "You have the list of paintings that the Manor lost?"

Safi stepped forward, drawing a paper from his breast pocket, and offering it to James.

"Yes, my Lord, I drew it up this morning. Seven in all."

"You are my brother's right-hand man, by all accounts," said Caro, smiling at the servant.

"I do as my Lord bids," Safi replied, falling behind as the crowds swelled around them.

"Which apparently includes confronting corrupt stewards. We are indebted to you for what you uncovered, I thank you"—Caro's tone turned from earnest to light—"and today, my Lord will do as I bid." She plucked the paper from James' hand and opened it.

"As will I," murmured Safi from behind her.

Caro turned, gave Safi a mischievous wink and said, "I think I shall like you, Mr Mamadou."

Safi closed his eyes in an expressively slow way, inclining his head.

"Ignore her, Safi, she is drunk with power," said James.

Caro gasped. "What? A joke. I had not thought it of you, brother. Do I take it from your good mood that you won the tennis match against Lord Avers?"

James grimaced. "I did."

Caro's fine brow puckered. "Oh? You don't seem happy about it."

"It doesn't matter." James waved a hand. "Tell me the size of the paintings so we might know what we're looking for."

A great cross-section of London society swathed the hallways and rooms in clusters. They chattered and pointed, some even collaring the artists who were present, demanding explanations of their work.

Couples in plain gowns and suits denoted the middling sort, while there were individuals whose fashionable fabrics and tailoring put them a step above. Standing out from these were those dressed in fashion of the first stare, with diamond buckles adorning their shoes and emerald pins winking from their cravats. Here and there a clergyman wandered through the rooms, avoiding paintings with nudity and focusing instead on biblical or historical scenes. It was a melting pot of ranks, all drawn by aesthetic beauty to this one place.

"I hardly know where to look," said Caro, gazing up at painting upon painting, hung cheek-by-jowl.

"Agreed," James replied.

His sister hurried forward, leaving the men in her wake and moving from one painting to another, her eyes scanning upwards and side to side.

"Tell me, James," she said, reaching a hand backwards, gesturing for him to follow. "What paintings do you like?"

"Landscapes mostly—I'm not one for allegorical works—"

"This one James!" she cried, arm outstretched to a painting just above eyeline. "It's called the Madonna and Child," she said, checking the Exhibition catalogue.

"Maudlin. I told you Caroline, no allegorical works."

"It isn't maudlin or allegorical!" she exclaimed. "Just look at the compassion on Mary's face—she shows such love. It's quite beautiful," she finished wistfully. "Don't you think it would suit the hall to the chapel."

"My Lord," called Safi, pointing to a painting about ten feet up.

James and Caro wandered over to gaze up at the piece.

"She's beautiful, is she not?" asked a drawling voice.

The party turned to see Lord Avers standing behind them, Lady Rebecca on his arm. James' chest tightened at the sight of her.

"Edward I's consort removing poison from his arm wound in Palestine," said Avers.

James noted that Rebecca was not looking at the painting as the others were. Her gaze was on the far side of the room. Avers' next words brought her back and James' eyes slipped quickly from her figure.

"It's by Kauffman, I believe. Such devotion."

The party stared up at the scene. After a few moments James felt Caro slip her hand from his arm and move towards Rebecca.

"I didn't know you were coming."

He saw a private smile pass between them.

"Are you here as observers?" Caro asked, speaking now to both Avers and Rebecca.

"I certainly am," Avers replied before Rebecca could. "With the most lovely of companions."

James was irritated when he realised he was clenching his jaw. He forced himself to relax. He had been over this in his mind. It was logical to let her go. Why weren't his feelings obeying?

"And you—collector or observer, Worth?" Avers asked.

"Collector," James replied, his voice monotone. It was the best he could do.

When he was away from Rebecca, it was easy to believe his feelings under control, but then she would appear before him, and all resolve bled away. It had taken all his strength at the tennis match to appear impassive.

"Ah—for your estate's restoration. My aunt was intensely interested in it."

James replied politely, introducing Safi as the overseer of the works, and soon after Caro and Avers began conversing on the benefits of the different artists' work present. James was not involved in the conversation and was thankful for it. It was proving more and more difficult to converse with Avers when the man seemed intent on provoking him.

He noted Rebecca was not engaging in the conversation either. It was unlike her, and as he risked another glance, he saw her attention was across the other side of the room again.

"You will excuse me for a moment," she said suddenly, cutting across everyone else's conversation. "I think I see a painting by Cosway."

She did not wait to take her leave but broke away from the circle immediately. James watched her go towards the other side of the room. She stopped before a painting of some Grecian myth or other. He frowned, checking the Exhibition catalogue he had taken from Caro and noting that the painting Rebecca was looking at wasn't a Cosway. Likely she had been mistaken.

But as James continued to observe her, he noticed she was not looking at the painting at all. In fact, she was looking at Lady Goring, watching intently as the Countess partook in a serious conversation with one of the Exhibition's auctioneers.

"Well, tell me why you will not offer more? It is a Boultbee after all, and of the finest quality. I was very much offended when my secretary came back with such a low offer from your house."

Rebecca feigned interest in the painting before her as she listened to Lady Goring's conversation. She had meant to look at the painting in an attempt to gain Lady Sophia's attention so she could speak with her, but on overhearing Lady Goring's words, she had stopped to eavesdrop.

"I am sorry, my Lady, but that is the highest we can offer at this time."

"I should like to speak to the individual in charge of your establishment," Lady Goring said with a sniff, looking down her nose at the man.

"I am afraid, my Lady," said the man, not cowed by the Countess' anger, "that I am the particular individual to which you are referring. We can offer you no more than what the painting is worth."

When Lady Goring's small eyes darted around the rest of the room looking for inspiration, Rebecca's own snapped back to the painting she had been pretending to look at.

She heard Lady Goring huff angrily. "I am most displeased about the matter, but I will accept."

The gentleman gestured towards a small office off the main room and Lady Goring followed him, precluding

Rebecca from overhearing any more. After the door closed behind them, Rebecca took a deep breath, staring unseeing at the painting before her, and mulling over what she had just heard.

Stirring herself, she looked over to where she had last seen Lady Sophia waiting for her mother, and observed the young woman speaking to a gentleman.

Rebecca didn't recognise the man, but from his body language he seemed familiar with Lady Sophia, even leaning in close to say something quietly to her.

Leaving her spot by the wall, Rebecca walked over to the couple.

"Good morning, Lady Sophia." Rebecca smiled at her, and then looked at the gentleman, who had visibly jumped at the interruption. "I had hoped to find you here."

"Oh, Lady R-Rebecca," Lady Sophia stammered, turning red. "How lo-lovely to see you."

Rebecca's smile broadened, but she kept her gaze on the gentleman, waiting to be introduced. When the event did not transpire, Rebecca took the situation into her own hands and broke etiquette. "Good morning," she said with a degree of authority. "My name is Lady Rebecca Fairing. Whom might I have the pleasure of addressing?"

The gentleman looked nervously at Lady Sophia, but when she did not give him a cue, he turned back to Rebecca, swallowing.

By this time, Rebecca had a fair idea who he was. This couple had been stealing a private moment together while Lady Goring was out of the way. Now they were looking sheepish that they had been caught. Oh yes, Rebecca was certain that this gentleman was the rumoured Mr Malvon.

He was a little over average height and build, making Lady Sophia look like a veritable fairy next to him. His wool coat, though not as finely cut as some, was of very decent cloth. His cravat was without lace, but crisp white and folded neatly. He wore boots and breeches rather than leather shoes and clocked stockings and it marked him out easily as a country gentleman rather than a Town buck.

"Mr Malvon—your servant, my Lady."

As she had guessed. When he straightened from his bow, Rebecca finished her survey on his face. It was slightly round and young, his eyes dark brown and earnest, and above his clear brow was a mass of curling hair drawn back by a simple black ribbon. He was quite handsome, Rebecca mused, and she could see why he might draw a blush from his amour, Lady Sophia.

"Ah! I have heard of you," Rebecca said, offering her hand. He took it and bowed. "You are keeping Lady Sophia company while her mother—"

"Purchases a painting," Lady Sophia said hurriedly.

Rebecca's brow rose a fraction, but she did not refute the statement. This was getting more interesting by the second.

"Mr Malvon was just going," Lady Sophia said, her face so etched with emotion that Rebecca thought her resembling some saintly statue in the throes of tragedy.

"You will—" Mr Malvon had turned to Lady Sophia, a look of pleading in his eyes, but she cut him off.

"Quickly." Fear flooded her large blue eyes. "Mama is coming!"

Rebecca saw Lady Sophia press a hand to Mr Malvon's arm. There was so much exchanged in their next look that Rebecca felt like an intruder. She glanced away and saw Lady Goring exiting the office. Making a quick decision, Rebecca marched forward.

"Good morning, Lady Goring," she said loudly. "Are you in the market for a painting today like the rest of Society?" She opened her arms as if to take in the room but in actuality to obscure the woman's view.

Looking irritated at being accosted, Lady Goring spluttered a little before replying in the affirmative. Rebecca waited for no invitation to launch into a monologue on the merits of Kauffman and Cosway, further delaying Lady Goring's progress. By the time the Countess had regained control of the conversation and led them back to her daughter, Mr Malvon was nowhere to be seen.

The Countess was fanning herself in an irritated fashion when a sudden look of delight transformed her features. "Ah!" she cried. "There is Lord Worth. Quickly, Sophia—we must greet him."

Lady Sophia shot Rebecca a look that was a mixture of gratefulness and distress as she was carted away by her mother in the direction of James, Caro and Avers.

Rebecca walked back behind them, retaking her place in the circle, and to her surprise, noticed James' eyes were on her as she did so.

"You are speaking of Worth Manor's restoration?" Lady Goring said after the greetings had subsided. "I am sure it is going well."

"Better now we have some paintings." Caro smiled up at her brother. "James' man is just settling our account."

"Splendid. Well, you know my brother-in-law's estate is not far from Worth Manor. When the renovations are completed we will come and visit."

It was not a request.

"Sophia, would that not be a lovely thing, to visit Lord Worth's home?"

The Countess was as subtle as a ton of the finest bricks.

"Lord Worth, what do you think?"

Rebecca waited for his response, as did the rest of the circle, but he said nothing. Upon his silence, she turned and saw that his eyes were still on her in all their blue intenseness. She flushed. Why was he staring at her like that?

"Lord Worth?" Lady Goring said sharply.

The spell was broken. James begged forgiveness and asked that Lady Goring might repeat her question.

She did so, much to her vexation, but Rebecca did not hear the rest of the polite conversation that transpired. She was too busy being torn between a desire to look at Lady Sophia after that intriguing encounter with Mr Malvon, and a desire to glance back at James and see where his gaze was now.

CHAPTER NINE

26 April 1776

D*ear Aunt,*

Your last letter contained within it wise words on silence. I am afraid, while I have endeavoured to take them on board, Lady Goring has yet to be given the lesson. Your guess at this moment is most likely right. She has already told Society of my rejecting Lord Worth. In fact, her cruelty knows no bounds, for she chose to do it when both he and I stood in a gathering at a party.

I hate to wonder on what his Lordship thinks of me now. It seems Lady Goring's wretched actions were a calculated attempt to push me farther from him to make way for her daughter. I might have saved her the trouble if only she would have been so good as to ask me if there were any attachment that still lay between Lord Worth and me. I should have told her there is not...

· · ·

Rebecca paused, staring at the words she had just written for so long that the nib of her pen, poised just above the paper as it was, started to dry. Before it did completely, she re-dipped it in the pot and continued.

If Lady Goring has her way, her daughter will be married to Lord Worth before the Season's end. I am happy for him, for although Lady Goring would prove to be a dreadful mother-in-law, I am sure Lady Sophia would be a fine wife. Yes, I am happy, though there is a slight wrinkle in Lady Goring's plan which makes me think I need to investigate.

It transpires, through an innocent overhearing of my own, that Mr Malvon has been sending letters to Lady Sophia. These letters—all from Mr Malvon and none in return—are not known of by her mother. I gather if her Ladyship found out she would be less than pleased. Thankfully I, unlike Lady Goring, know how to keep a confidence. The letters are secreted inside the house by a most resourceful maid—if I were not so dearly attached to Maisy, I should consider engaging her myself.

What I overheard was confirmed by a sight I beheld at the Royal Academy's Exhibition yesterday. I saw Mr Malvon stealing a moment with Lady Sophia when the Countess was otherwise engaged. From the way they spoke to one another— though I do not know what they said—and their embarrassment upon my joining them, I have a strong suspicion that all is not lost between those two. So, as you see, there is a mystery to be solved, especially if Lord Worth is to obey Lady Goring's wishes and become attached to the girl.

I do not want you to worry about my interest in Lord Worth's courting. I do so only to ensure his happiness. I may have rejected the gentleman, but that does not mean I do not care for him. In the sisterly way, that is.

· · ·

Images of James stripped down to his shirt and at play on the tennis court came to mind. Rebecca swallowed against the fluttering in her chest.

Yes, as a sister.

She wrote deliberately.

I have resolved to speak to Lady Sophia at the next opportunity to find out if her heart really is still engaged with Mr Malvon, or if the affection only resides on his side. That at least will set my mind at rest, and I shall keep out of Lady Goring's way from then on.
   Your ever-loving and inquisitive niece,
   Rebecca

By the time she had finished writing, the candle at her desk was burned halfway down. She sanded and blotted the pages. Folding them neatly, she sealed the letter, resolving to send it with Arleigh's daily correspondence tomorrow.

She rose and rang the bell, Maisy appearing a few minutes later to help her undress.

"No matter how I like fine dresses, Maisy, it is a great relief when I am released at the end of the day."

The maid smiled. "Yes, my Lady."

She removed the unpinned gown from Rebecca's shoulders, the petticoat and hip pads beneath going shortly after.

"I have sent for the scullery maid to bank the fire, my Lady," said Maisy, beginning on her mistress' stays, pulling methodically at the silk ribbon which laced them.

"Would you fetch another candle as well? I should like to sit up for a bit."

"Yes, my Lady, though please be careful. I had it from Lady Dover's maid that her mistress' bed curtains caught fire Thursday last. Barely escaped before being burned!"

"Yes, Maisy," Rebecca said, smiling reassuringly. "Put this with Lord Arleigh's letters for the morning."

Maisy nodded, taking the letter and directing the newly arrived scullery maid to see to the fire and fetch a candle. Maisy came back a short time later to see if her mistress needed anything else before she retired.

"No, thank you, Maisy, you may go to bed."

The maid lingered, a conflicted look on her face.

"Yes?"

Maisy came back into the room with uncertain steps. "You will pardon me for saying, my Lady, but you have seemed out of sorts of late. Is there anything the matter? Anything I might do for you, my Lady?"

The frank question was so out of character for Maisy that it caught Rebecca off-guard. Before she could stop herself, the honest answer came to mind—words that she had chosen not to write in the letter to her aunt. A flood of emotion Rebecca had been keeping at bay came over her.

"You are—" Rebecca couldn't finish her sentence with a lump forming in her throat.

The answers loomed in the front of her mind. Yes, there was a great deal the matter. James likely loathed her for allowing Lady Goring to find out about his rejection. The knowledge that he may harbour such feelings towards her rested like a lead weight on her chest.

In the meantime, Lady Goring had made it her mission to slight Rebecca at every turn. While she was usually immune to such pettiness, the Countess seemed to find the cracks in her armour every time. Worse still, she couldn't seem to rally in the moments after the Countess' attacks. That made it worse.

It had happened again yesterday at the Exhibition. Lady Goring had taken great delight standing next to Rebecca and pointing out how well James and Lady Sophia looked together. Not like Rebecca and James might look, the Countess had confirmed. No—Rebecca was too tall and dark next to Lord Worth.

Rebecca had remained silent. Silent! How had she not been able to think of one rejoinder? All that had been going through her mind was that James and Lady Sophia *did* look well together. Perhaps it was not just politeness on James' part. Perhaps his feelings were as warm towards Lady Sophia as they were cold towards Rebecca. It had paralysed her.

That same feeling of paralysis had just come back. What if Rebecca discovered Lady Sophia *was* free to attach herself to James? What then?

Before the feelings could engulf her completely, she cleared her throat to answer.

"You are too kind to a temperamental mistress," she said at last, her voice moving from uncertain to steady. "But there is nothing you can do for me more than you already do."

Maisy's face broke into a smile at the compliment.

"Might you want a hot chocolate, my Lady?"

"No, thank you. Now off to bed with you Maisy," said Rebecca, her imperious tones returning as the feelings subsided.

The maid bobbed a final curtsey and left Rebecca alone. She wasn't sure how long she stayed up staring into the fire. But it was long enough to gain mastery over the feelings that had threatened to overwhelm her and to refocus on the task at hand. She must speak to Lady Sophia.

Despite Society's general dislike of Lady Goring, whenever that lady chose to host an event and invite the cream of the ton, no one dared refuse the keeper of such salacious secrets. That was not the reason for James' appearance here this evening, however. No, James had suspicions. Thanks to Rebecca's behaviour at both the tennis match and the Exhibition, he believed she was up to something. He had known her long enough to see the look in her eyes when she caught the scent of some drama or other. Her behaviour at the Exhibition had been one of distraction and her interest in Lady Goring's affairs overt.

"Lord Worth, I am so pleased you chose to leave your estate accounts for an evening and spend it with my daughter and me," purred Lady Goring, elbowing Lady Sophia forward.

James took the young lady's hand, kissing the air above it, and saying something polite about the rooms.

"My daughter had so particularly wished to show you some of her late papa's painting collection, after your interest at the Exhibition—you will allow her, of course?" Lady Goring said without pause.

James looked about the room. Rebecca was standing with Lord Avers and several other gentlemen and ladies whom James was not acquainted with. He would have to bide his time to speak to her.

"Of course," he said, offering his arm to Lady Sophia.

"Splendid! Splendid! You two have fun," Lady Goring said.

James grimaced at the glee in Lady Goring's voice, hoping that Lady Sophia only saw his actions as polite, not anything more. Lady Goring's machinations were plain as day, but James was not entertaining them. He was being polite so as to save her daughter any embarrassment, but that was all.

"Over here," the young lady said quietly, pointing a gloved finger at a trio of paintings on the far wall of the room.

"This one is by Boultbee." She gestured to the first. "My father was a great admirer of equestrian art."

"He was a renowned horseman—my own father used to speak of his prowess," James said, the memory of his father coming out before he could check himself. He clamped his mouth shut behind the words, angry he should have exposed a vulnerability so easily, and worse, that he should make this woman feel uncomfortable with the reference.

"He would have been happy to hear it," said Lady Sophia, smiling. "He always enjoyed people complimenting it."

There had been no awkward look, no embarrassed expression. It was as if she did not know his father had been a wastrel Lord, too addicted to gaming to care for his own family, dying in penury. But everyone knew, and that meant Lady Sophia was choosing not to react. It spoke volumes of her character.

"What do you think of it?" he asked, voice softer than before.

"I think it fine," said Lady Sophia. "This next one is a romantic piece—Paris and Helen before the Trojans arrived."

The couple in question were suitably attired in ancient clothes and laid together on a scroll-sided chaise longue, fruit and drink scattered across the floor. A ship, likely the Achaeans, could be seen sailing toward them through a window. The lovers, oblivious to the fate their actions instigated, were looking into each other's eyes as if nothing else existed.

"What do you think of it?" Lady Sophia asked.

James studied it. "I am not one for classical works, but this is—" He broke off, looking again at the couple and finding himself caught by their attention for one another.

"Yes?"

"An emotional piece," he finished. "It certainly captures their love—as if nothing else in the world matters."

"Yes," she said softly, a far-off look in her eyes.

"Do you like it?"

"It is very fine," she replied.

A slight crease appeared between James' brows. She was a sweet girl, that was clear, but so reserved.

"This is the final piece."

"This one I like," said James.

"Oh good," replied Lady Sophia politely. "It is a view of Sussex by a painter my uncle had in residence. It is likely a view near your own estate. I expect that is why you like it."

The comment surprised James. Like Sussex? He had not thought that possible, but as he looked at the pastoral scene before him, he felt a faint twinge of nostalgia deep in his chest.

"I expect so," he said. "And do you like it?"

"If you do, I am sure it is worth my admiration as well."

The ease with which she gave up her opinion to another sent a wave of irritation through James. He checked himself. There was nothing wrong with this young woman being amenable. She was only being polite. Yet, he felt in that moment he would have preferred if she challenged him with her own opinion.

It made him think of another. A woman who did not hesitate to provoke him, with a mind full of mischief and a penchant for getting coiled up in another's troubles. He looked around the room—where was she? He needed a word with her. But Avers was alone, and Rebecca was nowhere to be seen.

At that very moment, Rebecca was treading carefully along the upstairs corridor of the Gorings' Town house in search of Lady Sophia's room. She had sent a servant with a note for Lady Sophia to meet her up here and she should receive it soon.

The heels of her silk mules clipped on a bare floorboard as she tried to keep in the side shadows of the passage. Not wishing to attract attention, she raised herself onto the balls of her feet. She didn't need a servant running off to tell the Countess that Lady Rebecca was wandering around her house unattended.

She was part way down the corridor now. To her left, a staircase led to the third floor. She discounted that—it would be the servants' quarters. Beyond this were several doors and she peeked in the first. A guest room. She moved on to the next, noticing a patch on the wall between the doors which was oddly bare—a picture hook in place with nothing hanging from it. The next room was equally unfruitful, so she tried the following. She passed another patch of bare wall between the doors. Rebecca frowned.

She reached the end of the corridor having checked all the doors along one side. Turning to try the other her gaze swept the length of the hall, the pattern of missing paintings now standing out to her in the candlelit space. It was odd. She shook her head. There was not time to consider the mystery, she must focus on the task at hand. Steeling herself, she approached the first door in the opposite wall, stretching out her hand. Just before she reached the handle, the door was opened, and a maid came out.

Rebecca jerked backwards and froze. The maid stumbled to a halt, eyes wide.

"Sweet Mary!" The servant gasped, almost dropping the linens in her hand.

"No," said Rebecca, schooling her countenance into one that contained no ounce of sheepishness. "Lady Rebecca Fairing." She extracted her fan from her pocket and wafted herself as if she were standing on some terrace with a handsome admirer, not in the dingy upper hallway of the Gorings' Town house. "If you will be so kind as to show me to Lady Sophia's room, she is expecting me."

"But Lady Sophia is at the party, Lady—Rebecca." The maid eyed her suspiciously.

Rebecca snapped the fan shut and pointed it accusingly at the servant. "You are her maid, are you not?"

"I am, my Lady," said the maid, forced onto the backfoot both literally and figuratively.

"Then you know the importance of discretion—for instance, with correspondence, or..." She let the hint drop into the water between them and slowly sink down. "...meeting a friend for a quiet word."

The maid looked at her with narrowing eyes, but after a few seconds she nodded.

"You're right, my Lady, that I do. That's Lady Sophia's door, just there." She gestured to the next one along.

At that moment, a woman appeared from the servants' stairs, her dress denoting her as another lady's maid. She paused at the bottom of the steps. Sharp eyes picked out the two women in the gloom, and she stared at them silently.

"Sweet Joseph," the maid breathed next to Rebecca.

"Miss Dent?"

The maid, so terrified of the other servant giving them the evil eye, nodded absentmindedly.

"Then you had better hurry and tell Lady Sophia to be on her way."

Rebecca looked back at the woman. Miss Dent was still staring at them accusingly. Rebecca raised her chin an inch higher so that she might look down her nose at the woman and then whisked past the maid and entered Lady Sophia's room.

As soon as she closed the door, she pressed an ear against it. She couldn't hear any speaking on the other side—only the sound of feet retreating rapidly down the hall. She hoped that the maid might reach Lady Sophia before Miss Dent reached her mother.

CHAPTER TEN

There was a timid knock at Lady Sophia's bedroom door.

"Enter," Rebecca called, placing her fan on the dressing table and looking up tentatively.

It was with an inward sigh of relief that she saw Lady Sophia come into the room. The young lady offered a polite curtsey before shutting the door, and then turned a bewildered expression on her summoner.

"Lady Rebecca, you sent for me?"

"Yes, and dreadfully rude it was of me too, to invade your bedroom and summon you like a servant, but I'm afraid it was the only way I could think to speak to you without your mama present. She does so love to interrupt." Rebecca rose. "Come, here, I can at least offer you your own chair."

There was no other in the room.

"Oh please," said Lady Sophia, going to sit on the bed and offering the seat back to Rebecca.

"No, no." Rebecca waggled her closed fan. "If you will permit me, I shall do quite well perched on the edge of the bed."

Lady Sophia reluctantly nodded and took the cushioned

chair by her dressing table. The light of the fire caught the side of the young woman's face revealing her fine skin and blue eyes.

"You really are rather pretty, my dear Lady Sophia."

The young lady blushed deeply.

"Oh, I am sorry—I did not mean to embarrass you. It's just that you don't seem to realise how pretty you are. I am a little forthright in my speech, and as you can see by my summoning you to your own bedroom, in my actions too."

"What can I do for you, Lady Rebecca?"

"I told you, Rebecca please." In truth, now that Rebecca was here, she suddenly felt the immense delicacy of the situation and hardly knew where to start.

"Rebecca," said Lady Sophia obediently.

"I have come—that is to say, I have come to speak to you about Mr Malvon." The name came out more bluntly than Rebecca intended, and she saw another blush overtake Lady Sophia's cheeks.

"I mustn't speak of him," the young lady whispered.

"Mustn't?"

"I—" she broke off, clamping her mouth shut.

"I am here because I know that your mother has set your cap, on your behalf, at Lord Worth."

"Oh, please, I am so sorry. My mama is insensitive some-times," Lady Sophia said before Rebecca could continue. "I have no desire to come between you and Lord Worth, I promise."

Rebecca's brows drew together, and she smiled softly. "Oh, my dear, you are the sweetest creature, but you need not worry on that count." She took on a look of impassivity and felt a little tension around her mouth as she prepared to say her next words. "There is nothing for you to come between. No, I am not here about that, but rather I am here about Mr Malvon."

"I mustn't speak of him," Lady Sophia repeated, her clasped hands twisting in her lap.

"You may with me," said Rebecca kindly. "I know he has been writing to you. You need not worry," she added quickly. "I shall not tell anyone. But it seems your Mr Malvon still cares for you very deeply."

At that, Lady Sophia burst into tears.

"Oh!" cried Rebecca, flying up from her seat and going over to her. "My dear, I did not mean to make you cry. Please forgive me for accosting you so bluntly. It is only that I wish to help you."

"Help me?" Lady Sophia looked up from the hands in which she had buried her face, tears still fresh in her eyes and a look of despair on her countenance.

"Why don't you tell your mother the truth?" Rebecca urged. "There is no lawful reason why you could not marry Mr Malvon."

"It is not that simple." Lady Sophia turned away, dabbing her face with a handkerchief.

At the sight of Lady Sophia's despair, Rebecca felt her heart lurch. The emotions she was doing so well at controlling roiled within her and she had a sudden urge to cry herself.

"I am determined that something may be done," she said, swallowing the lump in her throat.

Lady Sophia smiled weakly. "You sound like Mr Malvon, but he doesn't understand. Mama has made it clear—there are other things I must consider in the match I make." She did not elaborate. "But I have never had any intentions towards Lord Worth, though Mama may wish it. She cannot see, but he is nothing more than polite to me, and that is why she is so... why she treats you as she does. She can see the way he looks at you, just as I can."

Rebecca was stunned by the assertion.

"I think you are mistaken," she managed to choke out. She

fell silent soon after, the import of Lady Sophia's words making her forget her mission.

"Lady Rebecca," came a cold voice from the doorway.

Both women visibly jumped, having not heard the door open, and turned to see a most displeased Lady Goring glaring at them from the threshold.

"I find you have taken advantage of my hospitality by trespassing in our private rooms."

Rebecca jerked her head round quickly to Lady Sophia, whispering, "We must speak again," before Lady Goring could stop her.

"Lady Rebecca!" the Countess barked, like some lapdog whose territory had been invaded.

"You will forgive me for wishing for a private tête-à-tête with your delightful daughter." Rebecca rose, drawing her shoulders back as she turned to face Lady Goring.

She would not allow this woman to continually overset her. As she drew to her full height, the older woman, who had seemed so ghastly over the past few weeks, was shown to be at least five inches shorter than herself. It gave Rebecca a boost of confidence, and she put on her most imperious look, jutting out her chin and looking down her fine nose at the Countess —in spite of the embarrassing position she had just been caught in.

"You'll understand," Rebecca said casually, "that when one sees a dress one admires, one must simply find out all there is to know about its construction." She pointed a fan at Lady Sophia's cream botanical gown.

"You might have had a quiet word downstairs." Lady Goring's eyes narrowed, darting between the face of her daughter and Rebecca.

Rebecca risked a glance at Lady Sophia and saw the telltale signs of recently dried tears on the slightly reddened cheeks. Did Lady Goring see it too?

"Sophia, come—Lord Worth is asking after you."

Rebecca's face remained expressionless as Lady Goring searched it for a reaction.

"Yes, come, my dear," Rebecca said with sudden enthusiasm. "Let's rejoin the party." She reached down and took Lady Sophia's hand, leading both of them past Lady Goring whose eyes were now blazing with such anger, Rebecca thought herself at risk of catching fire.

As they walked back downstairs, Lady Goring snapping at their heels, Rebecca felt a flood of vindication. She had been right. Lady Sophia had feelings for Mr Malvon—that much was clear. Now all she needed to do was resolve whatever was stopping them from being together.

***

"Where have you been?" Avers whispered in Rebecca's ear when she returned to the party.

"Oh, nowhere really." She waved a hand around the room.

"Wherever it was, I hazard you found some amusement. There is a light in your eyes that was not there before."

"Perhaps you should look less at my eyes and more to the happiness of your cousin," said Rebecca acidly. "Wasn't it a concern for her heart that you spoke of the other day at the tennis match?"

Avers brows rose. "Ah, my cousin interests you?"

"Interests? You sound so heartless. Can you not see her suffering?"

"I see many things, Lady Rebecca," said Avers with an uncharacteristic coolness, "but there are some things in life one can do nothing about."

"I had not thought you so poor-hearted, Lord Avers."

"You mistake me, Lady Rebecca. I have no heart, as the ladies of my acquaintance well know. But your defiance is admirable. I take it from my aunt's furious countenance that you have been stirring up trouble where my cousin is concerned." His eyes moved in an exaggerated way to the other side of the room.

Rebecca saw Lady Goring glaring at her.

"Not trouble."

"I sincerely hope not, for my cousin's sake. Ah, speak of an angel and she shall appear. Sweet cousin, Lord Worth."

The couple joined Avers and Rebecca. Lady Sophia's eyes were on the floor, her face looking listless, no doubt forced by her mother back onto James' arm. When Rebecca looked at Lord Worth, she realised he was not attending the woman on his arm. No—he was looking at her with an intensity in his blue eyes that caused her breath to catch.

Rebecca had finally reappeared, and James had every intention of finding out exactly what she was up to. Even the sight of Avers murmuring in her ear did not put him off.

"Good ev—"

"Lord Worth." Lady Goring's grating voice came from behind him. He had just escaped that infernal woman.

"I think there is one more painting in the salon you may be interested in. Sophia, you will show Lord Worth."

Another of the Countess' unassailable commands.

James looked down at the girl beside him and saw the unhappiness on her face.

"In a moment," James said. "I wished to greet Lady Rebecca and Lord Avers, and your daughter is being good enough to accompany me."

"Well," Lady Goring said, fanning herself and casting a narrow-eyed glare at Rebecca. The Countess stayed where she was, apparently insensitive to the palpable tension in the circle.

"Aunt, you always know just what to say," Avers mocked and shifted his gaze to Rebecca and Lady Sophia. "You two are becoming quite bosom beaus are you not?"

"They are indeed." From the relish in Lady Goring's voice and the sudden look of concern on Rebecca's face, James guessed Avers had said the wrong thing.

"In fact, they have been scurrying away from the party to have little conversations without us. I am not surprised though," she said, continuing to fan herself—but the look in her eyes had changed from one of anger to one of predatory pleasure. She moved over to Rebecca as if she were about to whisper something quietly in her ear. The voice Lady Goring used, however, was nothing akin to a whisper. It was loud enough for the whole company to hear.

"It can be hard to see the success of other ladies when one is nowhere near to making a match oneself." Lady Goring turned to the others, "Please, chat amongst yourselves while I have a little word with Lady Rebecca."

Of course, with that command, all conversation that might have been attempted dissipated, and the three others were left listening as hard as ever to Lady Goring's words.

"One can hardly blame you for being a little jealous, especially where a certain gentleman is concerned, but I would ask you not to interfere with my daughter's prospects. There are gentlemen present who would appreciate her company and she can hardly fulfil those desires..." she said, looking pointedly over at James—though her words were as plain as the nose on her face, so the exaggerated look was hardly needed—"... when you're disappearing with her."

James felt Lady Sophia's hand tense on his arm. The trio next to Lady Goring and Rebecca exchanged gazes. James needed to stop this, but he could hardly do so without making Rebecca's position worse. It was clear Lady Goring was warning her off under some mistaken belief that James held affection for her daughter.

"Not that I wish to be uncouth, of course, only it is a little obvious, Lady Rebecca, and seeing as we are friends, and your mother and aunt are not here to guide you, I thought it best to mention it."

The woman's barbed tongue took no prisoners.

"Mama," whispered Lady Sophia, reaching forward to touch Lady Goring's shoulder.

"No, no, Sophia." Lady Goring brushed her off, turning back to Rebecca, her voice as loud as ever.

Avers tried to strike up a conversation on horseflesh as a distraction.

"Lady Goring—" Rebecca started.

"I say it for your own good, Lady Rebecca. I know you are used to having the sway of the eligible men present, but I think it time you realise you are several Seasons past, my dear. You must not ruin another's chances, even if you regret the decisions you have made."

She was going too far. James was about to step in when Rebecca rallied again.

"I had no intention of—"

But Lady Goring had full command of the conversation and she would not let it go.

"I'm sure not." A patronising smile took over the Countess' face. "But selfishness is such an ugly trait."

Lady Sophia gasped at James' side. His chest contracted. Were those tears in Rebecca's eyes or was it just the way the candlelight caught in them? The barb had drawn blood.

"That's enough, aunt," Avers snapped. He carried on in more moderate tones. "Will you not both rejoin the circle? We are eager for your conversation. I was just talking about the horse I've bought."

Lady Goring had flashed a look of fury at her nephew, but then a sly smile spread over her face. "I see you are not quite out of suitors yet, Lady Rebecca," she said in her false whisper, eyeing her nephew. "Shall we rejoin the party now we've had our little chat?"

Lady Goring turned with exaggerated movements towards the rest of the gathering, as if she really had been having a private word with Rebecca. The latter was frozen in her place. James saw embarrassment etched onto every feature of her face.

"You will excuse me," Rebecca said. Now her face had turned pale and pinched as if she were in pain.

"So soon?" Lady Goring asked innocently, stepping back so as to expose Rebecca to all their stares. "Well, if you insist. Sophia, I'm sure Lord Worth would like to see that painting now."

James saw Rebecca inhale, as if to say something, but then she let the breath escape, no words coming with it. His emotions, building throughout the exchange, were on the brink of boiling over.

He cleared his throat, but it was too late. Rebecca, having taken her leave, turned on her heel and departed. He saw an ugly look of satisfaction on Lady Goring's face. Lady Sophia looked horrified beside him and even Avers was grimacing. He watched after Rebecca's figure. He had never seen her retreat before.

Bowing quickly to Lady Goring, going only as low as civility dictated, he said curtly, "You will excuse me."

"But the painting—" cried Lady Goring.

"I shall come with you, Lord Worth," said Lady Sophia.

"No, Sophia!" Lady Goring snapped. "She is only making a show for attention. That's why I thought it prudent to be frank. Some ladies can be so sensitive to the truth." The Countess spoke the words with a wicked smile on her powdered face. "You will see the painting, Sophia!"

James felt his temper rising at the delay. When he had finally cried off sufficiently for Lady Goring to begrudgingly accept it, and he and Lady Sophia had made it to the door, Rebecca had already left the Gorings' home.

He cursed inwardly. Whatever Rebecca was up to, she had considered it worth risking the wrath of Lady Goring's vicious tongue, and she had taken the beating. He had an inkling Lady Sophia's upset was to do with it.

He must speak to her, but there was no way to do so tonight without causing talk. He could hardly turn up at the Arleighs' for a private interview with Rebecca at this time of night. That being said, he had no intention of staying here after what had just happened. Making his apologies to Lady Sophia, he left, resolving to call on Rebecca in the morning.

CHAPTER ELEVEN

When James and his sister were announced at the Arleighs' home the following morning, he braced himself for an awkward reception. He had not called on Rebecca since before he had proposed. At least Caro was with him. She had agreed, reluctantly, to leave little Anne at home and come with her brother after hearing the ordeal Lady Goring had put Rebecca through.

James had not explained his ulterior motives for calling on the Arleighs. Until he knew for certain what Rebecca was about, he did not wish to share his suspicions. Caro would try to dissuade him from getting involved. She had only spoken of Rebecca to him when she had absolutely had to over the last three months. He had noted her active avoidance of bringing her closest friend up.

Even when he had mentioned his wish to call on Rebecca, she had looked at him with deep concern in her large blue eyes and asked if he was sure, squeezing his hand, as if he were so fragile he might break. He had replied a little too gruffly that he was fine, and he merely wished to be polite after Lady

Goring had treated Rebecca so poorly. It would be ungentle-manly of him *not* to visit, he had argued. Caro had not appeared convinced, but she had agreed to go with him.

The morning room of the Arleighs' Town house was freshly painted in a powder blue with cream woodwork around the edges. A large Persian rug in reds and blues stretched across the floor, softening James and Caro's tread, and the furniture was all in powder and aquamarine blues complementing the decor. Rachel Arleigh was reclined on a chaise longue, her burgeoning figure wrapped in an oriental banyan, with a chemisette frothing out at her bosom, and her hair in a long braid hanging off the end of the chaise. If it had not been the eccentric Lady Arleigh, James might have been surprised at her dress. As it was, his eyes only rested on her for a moment before moving on to the others.

James' hackles rose as he recognised Lord Avers sat on a second chaise longue next to Rebecca. The gentleman was leaning in to her, murmuring with an amused look in his hooded eyes, and Rebecca replied with a faint laugh. The servant's announcement drew her attention and her eyes connected with James. Whatever polite smile had been on her face froze and cracked away.

"Good morning," James said, showing a leg and bowing to the room.

"Good morning," Caro echoed, her hand a little tighter on James' arm. "Rachel, how are you?"

"Dreadful, my dear—dreadfully happy and dreadfully waiting for this baby to arrive," said Rachel, waving a hand dramatically at her large belly. "You will forgive me for not getting up. It takes a great deal of time and I had other things planned for my morning."

Avers laughed.

"Of course, my dear," said Caro, leaving James and going

over to Rachel to squeeze her shoulder. "It will not be long now."

"Yes, I have just been telling Becky that we will be turning her out of the house before long. She is welcome to come to Somerset, of course, but she is insistent she stays on in London. Where she thinks she will stay with Aunt Etheridge still in Bath, I do not know."

"It would be a great shame to lose you now, Lady Rebecca," Avers said, his eyes not on the lady in question but rather on James. There was a little smirk about his mouth.

James shifted, drawing his shoulders back and levelling his gaze at Avers. He was growing tired of these games.

"I have no wish to go—perhaps your dear aunt may take me in," Rebecca replied, now avoiding James' eyes. "She took such an interest in me last night."

He saw a shuttered look on Rebecca's face. The previous day's vulnerability was hidden from view and in its place the armour of wit and humour.

"After yesterday evening's little drama, one cannot draw any other conclusion than that my aunt is obsessed with you."

"I've told you before, Avers," Rachel called over, "I have no idea how you can be related to such a ghastly woman. How no one has managed to put her in her place, I do not know. I would, but Julius is overbearingly protective at present and will not allow me even the mildest set-down for fear it will upset the babe."

"That is why I am here, Lady Arleigh, to commiserate with your sister and tell her to pay no attention to my aunt."

Rachel reached out to James, beckoning him towards her.

"He has been here half an hour already," Rachel whispered up at him, rolling her eyes expressively towards Avers. "Becky humours him, but in truth, I think she tires of him. You must go and relieve her."

James' face broke into a wry grin in spite of himself.

"Yes, you are very handsome when you smile," Rachel mused.

Before he had come back to London, he had been so focused on burying his father's shame and rebuilding his fortune he had never had time for humour. The shunning of his family's improper scandals had given him a dislike of anything unorthodox like the conversation Rachel was currently conducting, but over the past year something had changed. Perhaps it was the realisation that perfection, however hardly sought, was unattainable. No amount of propriety on his part would erase his past. Had that not been proven by Rebecca's refusal? He pushed the thoughts quickly from his mind.

"Go, off with you now," Rachel whispered commandingly. "Lord Avers," she called across the room, "come here and tell me about that horse you purchased." She shot James a mischievous look. "You had my husband's advice on the purchase, but not mine, and I shall feel slighted if you do not at least pretend to listen to it. Indeed, I am looking forward to telling you that you were wrong to purchase the beast and should have listened to me from the off."

Caro had already made her way over to Rebecca and was sitting in a chair nearby, holding her hand and speaking quietly and earnestly to her. James had no doubt Caro was offering comfort after last night's happenings. Avers rose at the command from Lady Arleigh.

"Such a queue of suitors, Lady Rebecca has," he murmured as James passed him. "Even the ones she's refused are coming back."

James bit his tongue, his fingers twitching. He wasn't sure which was stronger—the urge to deliver a set-down to Avers, or throw a hard right hook across the man's face. What was his game?

"You are set on provoking me it seems," replied James, pausing his step.

"It is my sole aim." Avers turned away, striking up a conversation with Lady Arleigh as he drew away.

James stretched his chin forward, rolling his shoulders back, and continued his stride towards Rebecca. Though appearing to listen to Caro, she watched his approach with wary brown eyes.

"Lady Rebecca," he said, bowing again as he came close.

"Lord Worth," she replied. "I trust you slept well after last night's soiree?"

He had not.

"Tolerably, I thank you."

"Caro?" called Lady Arleigh. "Come here and tell Lord Avers where he is wrong."

Caro rose from her chair, looking briefly between James and Rebecca, before obeying Lady Arleigh's request.

"Well-played of her, don't you think? She always has a way of commanding those about her," said Rebecca before James could speak. "How goes the restoration of Worth Manor?"

James did not immediately answer. Instead, he took a seat on the chaise longue where Lord Avers had been. Rebecca shifted as his leg pressed against hers through her skirts, and she glanced up at him.

"I have not come to speak about Worth Manor."

He believed, for the first time in their acquaintance, their roles were reversed, and it was Rebecca who looked nervous.

"Oh?" she said in an uncharacteristically small voice.

She *looked* small. Her normally bright eyes and fresh face appeared dull and drawn. Her shoulders, usually rolled back and ready for any encounter, were a little hunched, and she had faint shadows beneath her eyes.

"You do not look well," he said, digressing from his plan before he could stop himself.

"I should be offended," Rebecca replied, forced frivolity in her expression. "Aren't gentlemen who call supposed to tell a lady how pretty she looks? Oh, that is not—"

She looked embarrassed. He realised why. She was used to witty repartee that never cut beneath the surface, leaving the false veneer of Society unbroken and any true feelings hidden. But the veneer between them had been fractured that day she had refused him, and any careless word could hit the feelings below.

"I am not like that kind of gentleman," James replied, "as I'm sure you know."

She did not reply, and he again thought of how their roles were reversed. Her without words and him leading the conversation. What a difference a few months and a rejected proposal had made.

"I came to speak to you of last evening."

"Please," she sucked in a breath, pressing her hands in her skirts. "I don't wish to talk about it. Tell me about Worth Manor. Caro was saying you are planning a house party soon."

"I am here to talk about last night."

"Please."

He heard her suck in a ragged breath.

"Curse it!" she huffed, pressing careful fingertips just beneath her eyes to take away the tears before they could mark her cheeks.

"I'm sorry," James said, the sight of her distress causing the ache to return to his chest. He took a handkerchief from his pocket discreetly and passed it to her.

"I suppose it was only deserved, after what I did to you. Lady Goring has a penchant for upsetting us both." She gave a watery smile. "But Worth Manor, tell me—"

"Rebecca," he said firmly, his voice low. "I am here to speak of your tryst with Lady Sophia."

Her brow furrowed. "It's not what you think," she said. "I

am not doing as Lady Goring says and interfering. Lady Sophia is a lovely woman. I would never do such a thing—not to her... not to you."

The ache in his chest intensified. He pressed his lips together, his blue eyes searching hers to try and decipher the feelings that lay there, but she hid them too quickly.

"As Caro has told me before, I am drawn to the drama of others to a fault. Lady Goring did not take it well at all."

"Lady Goring," said James, enunciating every syllable, "should not have said what she said."

Rebecca smiled, the action cracking all armour from her face, and showing James the generosity which lay beneath. "You have been all that is kind to me when I have treated you very ill. I am not worthy of it." She smiled at him, her white teeth framed so perfectly by rose lips and her brown eyes open and honest as they looked at him. He saw a single tear run down her cheek and onto her lip.

It took everything within him not to reach up and wipe it away. He swallowed, looking away to regain his equanimity.

"Tell me why you went to see Lady Sophia alone," he said, focusing on a single blue swirl in the carpet. He looked back at her. "Tell me."

Her face was wrought with a warring look. She glanced over at the others.

"I have no intention of getting in the way of your suitors," he said, looking across at Avers. "I only wish to be of service to you, should you need it."

She looked sad again. What had he said? Was she thinking of Lady Goring's words?

"You are offering to help me?"

"Yes."

She stared across at him, her gaze slipping down his face, pausing on his lips. Her eyes darted back to his, a flash of embarrassment showing. What did that mean?

"Very well," she said finally. "I shall tell you the whole."

When Rebecca had finished her tale, she fell silent, watching James expectantly. She didn't just see him before her. She could feel him, his presence so large she thought it might overwhelm her. His leg had touched hers again while they were talking, and his fingers had brushed hers when he gave her his handkerchief. In truth, she was relieved she had finished the tale, because the way he looked at her with such direct earnestness set her heart whirring.

The chatter of Avers, Caro and Rachel drifted over to them. James' gaze had fallen to the carpet where he studied the swirls of blue and red again. Did he believe her? Or did he think she was lying to drive distance between him and Lady Sophia?

"You are sure of Lady Sophia's affections for Mr Malvon?"

Did James have real feelings for the woman? Perhaps what she had said had hurt him.

"I believe she would marry him, if her mother were not against the match."

James nodded, reaching up and running a hand over his jaw. She studied him, looking for any trace of sadness or disappointment.

"What do you know of Malvon?"

"Not a great deal. I know he is a gentleman of a small estate in Essex. Not the gentleman of title and fortune Lady Goring was hoping for, me thinks."

"Quite."

James had never accepted her outlandish speech so easily before. He was not daunted, either by speaking to Rebecca, or by her directness.

"And what is your plan?"

"I have not thought of one yet," she said, a little vexed at being caught out. "But I may well not have time to enact one. You heard I am to return to Bath."

James stuck out his bottom lip, his brow crinkling. The expression made him look like a puzzled little boy. Rebecca felt an unbidden smile curving her lips. She had never seen him look like that before.

He glanced at her, and a softness swept across his expression.

"You are concentrating very hard," she said, not knowing what else to say and feeling she must explain the smile she had been caught having at his expense.

"If we are to help Lady Sophia, you must stay in London," he said by way of explanation. "Caro will take you in."

"I would not want to impose on her. Not with the baby—they will hardly want me there." Rebecca wondered if this is what it felt like to be a spinster. Without a home of one's own, shuffled between relatives and friends.

"Anne's christening is next week. You will have to stay in London for that, no matter your sister and brother-in-law. Then the Feltons and I are for Worth Manor. I have put it off for too long, but I must return, and now that it is in a better state, I will not be able to keep Caro away." He smiled ruefully. "I will continue to entertain Lady Sophia in pretence. You may tell her it is a falsehood intended to help her, and Caro may keep inviting you as her friend to whatever engagements they attend."

Pretence? So was it a pretence on his side? Were there no feelings to hurt where Lady Sophia was concerned?

"You have devised this scheme quite nicely. Are you sure you are helping me, and it will not be the other way around?"

"You jest, but it is your awareness of others that found out Lady Sophia is in need of aid. I have always admired your generosity of spirit towards those around you. So no, it will not be you helping me—it is most assuredly my aiding you."

The breath caught in her throat. She wasn't expecting the compliment, nor the piercing gaze that accompanied it. How could he look so boyish one moment and so wholly manly the next?

"It is not me who is admirable." She pushed away the fluttering feeling in her stomach. "It is a great sacrifice you will be making. You know Lady Goring will not leave you alone for one moment, don't you?" She raised a brow amusedly at him.

"I can bear it," James said, an unreadable look in his eyes, "for the sake of love."

Avers called over to the pair then, and Rebecca realised how close she and James had become, their speech in whispers as they bent their heads together. She drew back.

The Boulle clock presiding over the gathering on its gilt mantel struck the hour. Shortly after, the party broke up with Avers and the Worth siblings bidding their farewells and departing.

After the guests had gone, Rachel retired to her room to rest. Rebecca stayed a while before following suit. As she ascended the stairs, she barely saw anything. In her mind, the conversation with James replayed. He had come to help her. *Her.* He had shown his disdain for Lady Goring's actions. He had complimented Rebecca. He had called his behaviour towards Lady Sophia 'a pretence'.

Was his behaviour only now a pretence, now that he had found out Lady Sophia's heart was engaged to another? Or had he never held affection for the girl? Rebecca wasn't sure. And even after all that had happened between them, he had said he admired her. That was more warmth of affection than she had expected.

What had passed between them this morning had caused a shift in their relationship. Gone was the stuttering and reserved James. Rebecca's own witty armour had been laid aside. What were they now—allies? Partners? Or even friends? The mere fact that there was an opportunity to move from cold and distant individuals to something closer sent a shot of hope through Rebecca. With that feeling came a new question —what exactly was Rebecca hoping for?

CHAPTER TWELVE

"I still don't understand how you could bear it, Rebecca," said Caro.

"I want to know," said Felton, interrupting his wife, "How you did not unleash your sharp tongue on the woman? You have by far the superior weapon."

Rebecca sat in the drawing room of the Feltons' London residence after they had dined together. She had arrived that morning to stay. James had been true to his word and Caro had sent a note inviting her last week.

"She is hardly worth the expense of energy," Rebecca said.

But that was not the reason. Lady Goring had managed to cut her to the bone. It was not the implication that she was on the shelf that had cut so deep. It was the truth Lady Goring had spoken about James. Rebecca had made her decision and would have to live with James finding another. If it were not Lady Sophia, it would be someone else. He was an eligible bachelor... and he was kind... and honest... and caring... and handsome.

In the weeks and months since refusing James, she had often reminded herself of why she had refused him to shore up her confidence that she had made the right decision. But that confidence was bleeding away. If she looked too closely at the wound, she knew what she would see there. Regret.

"She's a vile woman," said Caro with force. "I wish I had been there. I should have said something on your behalf."

Rebecca smiled. "I'm not sure it would have helped."

"It would have helped me," said Caro, fire in her blue eyes.

"On that note, I am for my club—you will excuse me, ladies."

Felton raised the glass in his hand to both of them before draining it and taking his leave.

"I have been dying to tell you—I never said a word to Lady Goring about... about what happened between James and me. That is—Lord Worth."

"Oh, my dear, I never thought you could have said anything. I know better than anyone how well you can be trusted."

"I was at Madame Depardieu's shop, speaking to Rachel, and Lady Goring overheard it. I could have died when she showed herself and made it clear she knew what had been said."

"I'm glad you didn't," Caro replied, an amused smile curving her full lips.

"I would have warned James, only..." Rebecca broke off. She glanced warily at her friend, but did not see any judgement in her eyes. Still, she decided to turn the conversation. "You are good to take me in."

"Take you in?" Caro chuckled. "You are not a stray dog, Rebecca, you are my dearest friend, and I could not have you missing Anne's christening for the world. James was most insistent too." She looked inquiringly at her.

That look meant that James had not told Caro the real reason for asking his sister to take her in. Should Rebecca tell

Caro what she and James were up to? But if he had chosen not to, then Rebecca should keep his confidence.

Wishing to steer the conversation into safer waters, she recalled the motherly talking points her aunt had sent her. Upon starting with the first, Caro was soon talking excitedly of Anne's growth, of her character which was coming out more day by day, and how Felton acted in the role of father. Rebecca found herself getting swept up in the wave of excitement and soon the talking points were left behind in favour of her own questions.

"And how are you, Rebecca? I have not asked that yet. How are you really?"

The question came out of the blue. They had been halfway through discussing the christening ceremony and the gown Anne would wear—one passed down through the Felton family—when Caro had asked it.

"Fine," Rebecca said too quickly. "I'm fine."

"It's only that, when I have seen you, you have seemed… sad. Is that a wretched thing for me to say?"

Sad? Is that how she seemed? Rebecca had hardly known how she felt for the past several weeks. Was she sad? She became aware of the dull ache in her chest that appeared every time she thought of James and what she had chosen not to have with him. For the first time, she did not shy away from it. She allowed herself to stare her decision full in the face. Yes, she was very sad.

Caro reached forward and took Rebecca's hand.

"You look upset now. I'm afraid I was not very understanding when you refused James. I was just so concerned for him, for he does not open his heart easily. He never has, even when we were children before all the business with my father. What happened with Papa only made him more closed. I understand now it is not my place to comment on what lies between you and James."

"You were honest," Rebecca cut in, her voice cracking a little. "You wished to protect him and for that you were right. I simply felt I did not know him then. I was not sure."

Rebecca was unaware of what questions her words raised. If she had been, she might have noticed that her friend did not pry.

Instead, Caro said gently, "You will both find love. I have hope for it. I'm only glad you are not at odds with each other. His ensuring you were not made homeless before your goddaughter's christening is proof." Caro chuckled.

"Your brother has always been over-kind to me," Rebecca agreed, the declaration of James' good qualities making the aching worse.

"And you are good to take Lady Goring's horrid verbal beatings in order to prevent him being any more embarrassed in public. It's admirable, what you're doing."

That word *admirable* again. It only made her think of James and the compliment he had paid her.

"But I can see that no matter the stupidity of Lady Goring's words, they are making you sad."

"No," Rebecca said with honesty. "I assure you, they are not."

It wasn't Lady Goring's words that made Rebecca sad. It was that—since her interview with James at the Arleighs'—she had realised just whom she had rejected. She had realised that the feelings for James which she had tried so hard to bury were not dead, but silenced, and now they were demanding to be heard.

"Lady Goring can be so very vile," Caro said. "Anyone would be considered human, and not weak, to be hurt by her words."

She was being kind and while Rebecca's true sadness did not come from the viciousness of Lady Goring's words, it was perhaps worsened by the truth of some of them.

"Yes." Rebecca broke into a grateful smile.

She wanted to tell Caro all the feelings running through her mind at that moment. The sadness. The regret. The fear. But she couldn't bring herself to. She had already hurt James once—she could not do so again. He must find happiness and love, even if it was not to be with her or Lady Sophia.

Besides, there were too many feelings, all clamouring for her attention, making it hard for her to breathe, to think. She did what she always did before they could overwhelm her. She forced them back, pushing them down, until they could not threaten to overset her anymore.

"And how could I not be happy when my dear godchild Anne's christening is tomorrow?"

"I don't know," Caro replied.

She pressed Rebecca's hand one last time and then expressed a desire to check on Anne before retiring. The women rose, but before they turned from each other, Caro reached forward and drew the taller Rebecca into a warm hug.

They said nothing, embracing each other in the candlelit room—a perfect moment. When it felt right, they broke apart, smiling, and bid each other good night.

Rebecca was unusually silent as Maisy prepared her for bed. After dismissing her maid, she sat and stared into the fire —an unread book on her lap. She opened back up the box into which she had forced her feelings earlier and before long silent tears tracked down her face, glinting in the firelight. She had refused James because she had not known him, but he had proven himself to her time after time to be a man of worth. A man who could admit his failings, who strove to do what was right, who cared for those he loved, and who did not hold her hurting him against her. He truly was a Lord of worth and she was a fool for rejecting him.

The christening was a lovely affair in St George's Church, Hanover Square. The vicar said all that was needed and was a friendly man who took great delight in Anne's gabbling throughout the service. Caro had shone with motherly beauty, Felton with pride—and there was even a misty look in his eyes.

Rebecca and James had faced each other across the font, promising to watch over Anne, to bring her up to follow God. Rebecca had only risked looking at him once. She had steeled herself for it, but she still wasn't prepared for those piercing blue eyes. They looked straight through her, and she was afraid of what he might see there.

The deed done and little Anne's life entrusted to God, the care of her parents and that of her godparents, the party left the church and returned to the Feltons'. There was a luncheon laid on to celebrate and they were just sitting down to it— baby Anne having been put down for a nap—when Lady Goring and her daughter were announced.

"Turn them away," Felton said in a low voice from the end of the table, his green eyes flashing at his wife.

Rebecca and James locked eyes and Felton saw it.

"We should not turn them away on such an occasion," James broke in. "They have no doubt come to offer congratulations."

The truth was, neither James nor Rebecca had managed to get Lady Sophia alone since their alliance. Lady Goring had proven a formidable opponent. She would not allow Rebecca near her daughter when they attended the same gatherings. Equally, the older woman threw James and Sophia together, but without giving them a moment's peace from her interfering ways. The Feltons, Lord Worth and Rebecca were due to leave for the Worth estate in two days.

"But it's a family affair," Caro said, faint surprise at her brother's words. "That's why we did not invite others."

"They will only be half an hour," Rebecca said, understanding the look in James' eyes.

"I smell something afoot," Felton murmured.

James ignored it, and Rebecca followed his lead, trying her best to look as if she did not care whether the Gorings came in or not.

"I'll be alright, Caro—I promise," Rebecca said, reaching across the table and pressing one of Caro's hands.

"Very well," Caro said, unconvinced. "Send them in, John."

The party rose, and Lady Goring swept into the room, wearing a dark blue polonaise whose bustles were large enough to knock a vase on a side table when she turned to face the room. Thankfully the bump only unsettled the vase and it wobbled back into its place.

"Oh!" she exclaimed, her gaze surveying the assembled party and the repast before them. Her small eyes lit with pleasure at the sight of James, and narrowed when they fell on Rebecca soon after. "We have interrupted... well, I hardly know what. Such an assemblage of persons." Lady Goring's eyes remained on Rebecca.

"Lady Goring, we were just celebrating our daughter's christening. I believe you know the godparents, Lord Worth and the *lovely* Lady Rebecca?" Felton was doing it on purpose, and Rebecca couldn't help but appreciate it. She flashed a secret smile at Caro.

"Lady Goring, Lady Sophia." James bowed.

Her daughter had walked in quietly behind her and was standing so close to the wall she might have been trying to blend into the paper.

"Won't you join us?" Caro asked as the footman added two more chairs to the table.

"We don't want to intrude," Lady Goring replied, already

taking one of the chairs. She settled, the rustle of her silks the only noise in the room. "Sophia!" she hissed. "Sit."

Lady Sophia obeyed, a shy smile on her lips for the occupants of the room. The rest of the table resumed their seats.

"Lady Rebecca, I hope you are fully recovered from our gathering last week?" Lady Goring asked, a pencilled brow rising.

She had chosen a direct attack.

"Very much so, Lady Goring. You are kind to ask." Rebecca raised her chin an inch.

Lady Goring looked vexed at the confidence of her reply and turned to James.

"And Lord Worth, how have you been since our little party?"

"I have very much enjoyed my niece's christening," James replied, smiling at Caro.

"Yes, of course. Felicitations, Mrs Felton."

"Congratulations," Lady Sophia echoed.

"Thank you," Caro said to the young woman, offering her a glowing smile.

"I suppose it makes you think to your own children one day, Lord Worth?"

Her lack of subtlety was enough to make anyone blush. But if it gave Rebecca the cover she needed to speak quietly to Lady Sophia, then she would not say any of the cutting remarks coming to mind.

"How are you?" Rebecca whispered, thankful that Lady Sophia's chair had been placed so close to her own. "We must finish our conversation."

Lady Sophia nodded, but had nervous eyes on her mother.

"What whispering is this?" Lady Goring said sharply. "Lady Rebecca, one would think after my words to you that—"

"It is fortuitous you arrived, Lady Goring," James said, cutting across her.

The Countess looked incensed but covered it quickly.

"We are leaving for Worth Manor in two days," James carried on. "The restoration is nearing completion, and we're returning to celebrate my niece's arrival. I have a mind to turn it into a house party, if you'll be so good as to host, Caroline? Both you and your daughter are invited, Lady Goring."

Caro would have replied if her mouth had not been gaping open. Felton spluttered in his tankard of ale. Even Rebecca was a little surprised, though she knew the reasons for the invitation.

"We would be delighted, would we not Sophia? What an honour to be invited," Lady Goring said gleefully, all animosity towards Rebecca dissipating. "We did have a few engagements—there will no doubt be some gentlemen Sophia will have to let down—but for you, Lord Worth, we will of course attend."

"That's good news," James replied, his voice as measured as Lady Goring's was excited. "And I had wondered if I could trespass on your goodness as well?"

"Anything, my Lord."

"As Anne's godmother, Lady Rebecca will also be attending, and I had hoped she might travel with you, for I am sure my sister and brother-in-law would want to come before the guests arrive. Will you do me that great favour?"

If Lady Goring was suddenly aware of the corner James had backed her into, she did not show it. She was all gracious smiles—though no doubt hiding gritted teeth—when she agreed to the request.

"Then it is settled."

"It is, isn't it?" Felton said, his green eyes widening at Caro. The husband and wife had already exchanged several frowning glances.

The Gorings stayed a little while longer, but Lady Goring surprisingly left at the proper quarter-hour, no doubt considering her visit a success that did not require extending. When they had gone, Caro turned to James.

"I had not expected that, brother."

"It is certainly a turn of events," Felton said.

"I wish to get to know Lady Sophia better," James replied bluntly. "She is a charming woman."

"In spite of her mother," Felton added.

"I'm not sure, James..." Caro trailed off, glancing at Rebecca.

"It's a splendid idea," Rebecca said cheerfully. His direct words stung a little in spite of the fact she had been expecting fabrication in aid of their partnership.

"But a carriage ride with *her*," said Caro. "Rebecca, are you sure that's wise?"

"If Lord Worth thinks so, I trust his judgement," said Rebecca, that particular surprise from James not one she had relished, though she had to admit its ingenuity. It would allow her a lot of time with the mother and daughter, and potentially some alone with the latter.

"Hopefully Lady Goring will trust that I am a good friend to her daughter," said Rebecca, in pragmatic tones equal to James', "and choose to be merciful with her tongue."

"I am not sure Lady Goring knows what mercy is," said Felton.

The group broke into laughter and soon the conversation took a superficial turn, driven mostly, and surprisingly, by James, until it broke up as he had to leave on business.

Rebecca escaped to her room, a feeling of weariness overtaking her. But the weariness within her was not alone. There was a tiny speck of something else, bright and warming. Was it hope?

Meanwhile, Caro and Felton were left to retire to their drawing room alone.

"They are up to something, those two," Felton murmured in his wife's ear as they reclined together on the chaise longue.

"I thought the same," replied Caro. She sighed, her head gently rising and falling on her husband's chest. "Do you think they'll ever realise they're both still in love with each other?"

CHAPTER THIRTEEN

Lady Goring had taken great delight in telling all of London of the invitation to Worth Manor. Whenever Rebecca visited an acquaintance to take her leave of them, they were quick to mention that Lady Goring had secured her daughter an invite from the eligible Lord Worth and that they expected a betrothal before the house party was finished. While Rebecca had determined not to allow Lady Goring's caustic words to get to her again, she was not looking forward to being enclosed in a carriage with the woman for hours on end.

The morning of their departure was crisp, the night having been clear, and a damp mist hung about the London streets. Rebecca had stayed with them for the previous night, since Caro, James and Felton had departed for Sussex a day earlier. Despite her best efforts to speak to Lady Sophia alone and find out more, Lady Goring had kept her daughter away from their unwelcome guest. When Rebecca had dined with them that evening, she had noted the three paintings present at their party only a week ago were no longer hanging on the walls of their Town house. The bareness of the rooms was explained away as part of the redecoration Lady Goring was doing. It was all the rage, according to the Countess, to have Chinese-inspired decor.

Rebecca settled into the carriage—a chaise and four hired for the occasion as Lady Goring explained their own equipage was being repainted. Rebecca had not commented. She caught a glimpse of Maisy, dressed in travelling clothes, looking unhappily up at the roofline of the carriage. Rebecca would have had her maid inside the vehicle had it been her own travelling coach, but Lady Goring had said quite firmly that the ladies' maids would do well on the roof, having hired no second carriage for the servants or the luggage. It was only two maids, after all. There was no sign of Lady Sophia's maid whom Rebecca had last seen in the upper hallway of the Gorings' Town house.

The coachman called something, and Maisy ran out of sight. A scuffling above could be heard as the coachman and footman took their seats, and the vehicle finally pulled away. The streets of London slowly rolled past.

"It is a great thing to have had my daughter singled out by Lord Worth," Lady Goring said to her.

Rebecca withdrew her eyes from the view reluctantly.

"You have been invited to this house party in deference to your role as godmother. Sophia has been chosen for her unique company. I feel it shows the true state of affairs. I hope you are not too slighted, Lady Rebecca, but you have made your decision. It will suit everyone well to have my nephew at Worth Manor joining the party. It should afford you some diversion."

A diversion that was not Lord Worth—that's what she meant. To allow an empty path to Lord Worth for Lady Sophia. Rebecca glanced at the girl, and she noted for the second time that morning that the young woman's eyes were rimmed with red.

"Avers is charming," Rebecca replied.

The more she thought about his behaviour, the more she wondered if he suspected his cousin's attachment to Mr Malvon was not as dead and buried as Lady Goring hoped.

"Charming, yes, but I'm not sure even you will be able to make him a marrying man."

Gracious! The Countess' tongue was vicious. Rebecca didn't know how her daughter bore it.

Responding with a smile, Rebecca ground her teeth behind her closed lips. If she did not keep firm control of her tongue, she would say things she ought not to. Any such outburst would be seen as an admission of Lady Goring's beliefs. The Countess would smell blood and go in for the kill. It would do Lady Sophia no good, and that was who Rebecca needed to focus on. Writing to her aunt the day before, she had said as much. Rebecca had informed Lady Etheridge of her plans to go to Sussex, of her suspicions surrounding Lady Sophia, and of the pact she and James had made to help the girl.

Lady Goring's spiteful conversation lapsed with Rebecca's refusal to rise to it, and by the time they had reached the outskirts of London they were travelling in silence. As much as Rebecca was relieved and looking forward to the mercy of a quiet journey, Lady Goring's frequent stares set her teeth on edge.

It was barely eight o'clock in the morning. Rebecca's eyelids began drooping as she watched the pastoral scene outside. The sound of the horses' hooves was steady and rhythmic. The turning of the wheels predictable. The carriage swayed and she had almost forgotten who she travelled with. Sway. Sway. Sway. Thud-thud, thud-thud. Rumble. Rumble. Rumble.

A gun cracked through the air outside. Horses whinnied in fear. The coachman cursed and Maisy screamed. The carriage lurched as the horses slowed faster than the vehicle. Rebecca was thrown forward, almost landing on Lady Goring's well-endowed bosom, and the woman screeched in response.

"Stand and deliver!"

Rebecca's heart raced when she heard the cry. A highwayman? But it was broad daylight.

A pistol rapped against the door a few seconds later making the ladies gasp.

"Open up!"

"Now, look 'ere!" cried the driver. There was a noise from up by the coachman's seat. Rebecca had no doubt he was retrieving whatever weapon he kept for just such an occasion.

"Halt!" came the highwayman's voice, a little more high-pitched this time. "Get down from there this instant! You and the groom—over by that tree, now."

The driver emitted some very crass curses, but in spite of his protestations, Rebecca felt the carriage lurch to one side as he climbed down from his box. The groom must have followed suit.

"You stay where you are, ladies," the highwayman called.

Ladies? Rebecca assumed he was speaking to the maids who sat on the roof. It was true she had never been held up by a highwayman before, but such manners!

"How dare they! How dare they!" Lady Goring cried, pressing a handkerchief to her mouth, searching for some-thing in her pockets with a shaking hand. She withdrew a bottle of smelling salts. "We shall be killed! Murdered!"

"Hush!" Rebecca whispered, a hand on her forehead as she tried to think. "Have you brought a pistol with you?"

Lady Sophia, who had frozen in fear, shook her head when her mother's only response was moaning.

"That good for n-nothing driver," Lady Goring wailed. "We shall be dead. Oh! Oh!" Lady Goring's breath came rapidly. A second later her eyes were rolling back in her head, and she'd fainted.

Rebecca exhaled a half hysterical laugh. "No," she told herself. "No, we shall be all right." She glanced at Lady Sophia who was looking miserable, tears running down her face. "They only want our money. We shall give it all over and they will let us go on."

The pistol rapped against the door again.

"Open the door," came the command.

Rebecca, hands braced on the seat and the door frame, looked Lady Sophia in the eye, her own clear of tears.

The pistol banged against the door for a third time. Rebecca jumped, and more from fear than any irritation, she threw it unceremoniously open.

"Yes! Yes! We've opened the door," she barked, panic making her voice sound angry.

The highwayman leapt out of the way as the door flew open and took a while to regain his footing. It made him seem entirely human, and if it weren't for the pistol that he kept thrusting in their direction, Rebecca wouldn't have felt an ounce of fear.

He was the stuff of the novels Rebecca had read as a school miss. He wore a tricorn hat pulled low on his brow, a muffler up to his eyes, and a heavy greatcoat hung from his shoulders. Rebecca could not help but think on such a fine morning that he must be very hot indeed. Moments of panic could do that to one—force the most inane observations to mind.

The highwayman's eyes were a dark brown In fact, thought Rebecca, they were rather earnest eyes for a criminal to lay claim to. In fact, thought Rebecca, they were rather handsome eyes. They took in the unconscious form of Lady Goring, then looked at Lady Sophia, pausing there longer, and finally looked at Rebecca. He was... surprised.

"Well?" Rebecca asked when he said nothing.

He shook himself, as if remembering just what he was doing—robbing from the rich.

"You." He pointed the pistol at Lady Sophia. "Come out here."

"Wait." Rebecca barred the woman's exit with her arm. "You need only take our jewels and our change purses and be on your way. There is no need for us to leave the carriage. We'll let you go without a fuss."

"No…" The highwayman hesitated. "I want her to come out here."

"What an impertinent thief you are!" Rebecca exclaimed, a rush of courage spurring her on. "My companion will go nowhere with you."

Rebecca caught sight of Lady Sophia just beside her, looking out of the carriage at the highwayman.

"My Lady, please come out here."

Those manners again.

"I've told you—"

"I can go." Lady Sophia interrupted in a whisper that Rebecca almost missed had her senses not been heightened by the situation. "I can go with him."

"What?" Rebecca exclaimed. Had the world gone mad? She swerved round to look at Lady Sophia and saw a most peculiar look on the young woman's face. She was staring at the highwayman—half in trepidation, half in hope.

"Let her come out," the highwayman commanded.

"Not alone," Rebecca snapped back at him, hardly understanding Lady Sophia's reaction. It seemed insane to let her get out of the carriage to be alone with a criminal so Rebecca started to get out of the carriage herself.

"Just her."

"No," Rebecca said firmly. "And you needn't keep brandishing that gun at me. I know very well you are in charge."

Where the courage was coming from, Rebecca had no idea.

"You're mad," came a garbled wail from Lady Goring who had apparently regained at least partial consciousness.

Rebecca ignored her, stepping down from the carriage. As she did so she caught sight of the highwayman's boots. They were... clean. Highly polished in fact.

Once Rebecca was outside, she turned to help Lady Sophia down, and the highwayman went to close the door of the carriage. Rebecca kept herself between Lady Sophia and the highwayman, never allowing her back to be towards him. She caught sight of the driver and groom sat over by a tree on the other side of the road. Maisy looked down at her mistress with terror in her eyes, but Rebecca gave her a reassuring nod. Why she thought she could reassure Maisy, she had no idea. They were on a deserted stretch of road and there was a man pointing a gun at them. It was not a good situation.

"What would you have us do?" Rebecca asked, fear rising as she thought of the possible answers.

But the highwayman wasn't holding his gun at them anymore. He had allowed the pistol to drop to his side, revealing the silver scrollwork down it's well-crafted barrel.

"I wish to speak to you over there," he said to Lady Sophia.

"Absolutely not," Rebecca replied without hesitation.

Their assailant sighed.

"Please," he said. "I give you my word I will not harm her."

The common accents he had been using disappeared from his voice. Rebecca stared hard at him. Polished boots, a silver pistol, those earnest brown eyes...

"It will be all right," Lady Sophia said quietly, her eyes fastened on those of the highwayman.

Could that be... surely not!

"I'm not leaving her," Rebecca said firmly, whatever suspicions she held not overriding her protectiveness.

"Sophia," the highwayman said. "Please."

It couldn't be…

"Lady Rebecca—" Sophia started.

Rebecca held up her hand, realisation finally dawning "I will wait by the carriage."

Once she was several paces away, she heard them strike up a whispered conversation. She could not make out any of it, even when she turned to watch them, but it confirmed her suspicions of just who had held them up.

The highwayman put his gun in one of the greatcoat's pockets and gestured to Lady Sophia as he spoke. She looked upset and when her shoulders began to shake, he took her arms in his hands, bending his head to hers, pulling his muffler down and whispering something close to her ear. Rebecca heard a movement in the carriage and moved to stand in front of the window to stop Lady Goring seeing what was taking place. Fortunately the carriage was blocking the coachman and footman from view. Maisy and Rebecca were the only audience to this tête-à-tête.

The highwayman then passed something to Lady Sophia, stepped back, bowed and turned on his heel towards his horse. He mounted quickly and before long was disappearing through the trees on the roadside. Rebecca waited long enough for him to fade from view and then strode quickly over to Lady Sophia, putting a hand around her shaking shoulders.

"Am I right in thinking we know the gentleman who just held us up?"

Lady Sophia's gaze was still on the retreating path of their assailant, and before she could reply, the carriage door was thrown open and Lady Goring's wail rent the air.

The rest of Rebecca's journey was uneventful in comparison to the first hour. They changed horses twice and reached the Worth estate by half past five that evening. Twilight was still some time off, and the late afternoon sun shone gold through the trees as they approached the house. Rebecca's attempts at speaking to Lady Sophia, whenever Lady Goring had been out of the carriage during the horse changes, had only resulted in the girl beginning to cry again. She had puzzled over what on earth had possessed Mr Malvon to hold up their carriage and surmised whatever it was he had passed to Lady Sophia held the key.

All these thoughts, however, fell away as she turned to look out of the window at the childhood home of Caro and James. Golden light shone on the landscape outside, she felt the carriage lean as they rounded a bend, and before it straightened again, there was a glimpse of Worth Manor. It was sitting in a pool of sunlight, its red brick warm, the stone mullioned windows dark and the myriad of chimneys and peaks of its roofline standing out against the blue sky.

Lady Goring, who had been moaning to herself almost non-stop since their unexpected encounter, perked up at the sound of gravel beneath the carriage wheels. She straightened in her seat, arranging her skirts and put a hand to her hair.

"What a mess I must look. Sophia, dear, re-pin your hat at once. It's sitting askew."

She looked over at Rebecca and as she did so, a scowl came across her face. Rebecca was none the wiser. She was too engaged in trying to see the house again now they had turned. This is where James had been a boy, and of this place he was now master. The glimpse she had seen, bathed as it was in warm light, had looked idyllic—hardly the site of an unhappy childhood and scandal. Appearances could be deceiving.

Rebecca herself had become adept at hiding her emotions and presenting instead an animated and charming front to Society.

The carriage finally eased to a stop before a covered archway and Rebecca saw a door open and several servants appear.

As she readied to descend from the carriage, she realised how stiff her limbs were. Rolling her shoulders back, she stretched, kneading her lower back with her fists.

"I will descend first," Lady Goring ordered, her bird-like eyes on Rebecca.

The carriage door was opened by the footman and the steps let down. No doubt Lady Goring wished to make a—

"Lord Worth! What a balm it is to see your person. We have been set upon by vagabonds and barely escaped with our lives!"

Lady Goring must have almost fallen from the carriage, for when Lady Sophia and Rebecca followed her out, Rebecca saw both her hands were on James', and she was leaning heavily against him.

The Countess sighed. "It has been a most unhappy journey."

"Vagabonds?" said Caro, who had just come outside with baby Anne in her arms, a concerned look on her pretty face.

"It was most dreadful."

"Clearly," said Felton from behind his wife, a protective hand on her back and his green eyes on Lady Goring.

"Set upon? Do you mean highwaymen?" James' tone was not the concern of his sister's nor the polite tones of a host. His words were clipped—his blue eyes fierce.

Rebecca was just about to say something to calm the situation when James' gaze sought her out.

"Are you hurt?"

The question could be for all of them, but his eyes were only on Rebecca.

"Oh yes, Sophia is fine, thank goodness," Lady Goring said, leaning even more heavily on James, making him look away from Rebecca as he attempted to keep his balance. "No thanks to the cavalier actions of Lady Rebecca."

After hours of listening to Lady Goring moan like a pitiful child, the lurching of a carriage journey, the tearful face of Lady Sophia, and the weariness that journeys could bring, Rebecca had had enough.

She opened her mouth to speak, but to her surprise, James handed Lady Goring to a much put out Felton, and came to her side.

He spoke as if to Lady Sophia as well as herself.

"What happened? Tell me." The look in his eyes, which Rebecca had mistaken for fierceness was... fear. It was to be expected, Rebecca reasoned, after such a revelation.

"We are quite all right, are we not, Lady Sophia?" Rebecca took the young woman onto her arm, the speech she had been rehearsing on the journey coming out clear and persuasive. "The scoundrel thought to rob us and held us up just outside of London. He demanded we come out of the carriage."

That part she wished she did not need to impart for it was highly unusual for a masked villain to make such a demand. Usually they just asked for trinkets and coins to be thrown out. But Lady Goring had already mentioned Rebecca's 'cavalier actions', so there was nothing for it.

"So we had to go."

Lady Sophia finally spoke. "Rebecca would not let me go alone. She was so brave."

"Foolish," Lady Goring corrected. "Your actions could have got us killed. You were so brazen with the fellow."

Apparently Lady Goring's petulant moaning in the carriage had not been the only thing she had been up to, and Rebecca was not the only one who had been rehearsing a speech.

"He didn't even take anything from our luggage," Lady Goring said, the realisation only just dawning on her.

"Yes," said Rebecca, thankful it had not taken her so long to realise. When they had last changed horses she had had the forethought to plan for this eventuality. "But he took my ring —see." She held up a bare right hand. "And my pearl bracelet. They are both valuable, and I've no doubt he thought it enough for his troubles."

"It appears you are the saviour of the day, Lady Rebecca," said Felton. "Paying off the rascal with your own possessions."

Rebecca forced a smile. Deceiving her friends made her feel as uncomfortable as the ring and bracelet hidden in her stays.

"It is a good thing he did not find my jewel case," Lady Goring said with a sniff, put out that her attempt at setting Rebecca down had resulted in her being proclaimed a saviour instead.

"A lucky escape indeed," said Caro. "Come, Lady Goring. I expect you wish for refreshments after your ordeal."

James had not stopped his study of Rebecca's face.

"Lord Worth," Lady Goring called, as if he were a lap dog.

A look of irritation passed over his countenance. He offered Lady Sophia and Rebecca an arm each, and escorted them inside the house.

CHAPTER FOURTEEN

After their journey the travellers went to rest. Not that Rebecca managed to do so. She was relieved when a servant came to tell her the guests were gathering for dinner, which had been put back until they arrived. After all, answers could not be found alone in her room. She needed to speak to Sophia.

Rebecca made her way downstairs. As she approached the drawing room, she saw James waiting outside.

"My Lord." She curtseyed, looking between him and the door which stood slightly ajar.

He looked up, the seriousness of his gaze arresting her footsteps.

"Are you hurt?" James asked, stepping towards her.

Had he been waiting here to ask her that? The sound of Lady Goring's voice floated through the doorway disrupting Rebecca's thoughts and causing her to glance in that direction. Her Ladyship was expounding on the craftsmanship of the mouldings on the drawing room ceiling and the fine paintings on display.

When Rebecca looked back, James was still staring at her.

She swallowed, the intenseness of his gaze making her stomach flutter.

"Yes, I'm quite all right—don't worry." She wanted to allay the concern in his blue eyes.

"Don't worry?" James looked bewildered.

"It was not a real highwayman," Rebecca whispered, eyeing Lady Goring through the partly open door to make sure she was nowhere nearby. "It was Mr Malvon. At least, I believe it was, though Lady Sophia has yet to confirm it. But I'm sure it was him. He didn't steal a thing from us, I had to lie about the ring and bracelet. I shall repent of it later and pray for God's forgiveness. Lying is a particular dislike of mine."

"What the devil was he about holding you up like that?"

Rebecca jolted with shock at the anger in James' voice. His face was contorted, and she imagined if Mr Malvon were present he might be feeling James' fist right about now.

"I suspect he heard Lady Goring and her daughter were on their way here. All of Society is betting on an engagement before the house party is finished. He likely got desperate."

"Desperate or no," James said, his voice tight with rage. "If he had caused any harm to come to you..." He trailed off and then added as if an afterthought, "Or Lady Sophia..." He trailed off again and it gave his words a distinct menace.

"I'm all right," said Rebecca. "I don't believe he even had a loaded gun. He discharged one to stop us, but I didn't see a second pistol, so even when he levelled it at me, I think it must have been empty."

"He what?"

This time Rebecca was actually frightened of the look in his eyes.

"But I'm not sure yet what the message he gave to Lady Sophia was," she carried on hurriedly. "They didn't just speak, you see—he handed her a note. To go to such extremes to give it to her makes me wonder what's in it. I've been trying to speak to her alone since it happened, but Lady Goring is determined to interfere every time I might manage it."

"You are held at gunpoint, in fear for your life, and yet your thoughts are still on Lady Sophia?" James said, disbelief in his voice.

"Well, it's—"

"Where is Lord Worth?" Lady Goring's voice came from the drawing room and precluded any further conversation.

James had been shocked by the strength of his anger when hearing of Mr Malvon's exploits. He had half a mind to quit his efforts to aid the man and Lady Sophia, had not the wildness of his own emotions given him the empathy he needed to at least partially understand Mr Malvon's actions.

He barely contained his impatience at the tittle-tattle of Lady Goring's dinner conversation and her incessant need to thrust Lady Sophia under his nose at every opportunity. All he wished to do was speak to Rebecca, even look at her, to be reassured she really was all right. What if it had not been Mr Malvon who had held the coach up? What if it really had been a ruffian and she had been in danger? What if something had happened to her?

James' conversation at the meal left much to be desired as these thoughts preoccupied him. The Countess was not to be deterred. She continued her dogged pursuit of his attention for her daughter when the party regathered after dinner. But she was to be left disappointed.

The party agreed they would retire early after their recent journeys. They all rose, the gentlemen allowing the women to leave first. James saw Rebecca whispering in Lady Sophia's ear.

"I don't think so," Lady Goring hissed.

James was sure the Countess had not meant for anyone else to hear. Her small eyes darted about the room and met his. She pasted a false smile on her face which he did not return.

"I am just telling Lady Rebecca she mustn't visit my daughter in her room. Silly chatter is not what's needed after a long journey. I shall send my maid to attend you, Sophia."

Rebecca sent a thwarted look to James.

"Of course not. I hope you will walk with me in the gardens tomorrow, Lady Sophia," Rebecca said, loud enough for everyone to hear.

Whatever Lady Goring's response was, it was lost to the hall outside as the ladies left and a servant drew the door to a close behind them.

"What a party," Felton drawled, resuming his seat, one arm hanging over the back of it and his legs stretched out casually before him. "I'd hoped it would go on all night."

James waved a hand at the servant remaining in the room as he walked over to the sideboard. By the time James handed Felton a glass of port, the two gentlemen were alone.

"You're enjoying the tension?"

"Come now, Worth—you can't seriously be entertaining any intentions towards Lady Sophia? Don't get me wrong—she's a sweet girl. But that mother of hers!"

"I am in no danger from Lady Sophia." James resumed his seat, studying his glass of port rather than drinking it.

"Ah, so it's as I suspected." Felton's brows raised enquiringly, a mischievous look in his eyes. "What possessed you to invite them here then?"

"I did so for Rebecca." James' hand tightened imperceptibly on his glass as he used her Christian name.

Felton took a sip of port, eyeing James over the rim of the glass. "And what am I to make of that?"

"Nothing. I didn't want Caro to worry so I didn't tell her

—or you," James added. Felton and Caro shared everything. "There was no need to. I'm only helping a friend."

James took a sip of port and then—as if the matter was closed—he turned the conversation. "Lord Avers arrives tomorrow."

Felton raised a sarcastic brow. "What a party we'll be then." He paused. "You know my friend Avers only flirts with Rebecca—he would never offer for her."

James' eyes left the glass and fixed on Felton. He tried to decide whether he believed those words. Avers had seemed intent on dangling his flirtation under James' nose for weeks. What other reason could he have for singling her out in such a manner unless he was seriously courting her?

"Perhaps Avers would suit her. He is a man of fashion and conversation."

"Oh, I don't know," Felton said. He rolled his glass round, watching the liquid swirl.

The image of Avers and Rebecca together, however fictional in James' mind, caused an unpleasant sensation in his chest. "Besides, what concern is it of mine?" The question came out more harshly than he intended.

"I'm not sure," Felton replied, unperturbed and suddenly acting nonchalant. He tugged loose the lace cravat at his throat and shrugged. Flashing a challenging look at James he said, "But then again, I'm not sure what concern it is of yours to aid Rebecca." There was a curve to his lips and then Felton winked.

"I am helping her—nothing more," James replied.

Felton had provided a comforting ear after Rebecca had rejected James all those months ago. They had not spoken of it since—only when it had come up in conversation—but he was always provoking like this when it did.

"If you say so." Felton winked again. "I think Lady Goring would beg to differ."

"Lady Goring—" James started with sudden gusto, but broke off. Nothing polite was about to come out of his mouth. "Trust me," he said after a time. "There is nothing between Rebecca and me. I have accepted it."

"I'm not so sure," said Felton. "Anyway, I'm for bed. This port has finished me off."He rose, patting James' shoulder as he passed him, and left the dining room.

James was left to ponder over Felton's words. Had he meant he did not believe James had accepted the status quo between himself and Rebecca? Or did Felton mean he thought there was still something between them?

Rebecca rose earlier than usual the following day. She was in a hurry to get downstairs and see if she could catch Lady Sophia alone. She instructed Maisy to leave her hair au naturel. They were in the country now and she did not have the patience for pomade and powder. Instead of the high coiffures she was used to, Maisy dressed her hair in loose, simple braids that she looped up onto the crown of her head, artfully but rapidly.

Rebecca fidgeted as Maisy dressed her in a simple white cotton gown, decorated with small flowers, and fixed a fichu around her neck. When she picked up her customary fan, Maisy told her that she looked as pretty as a pastoral painting.

"Nonsense—you are too complimentary, Maisy. Now off you go to breakfast."

Maisy did as she was bid, an unusually cheerful smile on her face as she beamed at her mistress before leaving.

In truth, Rebecca had been so preoccupied since Lady Goring's outburst on their arrival at Worth Manor, that she had not taken in anything of the house. Now, at eight o'clock in the morning before the other guests were up, the house was still, awaiting Rebecca's perusal. She walked down the upper hallway, the daylight having chased away the shadows of the previous evening to reveal a beautifully coffered ceiling. Dappled light shone through mullioned windows to illuminate the wooden panelling of the walls.

Dust motes danced in that cool morning sun. Rebecca passed a Gothic-looking carved chest on one side of the hall and on the other a far more recent addition of a marble-topped side table with scrolled wooden legs covered in gilt. This was unlike the London Town houses of Society which were remade along the lines of recent fashions. This house had the record of its age in the furniture and decor that still resided in its interior.

She came to the stairs—a wide oak set that came down in a squared spiral coming back on itself, and went down them, entering the antechamber of the great hall next door. She passed a wooden partition, similar to a rood screen in a church, all carved and dark, and the great hall stretched out before her high and wide, ready to welcome knights and ladies of some bygone age.

She imagined James and Caro as children in this house, running through this hall, their cries echoing up into the hammerbeam roof. It was difficult to picture it. The house seemed a little cold—unlike the warmth of her friend Caro—without the feminine touch. Its decor felt dark, heavy and masculine.

"Good morning."

Rebecca jumped. The place had been so silent—not even the sound of servants moving about—that she had felt all alone in the world. She turned to see James entering the hall behind her. He was dressed in a wool frockcoat, well-fitted, with a silk embroidered waistcoat beneath and an effusion of white lace at his neck. He wore breeches and leather boots, as befitted a country gentleman, and suddenly Rebecca realised how very much more this place suited him than the haunts of fashionable London.

"You approve?" James asked, a half-smile on his mouth as he looked down at himself.

Rebecca's hand came to her mouth, and she realised she had been smiling at him.

"Oh," she said faintly, then turned to look about her at the hall again—her eyes running up to the great portraits of Worth ancestors staring down on them both. "I was just thinking how well it suits you being here."

Silence fell between them. She turned back to him expectantly. All thoughts of Lady Sophia and Mr Malvon and what she was here for melting away.

"Would you like a tour?"

"Yes," she said happily. "That would be lovely."

James came to her side and offered her his arm. They started out together, their heels clicking on the wooden floor.

"This is my grandfather." James pointed up at a middle-aged gentleman whose painted countenance stared down at them from the great hall's high wall.

The figure wore a long wig, an embroidered coat with large cuffs and red-heeled shoes. He had a heavier brow than James, but Rebecca saw the man had the same blue eyes.

"My mother."

This woman looked just like Caro—the same heart-shaped face and alabaster skin, and the same disarming smile.

They came to the next painting, but this one James did not introduce.

"Your father?" Rebecca asked quietly.

"Yes."

He did not look much like James at all. He had a heavy brow, a more bulbous nose, and eyes that had none of the earnestness and warmth James' had.

"I admire you," said Rebecca, "for all that you have done

to restore your family's fortunes. It is no small feat. Your perseverance..." She trailed off, looking up at James.

His gaze was on her, but she could not read the look in his eyes.

"I'm sorry, I should not speak of it."

"No," James said, drawing them away from the portrait of his father towards the end of the hall. "I just didn't expect it."

They left the hall and came into a music room decorated in a vibrant green, with a pianoforte to one side and a collection of chairs around the fireplace. James pointed out several of the paintings and explained the piano had been commissioned from a German maker. He pointed out the view from the window which sped away over the grounds into the distant Sussex hills.

Next came a tapestry room, small and square and cosy. James said the tapestries had been purchased by his grandfather from Flanders. After this came a back entrance hall. It had the same panelling and coffered ceiling as the upstairs passageway, and a series of long, glass doors had been added to the room which opened onto the formal gardens. Rebecca could see a gardener at work in one of the flowerbeds.

"I don't consider what I'm doing any more than my duty. It is the least I can do for my family—for Caro and little Anne."

"But a lesser man," Rebecca countered, "would not work so hard, or so tirelessly. Look at half the young men in Society. They spend their days gaming and carousing."

"Like Lord Avers?" James asked, "He, like the others, does not have a sullied name to work clean."

Why had he chosen to mention Avers name in particular? Had he noticed the way that gentleman was flirting with her. Did it... bother him?

"Don't you see," Rebecca replied, wanting to wash the bitterness from his voice. "Your name is not sullied. You are a worthy man and that has been reflected in the name you carry. Everyone sees it. I see it."

She glanced up at him and saw a deep furrow in his strong brow.

"That was never why—" She broke off, her heart fluttering at what she had been about to reveal. She couldn't. Just because her feelings had changed did not mean she should reveal them. It was not fair to James.

Despite her stopping, James seemed to follow her line of thought.

"I fear doing my duty has not made me the man of Society others are," he said ruefully.

"Perhaps," she said hesitatingly. "Perhaps Society values the wrong things."

She could feel his eyes on her, but she dared not look back. He might see exactly what she was feeling at this moment. The desire to right all that was wrong between them. The need to tell him she had been foolish when she had refused him, thinking love rested on wit and conversation and not the character of a man.

"Rebecca." James' voice was husky and low.

He turned to her, the morning light falling across his face, picking out strands of his fair hair like golden threads. His blue eyes were unguarded as they looked down at her, his expression deep and open. She saw in them a warmth that had been hidden from her. Her lips parted, but no words came. His gaze fell to them, his head bending unconsciously lower. They were so close she could feel his breath on her cheek. Her heart raced. They were inches apart.

"Lord Worth!" Lady Goring's piercing voice came from the doorway.

James and Rebecca broke apart, looking at Lady Goring approaching and then with shock back at each other. Had they been about to...?

"Good morning," Lady Goring said. "My, you are up early, Lady Rebecca. I had thought you would be tired after your escapade yesterday. Lord Worth," Lady Goring said, coming between them, facing her host and cutting Rebecca from the conversation. "You will give me a tour while we wait for my daughter to come down. I'm sure she will be here shortly."

James bowed, offering his arm to Lady Goring, and looking over the woman's shoulder, he mouthed the words 'Lady Sophia' to Rebecca. Then he escorted Lady Goring back into the tapestry room to give her the tour he had just given Rebecca.

So, they must continue their ruse, and Rebecca must ignore whatever had just happened. She had understood James' command to go and find Lady Sophia while the Countess was otherwise engaged. He had turned from almost... kissing Rebecca... so quickly that she thought now perhaps it had been a trick of the mind. If it had, it had certainly had a very physical effect on her, for she wasn't sure she could move. Her legs felt like they did not belong to her. She took a sudden breath. How long had she been holding it? Pressing a hand to her chest to try and slow her racing heart, she turned to the view outside the glass doors.

Everything which had lain unsaid between James and her had been disturbed this morning. His protectiveness over the hold-up yesterday. Their almost kissing this morning. He had, hadn't he? Or had he just been listening to her attentively? Whatever the case, Rebecca had limited time, and now her heart was slowing she needed to pull herself together and go and find Lady Sophia. She shook herself soundly, took a deep breath, and strode from the hall to find her friend.

CHAPTER FIFTEEN

Rebecca left the back hall through the opposite door to the tapestry room, hoping she might find another way to the stairs that would not bring her into the path of Lady Goring and James. She opened a door which she thought may lead to a through room only to find herself in a study. She paused in the centre looking about her.

"My Lady," said a voice from behind.

She spun round to see James' steward, Safi, standing by a window with a paper in his hand. His brown eyes rested on her questioningly.

"Good morning," she said, cheerily. "I was just being shown over the house by your master, but now he is engaged with Lady Goring, and I had thought to—" He was James' servant not Lady Goring's. There was no need for subterfuge. "Find Lady Sophia upstairs."

"I am afraid this is my Lord's study."

"So I see." Rebecca looked around at the carefully ordered volumes of estate accounts on the shelves, the stack of corre-spondence, neatly addressed and sealed, laying on the desk, and the leather chair that must belong to James.

"If my Lady were wishing for an unobserved staircase, she might try the backstairs, back the way she came and right." He pointed with the piece of paper in his hand.

Rebecca felt the corner of her lips tug upward. "How observant of you, that you should think I might wish to be *unobserved*."

Safi bowed. "My master has told me a degree of discretion may be needed during your stay."

"Has he?"

How much had James divulged to the man? He must truly trust this servant if he was willing to give away an inkling of what was going on.

Safi nodded. "I have my orders." He paused, his dark brown eyes silently absorbing Rebecca's face. "He puts a high degree of... trust in your judgement, my Lady."

She couldn't help the immediate smile that appeared on her lips, nor the sudden need to dip her chin and look at Safi self-consciously through her lashes.

"I only hope I can deserve it," she said, inclining her head to the man and turning away.

She thought she heard him say 'so do I', but it was so faint, and surely he would not have the nerve. As she followed his directions to the back staircase, she believed that if he had said those words, she admired him for it.

Lady Sophia was already dressed and sat by the window of her bedroom when Rebecca entered.

"Out!" Rebecca ordered the lady's maid, Miss Dent, who was busy tidying Lady Sophia's dressing table.

"But my Lady Goring said I was to stay with Lady Sophia," said the maid, a defiant gleam in her eye. She stood her ground by the table, a horsehair brush in her hand, held as if it were a sword and she were waiting for an engagement.

Rebecca drew her shoulders back and looked down her fine nose at the servant.

"Lady Goring may have said that, but I am here to talk to Lady Sophia about my own private matters, and I will not have some nosy servant around to overhear. Out with you!"

She raised a hand and batted it in the air as if she might strike the woman out of the room with just the gesture.

The maid looked to Lady Sophia who was sitting open-mouthed on the window seat and then back to the intruder.

"But my Lady..."

"I tell you, Miss Dent, if you do not leave this minute, I shall tell Lady Goring exactly where her precious lace kerchiefs keep wandering off to. You don't think I'm as blind as your mistress, do you? I hear selling such items makes a pretty penny or two."

The maid looked shocked, her lined face going slack and her eyelids flickering.

"Yes, well, you should be surprised. I've heard of ladies' maids being sacked for less and with no references. Whose mercies shall you choose to fall on?" Rebecca was rather enjoying this. "Fall on mine now and I shall not say a word. All you must do is leave and not tell your mistress I am here. Or you may choose to fall on her Ladyship's, once I tell her of your sticky fingers!"

The maid gave one final look at Lady Sophia before making up her mind and leaving the room.

"Thank goodness for that!" exclaimed Rebecca when the door had closed. "Where is your own maid? I should much rather have my own than that dragon looking after me."

"Mama let her go. She said she couldn't be trusted after she was found with... with..."

"One of Mr Malvon's letters?" Rebecca finished for her,

and took the dressing table chair some distance from the window seat.

"Yes," Lady Sophia whispered.

"And it was Mr Malvon, was it not, who held us up yesterday?"

Lady Sophia had gone quite pale.

"I can't believe he did it, but he said he had no other way to get a message to me."

"And that," Rebecca said, nodding to the paper clutched in Lady Sophia's hand. "Is that his letter?"

Lady Sophia's eyes were wide, a look of terror in them

"Don't worry." Rebecca held up her hands. "I told you before, I only wish to help."

Lady Sophia shrugged, her shoulders shaking, and held out the quivering letter to Rebecca. She took it and began to read,

My dear love,

Forgive my actions, but I could think of no other way to reach you. You know that my heart is yours, in spite of what has come between us.

I wish you to consent to be my wife. I have made arrangements in the hope you will say yes.

Meet me in three days at the inn in Singleton. I shall wait there with a chaise to take us to Essex where you may reside with my sister until we can be married.

I hope and pray you will make the choice I wish you to in spite of circumstance.

Your love,

Edward Malvon.

· · ·

"This is splendid news," Rebecca said excitedly, folding the letter up and beaming at Lady Sophia.

"Splendid?" Her fair face crumpled as she began to cry.

"Why yes, my dear, for he loves you, and there is no reason you cannot be together."

"But I can't... Mama... "

There were voices in the hall outside. Lady Sophia flashed large, petrified eyes at Rebecca. Putting a finger to her lips, Rebecca re-folded the letter quickly and was just pushing it into her pocket when Lady Goring came into the room.

⁂

"A ball? What a wonderful idea," said Caro.

She, James and Felton all sat together at the breakfast table, awaiting the rest of the guests.

"I had thought it only fitting to celebrate baby Anne's arrival with our neighbours," James said, looking at Caro.

"That would be lovely, James." She smiled brightly back at him. "When is it to be?"

"I have already made arrangements for this Friday. I hope that does not put anyone out?"

"You have been a busy bee, dear man," Felton mused from his side of the table. "Quite the social butterfly you are turning into."

"I'm sure he doesn't appreciate being compared to insects, dear," Caro chided, a half-smile on her lips.

"Apologies. And Avers will arrive just in time to attend. Have you planned it so?" asked Felton, a crease at the corner of his mouth and a provoking gleam in his eyes.

"I'm sure he will be most welcome," James replied, his brow lowering a little at his brother-in-law.

The thought of Avers arriving today did not appeal to James, especially after the moment he had shared with

Rebecca. If Lady Goring had not interrupted them, they might have...

"And you shall have two ladies to show off to the neighbours—Lady Sophia and Lady Rebecca. A duo of beauties." Felton grinned at him.

James was deeply frustrated with himself for mentioning anything to Felton the previous night after dinner. A moment of weakness had made him feel the need for a confidant and now he was paying the price.

"Tobias," Caro said sharply, her blue eyes sending her husband a warning look.

James glanced between them and sighed.

"You've told my sister, then?"

"I could hardly keep it from her. First you organise a house party in a home you have told me yourself you did not wish to come back to, and then you invite... questionable guests. It's clear something is going on."

"Is it anything we can help with?" Caro asked, face all concern.

"No," James said through gritted teeth. "I am aiding Lady Rebecca, that is all."

Even as he said it, he felt a fraud. That is not all it had been this morning, when he had been so close to her he might have kissed her. She had seemed willing, the rejection of months ago forgotten, and the feelings between them rising up from the ashes of that first attempt at love.

"Throwing a ball for her too." Felton was still grinning.

"It is not for Rebecca—Lady Rebecca," James corrected. "I am stepping into all that my title requires. If I were not to have a ball to celebrate my niece's coming into the world, what would my neighbours think of me?"

It was not necessary to disclose that he was going to use the event to invite Mr Malvon, in order to force a meeting with Lady Sophia and bring whatever matters lay between them to a head.

At that moment, a servant came in and announced Lord Avers' arrival from London.

"The plot thickens!" Felton winked provokingly at his brother-in-law before jumping up from his chair and going to welcome his friend.

"We should go too," James said reluctantly, rising from his chair.

"Ignore Tobias. It is his way of helping you—saying awkward things—though it doesn't seem it." Caro sighed with satisfaction. "I am thrilled you'll be throwing a ball in Anne's honour. It is just as the Lord of Worth Manor should do," she said, taking his arm and squeezing it with both hands. "You will spoil her, I think."

"It is only fitting."

They began walking out together.

"Yes," Caro said. "And you will... you will speak to me, won't you, about the other thing? If you should need to, I mean?"

James glanced down. Caro's large eyes were fixed upon him.

"Of course, sister," he said, "but there is nothing to relate."

At least, he was not sure he understood enough of what had happened between himself and Rebecca this morning in order to be able to speak of it with any coherence. All he did know was that for the first time in months, there was the faintest glimmer of hope.

Caro did not reply. They both came to the entrance hall as Avers walked in, Felton slapping a hand on his back.

"Well, Lord Worth. Good of you to invite me. Tell me, what have I missed thus far?"

"My man has been making enquiries," James said to Rebecca in a lowered voice.

They were stood together a little way from the rest of the house party who had gathered on the lawns behind the Jacobean manor house. A collection of chairs and tables had been placed under a canvas tent with a good view of the area where a game of bowls was being played.

The party, completed by Avers several days ago, had been proceeding with the same amount of unspoken tension and sharp set-downs from a certain Countess. Rebecca had managed to engage in several conversations with James over the matter of Mr Malvon and Lady Sophia, but neither of them had raised that first morning and the almost-kiss that had occurred.

"Yes," Rebecca replied, keeping her eyes focused on Lord Avers who was taking his go.

"He has found out that Mr Malvon is staying not far from here, in Singleton."

"Oh yes," said Rebecca, forgetting to sound surprised

She had told James about Mr Malvon's letter but not the contents. In truth, she had been worried that James would not respond well—that he might refuse to help them with such a clandestine activity on the cards as elopement. When he had told her of his plan to invite Mr Malvon to the ball, she had reasoned that the elopement was a last resort and need not be discussed unless absolutely necessary. Even then, she was not sure Lady Sophia would have the stomach for it after her initial reaction the other day.

"That would make sense." Then she added quickly, hoping he would not notice the slip in her tone, "He would want to be nearby."

"My thoughts exactly," James said, a note of excitement in

his voice. "According to the landlord, he has been staying there awhile, I expect since his escapade as a highwayman. It was only a matter of time before Safi tracked him down."

"A genius stroke," Rebecca called to Lady Sophia who had just rolled her ball, but she looked directly at James as she did so, a gleam in her eyes.

"I'll take the compliment," James replied, a smile hovering over his lips.

This is what it had been like since that morning in the back hall. An ease of conversation had been born between them.

"I have relayed a message to him, through Safi, that I request his attendance at the ball."

"Excellent. Then it is just up to us to get him an opportunity to speak to Lady Sophia when he is there. As soon as Lady Goring spots him, our game will be up."

"There will be plenty of side rooms in which we might arrange for them to meet," said James, "and in such a public setting, should he re-propose, it would be difficult for her mother to refute the engagement. We shall make witnesses of all the attendees."

This was very promising indeed. Perhaps an elopement really wouldn't be the only recourse for the couple.

"How can you be sure he'll do so?"

"Safi was clear that my invitation to the ball was on behalf of Lady Sophia. He passed on a rather... effusive message to the man."

"Effusive?" Rebecca quirked a brow at him.

"Yes."

James offered nothing more and Rebecca was left to wonder just what words Safi had used to persuade the man to try again at love.

"Your man Safi is a servant to be reckoned with."

Rebecca pulled her handkerchief from her breast and

polished the ball in her hand to have something to do that would stop her staring at James. During their encounter in the hall that first morning, the old tension of discomfort between them had been replaced by a new one. But this was far different in nature. It crackled and fizzled when they were together, and when the easy conversation between them dropped, and all that was left was looks, the feeling heightened.

"That he is," James replied. "I shall tell him of your approval."

"Please do." She sighed inwardly, thinking of the servant's challenging words when she had seen him in the study. And then she murmured to herself subconsciously, "I am not sure he likes me just yet."

"I can assure you," James said with sudden feeling, "he has heard no cross words from me on your account."

"Oh no! I did not mean to imply that—dash it!" Rebecca dropped her ball and it landed very near James' booted toe.

He bent to retrieve it for her, and when he placed it back in her hands, she felt his gloved fingers running over hers sending a tingling sensation up her arms.

"You have hope then—for the couple's second chance?" she asked, realising all too late her attempt at diverting the conversation from her awkwardness had terrible echoes of their own past.

"Hope, I think, is an undervalued commodity. I myself have not had much of it in my life, but now—yes, now I have hope for them."

"Lord Worth." Lady Sophia's gentle voice came from the playing green. "It is your go."

James left Rebecca to take his turn on the pitch. She gazed after him, trying to understand who he had been talking about. Her mind ran forward—was he talking about them? A wave of hope raised her. Surely not. It ebbed away. He couldn't be speaking of them.

She might have stayed like that for quite some time, pushed between hope and anguish, had Lady Goring not appeared beside her.

"Lady Rebecca, you are forever a thorn in my side, are you not?"

Rebecca turned to her, but the woman was all painted smiles directed towards the players on the bowling green.

"I hardly know what you mean."

"I thought I had made myself clear when it came to Lord Worth and my daughter," said Lady Goring.

"You are intent on making a great many of your opinions clear, Lady Goring. It is difficult to keep up."

Lady Goring's countenance puckered as if she had sucked on a lemon. It was the first time Rebecca had managed to push back at the Countess' attempts to crush her underfoot.

"You have a high opinion of yourself, but remember—" Lady Goring allowed a malicious smile to creep across her thin lips. "The higher you are, the further you fall. I've warned you one too many times already and you have obstinately chosen to ignore me. What happens now will be on your own head."

The Countess finished her ominous pronouncement and turned her false smile on Rebecca, letting it widen until she almost looked a little crazed. Then she wiped it off her face in a second and turned away, swinging her wide skirts around, her false rump dipping and rising as she approached Caro, Felton and Avers who sat chatting beneath the canopy.

A shiver ran down Rebecca's spine in spite of herself. She glared at the back of the Countess, who was now cutting across the trio's conversation with some inane comment, and then shook herself. The woman was all hot air and threats. What could she possibly have over Rebecca?

CHAPTER SIXTEEN

The day of the neighbourhood ball arrived with rain and then bright sunshine. While Worth Manor would never be as modish as the fashionable residences in Town, Rebecca thought James had done a magnificent job of restoring it to its former glory. It had been beautified with garlands from the estate and a thorough clean had lifted the dust from the gilt portrait frames, candelabras and wood panelling. If it did not exude the elegance of the latest fashions, at least it glowed with warmth, and the neighbours of the estate were enchanted.

They flocked to the manor from several miles around. Some were driven by curiosity to see the new Lord Worth's endeavours in the flesh—others to renew their acquaintance with a family they had shunned many years before. Rebecca watched James welcome them all—the perfect host next to his glowing sister Caro.

James had appeared apprehensive as the time drew near for the first guests to arrive, but as they filtered in, many offering kind words and happy smiles, Rebecca noticed him visibly relaxing. He became cheery and generous with his own smiles, and he looked the ideal Lord of the place. The Worth siblings presented a unified front and a new beginning for the Worth name.

"Quite the gentlemanly host," Lady Goring was saying. "We are most gratified to have been included in this select party." Rebecca could see the Countess gesturing with a glass of wine in her hand at herself and her daughter. "Then again, my daughter Sophia is much sought after in Society. She is, after all, a great beauty. It is hardly surprising Lord Worth should include her."

Various members of the local gentry had gathered around Lady Goring to listen as she spouted tainted truths to bring them under her spell.

It was so very obvious and tasteless. Rebecca resisted the desire to roll her eyes. She would be glad when Lady Goring's designs were finally thwarted.

"Though I am sure," Lady Goring continued, "we shall be hearing quite a few announcements when this party is at an end."

A few? Lady Goring might be expecting an engagement between Lord Worth and her daughter, however much in vain. But more than one such announcement? Rebecca didn't have time to mull over Lady Goring's claim for, in the next moment, Lord Avers was requesting that she partner him in the first dance.

"You are looking ravishing this evening, Lady Rebecca, but I'm sure you know that already." He guided her onto the dance floor.

"Your superficial flattery holds no water with me this evening, my Lord," she said ungenerously.

"Oh, how your words sting, but from so pretty a face they do not sting for long." He smiled sleepily at her. "Tell me, without so much venom, what have you done to make my aunt so giddy? She has a veritable spring in her step this evening."

The pianist, a local player who had been engaged on short notice, was tinkling on the keys waiting for the rest of the dancers to take their places on the floor of the great hall.

"I do not believe I could ever be accused of making your aunt giddy, Lord Avers."

Rebecca took in the other couples joining the set and then glanced up at the faces of the Worth ancestors looking down upon them. Tonight, whether it was the glow of the candles or the mastery of the long-dead artists, their painted expressions —which had seemed mostly dour in the morning light—were soft and happy this evening, in keeping with the event.

The piano began to increase and fall into a regular melody and soon they were dancing, Avers coming forward and moving his stockinged legs deftly. Rebecca copied the pattern and then moved around her partner.

"Have you not noticed? She is looking positively gleeful."

"I had not." Nor, in this moment, did Rebecca care. Her eyes were flying over the growing crowd as she moved about the floor.

"I should be more concerned than you appear, if I were you. There are few things that make my aunt so pleased, and it is more often than not the imminent downfall of another, usually instigated by her vicious tongue."

"Now you wish to stop your aunt's machinations?" Rebecca asked. "I thought they amused you."

"Apparently more than I am amusing you in this dance. Will you ever turn from the crowds and look upon my face? Have you not noticed the patch I have donned this evening? A wonderful moon in homage to you as the sun in my life."

Rebecca resisted the urge to deliver him a resounding set-down and tell him to jolly well shut up. She had suffered enough of his flattery and witty conversation. She had had enough of that from the fashionable young men of Society to last her a lifetime. It was all hollow and false.

The main reason she did not rebuke him there and then was because he had quite rightly pointed out her lack of interest. She had been scanning the crowds for any sign of Mr Malvon. It was not Mr Malvon she glimpsed, however, but Lord Worth, and the sudden directness of his blue eyes across the crowd caused her to miss her step.

"That is not the step, Lady Rebecca."

She caught herself up quickly, correcting her move, and paying closer attention to the next few movements. She had never made such a faux pas on the dance floor before.

"Ah, I see his Lordship has entered the hall. Done with greeting his guests. Enough to overset any lady."

Lord Avers swept around her, offering a charming smile to the crowds at the edge of the dancefloor, and did much to cover her misstep. Still, Rebecca caught several gazes looking interestedly over at her, and here and there a smirk.

"Don't worry," Avers murmured in her ear. "I am sure they look admiringly at my dancing ability."

"Confound you!" Rebecca hissed at him.

She turned about in the dance and saw James again. This time, he was not looking at her as he had been when she had stumbled. He was standing with Caro, enveloped in a buzz of gentlemen and ladies who swarmed around them, hoping for a second conversation with the handsome Lord.

"Finally, a little colour in those cheeks," Avers said. "Though I should like to have been the cause."

"Oh! Do stop talking such nonsense! You have no intentions towards me, and I wish you would cease being so intolerable."

"Yes, but I see that my intolerable actions have led to some rather excellent progress while I've been tardy in coming to Sussex. Am I to guess correctly that my little cousin has some competition for the eye of Lord Worth?"

"What?" Rebecca said, sucking in her breath. She spun

away from Avers in the next move of the dance. It gave her enough time to regain her composure. "What game are you playing, that you see my getting in the way of your cousin as progress?"

Avers smiled at her, his hooded eyes twinkling. "I am always playing some game or other." He broke away from her, and when he returned, his face contained a seriousness that had not been there before. "And if it is for my cousin's happiness, then I shall play hard and fierce."

"Your cousin's happiness? Then we are—" Rebecca broke off.

The dance was drawing to a close. She had assumed he was on the side of his aunt where his cousin's match was concerned, and his funning was only to annoy her and James. But if he was happy about them...

"It does not explain it, then—the spring in my aunt's step —if Lord Worth is looking at you like that."

Rebecca felt herself colouring more hotly than ever and wished she had her fan to hand to swot the insufferable gentleman.

"Ah," he murmured, slowing his step for the end of the dance. "I fear my aunt's giddiness may be short-lived."

He bowed to her, and she returned a curtsey, keeping her eyes on him as he jerked his chin over her shoulder at whatever he had seen.

"I take it that is your doing?"

Rebecca rose, turning gracefully to take up Avers' arm, scanning the room as she did so. It took her a few moments to discover in the crowd the object of Avers' attention. A tall dark-haired gentleman had just entered the hall and was slipping between the ball-goers until he was against the wall of the room. His back to the wooden panelling, he looked out across the crowds, searching for someone. Rebecca knew exactly who he was searching for, and she had every intention of ensuring he found her.

"You must excuse me, Lord Avers."

"Of course, my *incomparable*, but I urge caution. In the case of my au…"

Rebecca heard no more of his warning. She was already half-way through the crowd, on her way to Mr Malvon.

***

"Mr Malvon," Rebecca said a little breathlessly as she finally came upon him.

The man looked startled at her accosting him. His expression turned to one of embarrassment as he recognised her, and his cheeks blushed a deep red.

"You'll remember me—Lady Rebecca," she said, introducing herself, inclining her head quickly. "You needn't worry about holding me at gunpoint when last we met. I shall not hold a grudge. But perhaps you will make it up to me by escorting me to the drinks table and procuring a glass for me. Dancing does make me so thirsty."

The man's mouth opened and shut without a word being uttered.

"Excellent—you do not object." She took his arm without him offering it and began steering them through the crowds.

The room was full now, most of the guests having arrived, and the next dance was already part-way through. Rebecca caught sight of James on the dancefloor partnering a woman she did not recognise. Felton and Caro were there also, laughing as they danced down the line of the country jig, oblivious to what others thought of them partnering each other. There was something wonderfully informal about the setting which Rebecca thought was absent from the London balls. It felt far more an occasion for laughing than those gatherings, which were so often filled with drama and intrigue from the latest *on dits*. That being said, she thought ruefully, she had a mission to fulfil if she was to help Lady Sophia and Mr Malvon find each other.

"I hope you do not mind me being forward, for I'm afraid it is in my character, and I wish to speak to you on behalf of Lady Sophia."

"You do?" He looked down at her.

"It's best if you look around and smile," Rebecca said, "for then it will not look like we are discussing anything of import. After all, you are a new acquaintance of mine whom I have not seen in some time. We are just catching up."

"Of course."

Mr Malvon appeared to be regaining his equanimity after being confronted by the woman he had held up on the road. Rebecca expected nothing less from a man who was willing to become a highwayman just to gain access to his lady love.

"I apologise for my surprise," said Mr Malvon. "It is just that I was invited by his Lordship this evening."

"Yes, Lord Worth has done an admirable job of bringing you here on behalf of Lady Sophia."

"You both work in aid of Sophia?"

The Christian name on his lips made Rebecca glance at him. It was an intimate thing to do and usually reserved for betrothed couples.

"You were travelling with her Ladyship, though," he carried on, thinking aloud. "How am I to trust you?"

"Seeing as I did not betray you to her Ladyship, even when your fine leather boots and silver scrolled pistol gave away your identity, I should think that proof enough of the confidence you may have in me, do you not?"

They reached the antechamber in which the drinks table was set, and Mr Malvon ordered two glasses of punch. When he was given them, he guided Rebecca to a quiet corner of the room. The majority of the ball-goers were in the main hall now as the dancing had recommenced. He handed a glass to Rebecca and studied his own thoughtfully.

"Why do you help us? Surely you know my plight is dire."

Rebecca pushed out her full lips in thought, her dark brow crinkling, and then said, "I think the course of love does not always run smooth. Sometimes a second chance is needed. It is clear she loves you."

"Love has not been the issue."

Thinking he meant Lady Goring, Rebecca's thoughtful face broke into a smile.

"Yes, we both know what the obstacle has been, but that is why you are here. You have another chance to declare your love for Lady Sophia, and this time you will overcome it."

He looked at her sceptically. "You are very sure."

Mr Malvon was a plainly dressed man, without the dash of the dandies in Society. He wore a blue suit, with a little lacing at his throat, and no diamond pin. His hair was plainly styled as well, without the artificial curls of so many of the young men of fashion. And there was an honesty in his open face that Rebecca was drawn to.

"I do not have much to offer in the way of material goods —a small estate in Essex and no title. As such, I had thought my cause lost."

"Lady Sophia has not forgotten you as much as her mother might have wished it," said Rebecca. "I have seen the conflict within her. Your cause is not lost."

"But to be invited and helped by Lord Worth," said Malvon in disbelief. "I had heard from several of my acquaintances that he was courting Lady Sophia with a hope to wed her. I had wondered if his invitation here was some cruel jest to make me see that which I dread. Perhaps at the instigation of Lady Goring."

"His Lordship would never do that," Rebecca said quickly.

Mr Malvon studied her, his gaze not faltering.

"And yet, you came," she mused, looking back at him, and thinking again that this man was indeed courageous for his love. "Lord Worth offered to help me in my mission to free Lady Sophia from the cage that has been keeping her."

"What do you both have to gain from it?"

"My, you are a suspicious man when aid is offered," Rebecca said a little testily. "We do not have much time before Lady Goring discovers you are here and makes our attempts to bring you and Lady Sophia together doubly difficult. Are you to question me all evening or are we to find Lady Sophia?"

"You'll have to forgive me," he said, frowning at her. "But I find your interest in our story a little hard to reconcile, that is unless—"

"I wish you had more faith in the goodness of others. Now, I have a plan. His Lordship's study is nearby. If you wait there, it will keep you from Lady Goring's prying eyes, and I will send Lady Sophia to you."

He was still frowning at her, clearly undecided as to whether to trust her or not.

"I know what it is like," she said, sighing under his scrutiny. "To wish for another chance to... to express your feelings for another. What do you have to lose?"

Rebecca wasn't sure if it was the honesty in her words or the earnestness in her face that won him over, but he nodded slowly, setting down his glass.

"You will be so good as to show me to the study? If you are in earnest, then you have all my gratitude."

They left the antechamber for the main hall again. Rebecca told Mr Malvon to keep to the sides of the room to prevent them from being seen. If Lady Goring caught sight of him, she would likely not let her daughter out of her presence for the rest of the evening. It would also expose James and Rebecca's plans and likely preclude them from any further plotting.

There was another country jig taking place on the dance-floor. The pianist was playing the quick merry notes with a vibrancy that was setting the whole room off. Laughter and chatter had risen to the point where individuals were having to shout to each other to be heard. Even the sound of wooden heels dancing on the floor was swallowed up by the general hubbub. Rebecca's eyes roved over the crowds continually. On the far side, she saw Caro and Felton chatting with a couple and their young daughters, Caro laughing and exclaiming and Felton's eyes all for his wife.

James was on the dancefloor with another young woman. He would likely have to dance with half the neighbourhood before the night was out. Rebecca wished she could speak with him and let him know she was arranging the tryst for Malvon and Lady Sophia now, but there was no way she could. Besides, there was part of her that did not wish to take this night from him with her preoccupations. It was a grand success and a wonderful step forward for his family name. He should enjoy what he had worked so hard for, even if the ball was also being used as a ruse on Lady Sophia and Mr Malvon's behalf.

Just as she thought of the young woman, Rebecca saw her, standing by the edge of the dancefloor with her mother. Lady Goring was whispering something into her ear and pointing to Lord Worth. Lady Sophia obediently watched his Lordship, no doubt her mother telling her to push herself forward to be chosen by him for the next dance.

Rebecca was just about to turn to tell Mr Malvon to lower himself as he walked through the crowd when the most curious thing happened. Lady Goring, who had appeared entranced by the dancers just as her daughter was, looked directly across the floor between the crowds at Rebecca. She smiled, that slow feline smile of hers, and wafted her fan, inclining her head a little in acknowledgement.

Rebecca passed behind another group of ball-goers, and when she came out the other side, Lady Goring was no longer looking at her and she wondered if she had imagined it. Surely, if Rebecca had been seen, Mr Malvon would have been also, and Lady Goring would not be smiling. She must have imagined it. No doubt her ladyship was looking at someone else near Rebecca.

They finally came to the far end of the hall, and Rebecca led Mr Malvon through the music and tapestry rooms where people chatted over glasses of wine. These quieter rooms were the preserve of the married and elderly who had no need to partake in the dancing which was the main courtship ritual of such events. Instead, they caught up on the latest goings on in the neighbourhood and chatted about how different the house was now that the new Lord Worth was installed.

At last they came to the door of the study. Mr Malvon entered and turned back to Rebecca who stayed in the doorway.

"I shall contrive some reason for her to leave her mother's side and bring her to you. No one will know that you're meeting here. It will give you both a chance to speak."

Mr Malvon bowed low. "You have my heartfelt thanks, Lady Rebecca."

She curtseyed in return and then closed the door behind her. Walking back through the empty rear hall to the rooms of chatting ball-goers, she came again to the main hall. With Mr Malvon installed in the study, now she needed to extricate Lady Sophia from her mother's clutches, and that would not be an easy task.

CHAPTER SEVENTEEN

Lady Sophia had just stood up to dance with James. She was looking particularly lovely in a cornflower blue silk gown, white lace at her neckline and three-quarter length sleeves showing off her pale arms. There were pearls threaded through her powdered hair and one might have expected her to look happy. She was dancing with the host, an eligible bachelor with a fortune, looking lovely at a ball, and yet there was no pleasure on her face. At least, that was Rebecca's assessment when she returned to the great hall and sought her out.

James was speaking to his partner as he danced, and Lady Sophia returned a smile. Rebecca felt pressure on her chest. Even in the midst of the charade, James was being a gentleman.

Rebecca could do nothing until James and Lady Sophia finished their dance. She waited near a columned plinth with a classical urn on it. On the other side a middle-aged couple were talking loudly enough for her to overhear. Judging by their clothes, Rebecca surmised they were neighbours here in Sussex.

"I've had it from the Countess of Goring herself. She predicts an engagement before the ball is out."

"My dear, what excitement you show when London Society comes to Sussex. Next you will be requesting we attend the Season."

"No, dear." There was humour in the woman's voice. "You know very well it is quite out of our reach. I just can't help but enjoy the fashionable *on dits* while they're here! That Lady Goring seems to know everything. She says the Lady Rebecca Fairing—that tall, dark-haired one— is pining."

"You seem to have become bosom beaus in less than a quarter of an hour," her husband replied.

"She must have taken a shine to me. According to her, Lady Rebecca is pining after a gentleman she is very much in love with."

Rebecca rolled her eyes at the pronouncement. No doubt Lady Goring was revelling in telling the ball-goers that Rebecca had lost Lord Worth to her superior daughter.

With James and Lady Sophia still well involved in the dance, Rebecca risked peering discreetly around the urn to observe the speakers. She saw the lady smiling smugly at her husband and recognised them as a couple from a nearby estate —an untitled gentleman and his lady wife.

"And don't you think the new Lord Worth is handsome? I should have liked him for Eliza, if she were not so young."

The wife must be referring to one of their children. While Rebecca disliked very much that she and James were the object of their gossip, she heard no malice in their voices. Just curiosity, and that, she supposed, they could not be blamed for.

"He is not tested yet, my dear. There is badness in the Worth blood. Don't you remember his father and the way he used to be at the local assemblies?"

"Yes, but I also remember his wife, my dear. Lady Worth was a charming woman. She bore a great deal for so long. One cannot see how she did it, but it was a testament to her character."

"She didn't bear it," the gentleman replied. "Why else did she die so young?"

"That is cruel," his wife whispered. "And don't you see, if the young Lord Worth has his mother's blood, perhaps he really is as pleasant as he appears."

"I'll own he's done more good for the estate in the last few months than his father did in years. Have you heard about the new farming techniques he's implementing?"

"If you are about to speak on *that* subject, you will have to fetch me another glass of wine first."

"Your wish is my command."

A moment later, the gentleman in question walked in front of Rebecca, passing her on the way to the drinks room. Well, that was enlightening, Rebecca mused. At least she knew the sort of tales Lady Goring was spreading and none of it was a surprise.

The distraction at an end, Rebecca looked again to the dancefloor and saw the final movement taking place. She stepped forward, walking past the woman whom she had overheard, and smiling as she passed. The woman returned the gesture and seemed none the wiser that Rebecca had overheard her.

Rebecca made it to the edge of the dancefloor just as James and Lady Sophia finished the last movement. The Countess was waiting nearby, holding court with a selection of the neighbours. From the look of their clothes, Rebecca guessed these were the richer, titled neighbours, hand-picked by Lady Goring to listen to her gossip.

James said something to Lady Sophia—it looked like thanks—and she replied with a polite smile. As they turned to make their way off the dancefloor, a gentleman, seemingly an old friend of James, took his Lordship's arm to pull him round and greet him in a boyish manner.

Lady Sophia was released. Now was Rebecca's chance. She stepped forward, but as she did so, she felt a hand on her elbow.

"We are both wanting to speak to my cousin," Avers murmured.

Rebecca looked back at him in irritation, but before she could deliver a rebuke to shake him off, they had reached Lady Sophia.

"Sophia," Rebecca said lightly. "Your dancing is enviable, but I wondered if you might come with me for a little walk."

"A walk?" Avers said, his hand still on Rebecca's elbow as if he were escorting her. "It wouldn't perchance end in meeting a certain gentleman?"

Lady Sophia's expression changed to one of bewilderment as she looked between Rebecca and her cousin.

"Will you stop provoking matters?" Rebecca snapped in a harsh whisper. "I thought you cared for your cousin's happiness, and I have every intention of trying to secure it in spite of your aunt."

"My happiness?" Lady Sophia's voice wavered, blue eyes wide with anxiety. "But I've told you, Lady Rebecca, if you are speaking of... of Mr Malvon, it cannot be."

"But my dear, he is here," Rebecca said, her face lighting up with a smile. She discarded Avers' arm in favour of taking Lady Sophia's hands, pulling her from the edge of the dance-floor to the side of the room where they could speak unobserved. Avers followed. "Mr Malvon is here to see you so you may settle matters with each other."

"What?" The colour drained from Lady Sophia's face.

"Sophy, please don't be anxious." Avers put an arm around his cousin in a more affectionate move than Rebecca knew the man was capable of. "I know you mean well, Lady

Rebecca, but I told you it was more complicated than you believed. Your intentions are pure, but your plan won't succeed."

Rebecca looked from Avers to Lady Sophia.

"But why? He is here waiting for you. Don't you see?" Rebecca's eyes pleaded with the young woman. "He loves you and is a gentleman worthy of your affections. I know you care for him. It is as plain as day. You needn't be controlled by your mother."

"May I suggest," Avers cut in, "that we move over there so as not to attract attention. My aunt is already looking over."

Rebecca, surprised by the resistance she was facing, obeyed Avers and followed both of them to the little alcove next to the plinth where she had been standing before.

"She doesn't understand, John, and it is too awful for me to say it."

"Don't worry, sweet Sophy. I shall explain." Avers patted her hand and then turned to Rebecca.

"It was not my aunt who broke off the understanding between Mr Malvon and my cousin. It was Sophy."

"Oh!" Rebecca gasped. "But I was sure of your feelings for him. And you—" She turned to Avers, "Why have you been driving a wedge between your cousin and Lord Worth if she does not love Mr Malvon?"

"I d-do." Lady Sophia sniffed against the tears that threatened.

The questions in Rebecca's mind multiplied as she looked between the two cousins.

"I will not see my cousin forced into a loveless marriage she does not want," Avers explained. "She's not ready. So it seemed simpler to stoke whatever lay between yourself and Lord Worth. Finding out from my aunt of your refusal to marry the man was a boon for my plans."

But why would Lady Sophia not consent to marry the man she really loved?

"If I were to m-marry Mr Malvon, mother would be left destitute. I could never do that to her. Since Papa died, Mother has not been very good at managing her money, though she will not admit it. She says if I do not marry a gentleman with a fortune, she will lose the Town house. That is why she is so set on Lord Worth. But I... I cannot."

Lady Sophia finally broke down into tears, turning into Avers' arms and burying her face in his chest like a little sister. Avers patted her back gently.

Rebecca's mind ran over all the memories of the past weeks. She remembered the unpaid modiste's bills, the paintings Lady Goring was selling, the bare upstairs of their London home, and the missing furniture and artwork.

An awful feeling started to grow in the pit of Rebecca's stomach. "I had no idea." She and James had raised Mr Malvon's hopes so high. Now, she must dash them, for she could see no happy resolution to their story.

She reached out a hand to touch Lady Sophia's shoulder lightly. "Forgive me, Sophia. I only meant to help."

The girl continued to cry softly into Avers' chest.

"I must go and break the news to Mr Malvon," Rebecca said listlessly.

Shaking herself free from the sudden melancholy, she turned away from the embracing pair and started back through the crowds, overshadowed by a feeling of immense regret.

⁂

James had been unable to get near Rebecca all evening. The reunion of so many old family friends, under far happier circumstances than he had thought possible, had monopolised his time. There were so many individuals he had forgotten in his long sojourn to the West Indies. The past he had intentionally put out of mind in those years was coming rushing back. There was the Robbins family from a nearby estate, his childhood friend Lord Carey, and the Kimber family and their four daughters who had only been children when he'd seen them last and were now partnering eligible gentlemen on the dancefloor.

James had not seen these people since before his time abroad. Many had shunned the family even before that. They had slowly filtered away as the dirt on the Worth name had grown darker. James could not blame them—not when so much of the censure was deserved. If he had been in the same position, with young children, he would not have wanted them around his dissolute father.

Now here they all were, together and under the Worth roof—something James had never thought possible. It finally felt as if the family might once again take its place in local society. His chest swelled at the thought of it, and the knowledge that baby Anne would grow up with a family she could be proud of—that she would never know the shame that James and Caro had.

As his sixth dance came to a close and he walked his partner from the dancefloor, Safi approached.

"My Lord," he said quietly to his master.

James returned the young woman to her glowing parents, and came back to Safi.

"He has arrived, my Lord."

In the melee of the ball, James had almost forgotten Mr Malvon would be coming. It had only been in the brief glimpses he had caught of Rebecca that it had come to mind. But those remembrances had not lasted long when he'd looked at her. His mind had quickly been taken up by the recent happenings between them. Dressed as she was this evening, the deep crimson of her gown setting off her creamy skin and the gold lace picking up the light in her brown eyes, she was breath-taking. It set off a deep ache in his chest, one that caused his breath to catch, and all he could think about was going to her and finishing what he had begun several mornings ago.

"You will not see him here, my Lord," said Safi.

"No? Where is he then?" James had not been looking in the crowds for Mr Malvon. He had been looking in the crowds for her.

Safi glanced away before replying. What was this? James had never known his stoic servant to be anything but bravely candid before him.

"Lady Rebecca has taken him to the study, my Lord."

"The study?" James frowned.

Another neighbour interrupted then, congratulating Lord Worth on his return to the Manor and saying he had not seen a ball like this since the days of the late Lady Worth. James thanked the local magistrate and sent him off to sample the wine on offer from the newly stocked Worth cellar. Before the gentleman had taken half a dozen steps towards the drinks table, James was already striding in the opposite direction, with Safi following behind.

He slowed his pace once he realised many eyes were following his movement. It was not so easy this evening to be inconspicuous as it had been in the great balls and halls of London Society. There, he had been a lesser figure among the fashionable ton, but here he was the master. He slowed until he appeared as though he were just wandering through the crowds, greeting guests. He did not let any individual waylay him entirely, offering comments and compliments while walking, and eventually he negotiated his exit at the far end.

The music and tapestry room were easier to navigate. There were fewer people here, mostly sat down or standing at the edges of the room talking, too far away to easily catch him up in conversation. With Safi following behind him, he hoped he looked as though he were responding to some issue with the ball's arrangements.

As he came to the back hall, his eyes fell on the glass doors to the lawn. In his mind's eye, Rebecca appeared there, looking up at him. Those full lips, aching to be kissed, and that fine skin waiting for his fingers to trace the line from her collarbone to her chin before he caressed her face. But the memory of her dissipated when his eyes fell on the study door. He was just about to reach out for the handle when Lady Goring called him from behind.

"My Lord, I have some quite shocking information that I hardly know what to do with."

James swivelled on his heel, barring her from the door, eyes flashing at Safi to be quiet.

"Lady Goring, can't it wait? I have an urgent matter to attend to."

"I do not think it can, my Lord. Perhaps we might go in your study and speak of the matter?"

James' mouth opened a fraction and then firmly shut again. His eyes searched her face for signs that she knew who lay behind the study door.

"It is only that it involves Lady Rebecca, my Lord, and I am afraid it is quite damaging."

James' heart sped in his chest. How could she know that Rebecca was in the study with Malvon? Had she followed her here and been waiting until someone might come along to be a witness? Horror filled James as he realised just how dark the Countess' machinations might be. If Rebecca were caught alone with Malvon, with no chaperone, her virtue would be compromised.

He could not allow the Countess to enter the room. Just

as the thought came to him, he noted Safi's presence by his side. Two men blocked the doorway.

"Is Lady Rebecca your concern, madam?"

"Well," said Lady Goring, fanning herself in an effort to regain her footing, creases of shock on her powdered face at James' curtness. "I hope I should never be accused of ignoring the plight of a woman, even if it is of her own doing, when her reputation is at stake."

"What plight is that?" James asked. If she could not barge into the study and show Malvon and Rebecca alone together, she had no card to play.

Lady Goring spent a few seconds studying James' face. Her narrow eyes darted to Safi and back.

"A plight," she said slowly for effect, "that would see her reputation ruined for a man she is infatuated with."

James refused to allow his expression to betray any hint of his surprise. He said nothing, knowing Lady Goring would need no encouragement.

"Miss Dent!" Lady Goring hissed.

From the shadows on the far side of the hall, her Ladyship's maid materialised. She looked like some phantom, holding a letter in her outstretched hand, her face cloaked in shadow. James had not expected anyone to come to this part of the house this evening. There were barely half a dozen candles in the large space, throwing all of these goings on into an ominous half-light.

"This," said Lady Goring dramatically, snatching the paper from her maid's hand and holding it aloft, "is a letter my maid found, quite by accident, in Lady Rebecca's rooms earlier today, when she was returning a pair of kid gloves Sophia had borrowed. It fell open in my hand as she gave it to me."

If the situation had not been perilous to Rebecca's reputation, James would have scoffed.

"I became privy to far more than I should want to know of Lady Rebecca's plans—plans which threaten to ruin her. I thank God for the providence of it, for now I am able to give it to you, for I know being the gentleman you are, you might help."

Lady Goring held out the letter, apparently unwilling to give clear facts and sticking instead to ambiguous theatrics.

By this time, James doubted Lady Goring knew Rebecca and Malvon were in the study. If he could only keep her occupied and away from the room, all might be saved, but with the accusations she was throwing out about Rebecca, he could hardly take her back to the main hall.

He took the letter reluctantly from Lady Goring's hand. Safi reached out to one of the sideboards and took a candle from it to give James light by which to read.

My dear love, it began, *Forgive my actions, but I could think of no other way to reach you. You know that my heart is yours in spite of what has come between us.* James felt a shiver run down his spine. Questions flooded his mind as he absorbed the words. What was this letter? Did Rebecca really have another suitor? Was she in love with someone else?

It carried on, *I wish you to consent to be my wife. I have made arrangements in the hope you will say yes. Meet me in three days at the inn in Singleton.*

Singleton. Understanding dawned in James' mind. He finished reading, saw Malvon's name at the end, and then his eyes flicked back to the top. It was not addressed to anyone—a careful choice on Malvon's part to protect Lady Sophia should anyone find the letter. A choice which had left the letter open to interpretation and abuse by the Countess.

"Who is this Mr Malvon?" he said, feigning ignorance to buy time.

Looking up from the paper, he saw a malevolent look in Lady Goring's eyes. They watched his face keenly. Was that...

pleasure in them? James thought quickly. The letter was clearly the one Malvon had given to Lady Sophia when he had held up their coach. He did not know how it came to be in Rebecca's possession, but he could take an educated guess. With this maid of Lady Goring's rifling through rooms, it was no great leap to assume Rebecca had taken it into safekeeping for the young woman. But why hadn't Rebecca told him of its contents?

His ignorance left him unprepared to combat the Countess' obvious lies. If the letter had been found in Rebecca's possession, why wouldn't it be hers? Lady Sophia and Mr Malvon's liaison was cut off months ago.

"He is a gentleman of the county of Essex. He once entertained ideas towards my daughter, but Sophia refused him on account of his being below her station, and it appears he has now brought Lady Rebecca under his sway. Or perhaps it is the other way around." Lady Goring's thin lips curled back to reveal her teeth. "While I do not pretend to understand it, she does seem to attract the attention of gentlemen."

James ignored the jibe. "How did they meet?"

"My Lord, how would I know such a thing? All I know is that the letter was found, and its contents could cause a scandal that would ruin the woman's reputation."

That answered at least one question. Lady Goring could not have seen Mr Malvon this evening.

"I brought it to you, for you are the host and it is to your name that this scandal may become attached. I believed you might wish to know to distance yourself."

What a very clever game the Countess was playing. She plucked all the strings she had observed and understood over the past few months to get the tune she wanted.

"Your timing is inconvenient," James said caustically.

She inclined her head in an uncharacteristic show of acceptance. "I know it may seem so, but I am only a woman, and it pressed on my heart so heavily that I could bear it no more. I wished to spare you from the conversation this evening, but when I saw you so joyful with your neighbours and the young women who danced with you, I could not stomach the thought of all of that being stripped away by the selfishness of a woman who associates with your family."

In this moment, it was not his own reputation that James worried about.

"You will leave it to me to deal with this?" he asked, his expression dark.

Lady Goring smiled at him. "Of course, my Lord. Whatever you think is best."

Perhaps she thought she had won. That the look on James' face and the heaviness in his tone was proof of the wedge she had finally managed to drive between himself and Rebecca. She could hardly know it was barely contained fury on his part.

There was a noise by the study door. James jumped. The handle was turning.

"Your Ladyship, I believe it is time to return to—"

He felt a gust of air as the door behind him opened. Lady Goring's eyes widened.

"Oh!" he heard Rebecca exclaim.

"Mr Malvon," Lady Goring gasped.

James turned to see both Rebecca and Malvon coming from the study, and before his very eyes, any hope of resisting Lady Goring's machinations disintegrated. They were all dancing along to her malicious tune.

Rebecca had been found alone with Mr Malvon. A letter proving their previous attachment was in James' hand. His Lordship and Safi were the witnesses to this compromising tryst. And there Lady Goring stood, the supreme conductor of it all, no surprise on her face—only a barely disguised look of devilish glee.

CHAPTER EIGHTEEN

A feeling of cold terror overwhelmed Rebecca as she stared into the eyes of first James and then Lady Goring. She tried to back up, as if returning to the study would turn back time, but all she did was bump into Mr Malvon. She stumbled a little, and the gentleman took hold of her upper arms to keep her stationary. It grew worse.

James, who had turned upon the door opening, was staring at Mr Malvon's hands on Rebecca's arms. She stepped forward, shaking free of her supporter, and opened her mouth, but no words came. There was no clever quip, no artful explanation. She had been caught alone with Mr Malvon by two of the worst people who could have found them.

At least James might aid her against any salacious gossip Lady Goring was conjuring in her head.

"Lord Worth, I found your friend Mr Malvon in the study. I believe he has been waiting to see you for some time."

There was no need to bring Lady Sophia into this. It would be obvious to Lady Goring what was happening—that

Rebecca had arranged a rendezvous for Mr Malvon and her daughter—but it did not need to be acknowledged aloud.

But when Rebecca's eyes focused on Lady Goring, she saw the woman looking darkly happy, not angry at all.

"See, Lord Worth," Lady Goring said. "She lies to cover up her improper behaviour."

"Lady Rebecca," James said.

His expression was one of brokenness. Surely he did not really believe that she had rendezvoused with Mr Malvon for herself?

"Ever the compassionate gentleman, Lord Worth," the Countess said before he could continue, "but I hardly think compassion is what is needed in this situation. We know everything, Lady Rebecca. And you"—Lady Goring stabbed a thick finger at Mr Malvon—"are neither gentleman nor worthy of address. I only thank God my sweet, innocent Sophia did not fall prey to you."

"What?" Mr Malvon gasped, as far behind in whatever was going on as Rebecca felt. "Did you bring me here only to humiliate me?" he whispered at Rebecca's back.

She whirled around. "No, of course not, you were brought here to—" But she could not continue without putting Lady Sophia in a terrible position.

"We know exactly what you have been doing," Lady Goring said. "Lord Worth has the letter planning your elopement, and here you are meeting with no chaperone on the day of his ball, bringing scandal on his name. You should be ashamed of yourselves. Especially you, Lady Rebecca, after he has been so gracious towards you. I am afraid your reputation is in tatters."

"That's enough!" James barked, his voice not raised but firm enough to brook no refusal.

The party fell silent. Rebecca turned anxious eyes on

James. He looked so angry and now he would not look back at her.

"What letter?" she demanded when her courage finally returned.

James handed her the letter silently. She took it, holding it to a nearby candle, and recognised the script almost immediately. But there was nothing she could say. If she denied it, she would be sentencing Lady Sophia to the wrath of her mother and any hope that still remained for the couple might disappear forever. There must be another way out of this. Rebecca wouldn't give up the lovers.

She folded the letter precisely and dropped her hands to her sides.

"Where was this found?" she asked, looking accusingly at Lady Goring.

"Ha! You are to play the victim because my maid accidently found it in your belongings? The cheek of you is beyond comprehension. It is fortuitous that my maid found it, for it's his Lordship who will suffer from this. To have scandal attached to his name again after recovering so recently from his father's past. Selfish girl!"

"Lady Goring." James turned on her, his shoulders drawn back, his height dwarfing hers and his blue eyes hard as ice. "You will be silent."

Even the relentless Lady Goring was cowed at the sight of James. Rebecca tried hard to read his expression, but couldn't understand it.

"I should hope in the future you will not be so curt, my Lord, when we are likely to be closer if... Well, I shall not be crass, but I will forgive your upset at such a situation."

James did not respond to Lady Goring. He had stopped looking at her the moment his rebuke was at an end and was staring hard at Mr Malvon now. Rebecca looked back at the gentleman behind her. All colour had gone from his face as he realised just what a predicament they were in.

The whole, horrible truth hit Rebecca so hard she could hardly breathe. Lady Goring had painted a very fine picture indeed. Rebecca was the one courting Mr Malvon in secret. They were the ones arranging an elopement. Now they had been caught alone together with a witness who would not hesitate in spreading this damaging rumour abroad. Rebecca's gathering dread grew so strong within her that she began to shake. There was only one recourse for this.

"Mr Malvon," James said, his words like chips of ice. "You will leave the ball now. Safi, escort this gentleman through one of the servants' entrances so he will not be observed. I expect you to call on me tomorrow morning at eight o'clock."

Without hesitation, Mr Malvon moved past Rebecca to stand beside Safi, waiting to be led away. James leant so close to him Rebecca thought he meant to hurt him.

"If you do not return tomorrow morning, I will hunt you down. Do you understand me?"

Mr Malvon nodded nervously. Safi stretched a hand towards a second door that would take them away from the main ballroom and both men left.

"There is only one thing that can be done to save your ruined reputation," Lady Goring said, her last words spoken with a sick pleasure.

James passed a hand over his eyes. How much in this moment did Rebecca wish they were alone, that she might explain what had happened. That the note was not hers and she had only had it in her possession to protect Lady Sophia. But they could not be alone.

"You will return to the ball, Lady Goring, and not speak of this incident."

Rebecca doubted very much Lady Goring would obey the

command. This would seal Rebecca's fate and secure her daughter on the road to becoming Lord Worth's bride.

"And me?" Rebecca said in a voice so small she felt like a child.

James shook his head looking utterly hopeless. His eyes finally rested on hers and they were filled with so much sorrow, she thought her own heart might break in response.

Lady Goring was whispering something to Miss Dent. It gave them a few seconds unobserved, and all James could say was, "Rebecca, what have you done?"

The tears that had been building as she realised just what a position she had placed herself in finally came. They rolled large and unbroken down her face as she looked at James. The answering sorrow in his expression was quickly covered when he saw her tears. He straightened his jacket.

"You may wish to retire early if you feel unwell, Lady Rebecca."

He turned to go back to the ballroom and Lady Goring placed a hand through his arm though he did not offer it. They walked out together, Lady Goring looking over her shoulder at Rebecca with one final expression of triumph.

When the door to the tapestry room closed behind them, and the half-lit hall was empty of everyone except her, Rebecca finally felt her knees give way. She crumpled in a pile of silk and tears and allowed the sobs to escape her. She was ruined.

James returned to the ballroom, his mind wholly preoccupied. Lady Goring's incessant prattle beside him was like raindrops rolling off him. He didn't take a word in. All he could think about was the shock on Rebecca's face and the anger he felt at the situation they had been placed in. He knew if he responded to the Countess' chatter, he could not be held accountable for his words. While he did not take in what she said to him, he did understand the tone. She was pleased. It had all worked out according to her dastardly plan. She had tied up James and Rebecca's intentions for Lady Sophia and Mr Malvon in such a knot that he could see no way for it to be undone.

The feeling of despair was the same as he had felt when his father had first died, and he had learned the true extent of the debts and scandal that sullied the Worth name. He had been standing in front of a mountain with no view of the summit nor of the path that needed taking to gain it.

"Ah, there are my daughter and nephew. We should go to them," Lady Goring said, pulling James in that direction.

James reluctantly acquiesced. Lord Avers and Lady Sophia were standing beside one of the Grecian urns his grandfather had picked up on his Grand Tour in the early part of the century. James had bought it back from his father's creditors several months ago, along with a few other family heirlooms he had managed to track down.

"Why, Sophia, you look quite red. What have you been doing with yourself?" Lady Goring asked sharply.

"I'm afraid I am to blame," Lord Avers replied. "I have been forcing my cousin to dance rather too exuberantly with me and it is getting quite hot in here."

James took in Lady Sophia's face and determined that those were not red blotches of heat but rather of tears. He glanced at Avers who held his gaze, the look piercing from those hooded eyes.

"Ah, you will have to excuse her complexion, my Lord," the Countess said. "My daughter is not used to the Sussex air yet."

Yet. Lady Goring's words made a cold shiver run down James' spine.

"And the *incomparable*—where is she?" Avers asked.

James felt whatever rein he still had on his temper fraying.

"She has retired with a headache, has she not, my Lord?" Lady Goring was taking control of the conversation. "But seeing as you are both here and family, we may tell them, may we not Lord Worth? For the news will abound soon enough. Lady Rebecca has been caught with a certain gentle—"

"Shut up!"

The barked command was a surprise to James himself, even though he uttered it, and it caused Lady Goring to draw up short and glare at him. Lady Sophia gasped and Lord Avers raised an interested brow.

"Apologies," said James, finally relinquishing Lady Goring's arm, and pulling his jacket straight in an effort to calm himself, "but Lady Goring speaks out of turn. I was very clear in my command."

"Well, yes, but—"

"What has the *incomparable* done to you now, aunt?" Avers asked, James noting a hardness to his tone.

"What do you mean done to me?"

"Come now, aunt, your games are too much. What vicious rumour are you spreading?"

"It is not a rumour," she replied peevishly. "Lord Worth and I saw it with our own eyes. And there was a letter."

"What letter?" asked Lady Sophia, her voice wavering. "What letter are you talking about, Mama?" she asked a little more strongly, her blue eyes searching her mother's face.

"One," Lady Goring started, looking at James to see if he would stop her and then carrying on too quickly for him to intercede, "in which she planned to elope with a certain gentleman. And tonight she was found alone with him." The words she was forbade from saying now out, she slowed and raised her nose imperiously. "All I can say, Sophia, is that you made a lucky escape from that gentleman."

"Oh no, oh no, no, no," Sophia said, the protestation

becoming a sob as tears started in her eyes. She began wringing her hands before her, the handkerchief in them dancing about as she did so.

"Stop it, Sophia! Do stop making a fool of yourself."

"Aunt, please do as our host says, and shut up," Avers drawled, turning to Sophia and taking her hands gently but firmly in his own. "It's all right, sweet cousin, don't worry. Just take a breath. I'm sure it is not as bad as your mother is determined to make it. We know how she is for a tale. Is that not right, Lord Worth?"

James, whose mind had been running in multiple directions, trying to find a solution to this tangle of Lady Goring's making, looked at Sophia and then Avers, but said nothing. What could he say? Lady Goring's summation was correct, and he could not refute it without it becoming a war between their versions of the truth. And in the end it would not matter. If Lady Goring's version came out into Society, Rebecca would be ruined along with any chance of Lady Sophia marrying Mr Malvon.

Uncertainty flickered across Avers' impassive face.

"No, oh no, oh no," Sophia carried on whispering.

Avers turned on his aunt. "What have you done?"

"Me?" she pressed hands to her heart innocently. "Nothing, nephew, and I would thank you to alter your tone towards me. Now I'll take my leave of you, if you insist on being so uncivil, when all I have done is averted a scandal for his Lordship's name. Sophia, you'll come with me." She reached out and snatched her daughter's hands from Avers, dragging her away and scolding her as she did so.

"I think it time we formed an alliance," Avers said to James, his usually sleepy face alert and serious. "Would you care to join me in a quieter spot?"

James stood by the window and looked out. The terrace was illuminated by torches, and several guests were taking a breath of air. He was vaguely aware of Avers ushering everyone else out of the tapestry room with false promises of refreshments elsewhere. He barely noticed when Avers poured two glasses of brandy from the decanter on the sideboard, but came back to the present when he was handed one of them.

"I would like to apologise for goading you so much over the last few weeks." Avers took a sip of brandy, an amused smile on his lips. "I did it solely to aid my cousin Sophia."

James took a gulp of the brandy, the liquid burning its way down his throat before settling warmly in his stomach.

"You've been goading me?"

"Ha!" Avers chuckled. "You play so coy, like a miss fresh from the schoolroom, but you know to what I refer. I have been making love to Lady Rebecca in an effort to enrage you. I have been quite effective, I think." Avers looked at his nails, flicking some imaginary dust from them.

"And how has that aided your cousin?" James asked, his teeth gritted in spite of his efforts to remain impassive.

It was all a game to this man. His whole life in Society was one amusement after another, no thought to feelings or principles. The thought that all the times he had seen Avers flirting with Rebecca—which had stirred up James' own feelings— had been a lie caused the anger he was already bridling to slip out of his control.

"I suppose it is a family trait," he said before Avers could reply. He gulped down the remains of his brandy. "To meddle in the affairs of others for your own gain. Does Lady Rebecca know you are not in earnest?"

"Lady Rebecca," Avers said, leaning back on one leg and studying his glass, "does not have eyes for me, I assure you. Any such attentions I showed her were only to engage your attentions in return and divert them from my cousin."

"What?"

Avers sighed. "A cheap trick, it's true, but any fool could see whatever lay between you and Lady Rebecca was not dead and buried. That's why my aunt has done... well, whatever she has done this evening. To seal Rebecca's fate so you might be free to marry my cousin."

"And you do not yearn for the match?" James asked harshly. "Even with Society ringing with news of my grand fortune?"

"As attractive as that appears for my cousin's security, no. It is the object of my aunt's desire, that's true, but not of Sophia's, and I do not wish to see her pushed into an alliance she does not want. Without being overt in a way to attract my aunt's ire, I wished to be a barrier to that happenstance. Sophia has always been... a dear friend of mine, not just my blood. She is a gentle and loving soul and I wish her to be happy."

James did not know how to respond to this revelation and sought refuge in pouring himself another brandy. He looked up, nodding to Avers' now-empty glass. The gentleman passed it to him to be refilled.

"What makes you think she would be unhappy with the match?" James said, pouring a generous amount of the fine brandy into Avers' glass.

Avers smiled, one corner of his mouth drawing up more than the other, and the look of characteristic amusement back in his hooded eyes.

"To be married to a man who loves another? I'm not sure that is an enviable position to be in."

James passed Avers his refilled glass and turned back to fill his own. Had he been so obvious? Had the feelings he had for Rebecca—that love that had never gone away even with the extinguishing of the hope that it might be returned—been so obvious on his face, in his actions, in his eyes?

"You're very confident of my feelings."

Avers rolled the brandy around in his glass, the dark gold liquid running in a pool around the bowl, the scent of the beverage emanating out. He looked up from it and James saw on his face a sudden bareness. As though whatever mask Avers was wont to wear in Society had been removed.

"I am a confirmed bachelor now, but I wasn't always. Let us just say, I know what it is to love."

James considered denying it. But what did it matter? In the current situation, there were far bigger things to worry about than Avers figuring out that James still felt for Rebecca.

"She has been consistently telling me off for my love-making anyway." Avers sighed humorously. "She knew I could not be in earnest. I told her this evening, before—ah, the fracas —that I was trying to help my cousin with my unwanted attentions. Mr Malvon's appearance only confirmed my theory that she has been trying to aid my cousin also."

"I invited him," James said.

"Oh." Avers looked genuinely surprised at that.

"I have been helping Rebecca to see Lady Sophia reunited with Mr Malvon."

"The puzzle pieces are falling into place," Avers said, fingers from one hand tracing invisible objects falling through the air. "Unfortunately, you and Lady Rebecca have not been in possession of all the facts surrounding the broken attach-ment. You have both been labouring under the false assump-tion that my aunt forced my cousin to cry off from her love. That misapprehension is what led to Lady Rebecca being alone in the library with Mr Malvon this evening. Upon hearing he was here, my cousin refused to go to him."

James waited for him to go on.

"You see, my aunt is in financial straits—severe financial straits. I believe—although my cousin has always been euphemistic when speaking about her mother—that my aunt was clear that if Sophia did not marry well, she would be leaving her mother destitute."

"She broke it off—not Lady Goring?"

"And therein lies the crux of the matter. When Mr Malvon appeared this evening, Sophia did not wish to see him, and so Lady Rebecca returned to tell the man as much. Her unwise decision to put herself in such a position of vulnerability was my aunt's triumph."

"It's the letter that has sealed her fate."

"Ah, yes, that is most unfortunate."

"She should have told me what it said," James muttered, more to himself than Avers.

"Perhaps she thought you would disapprove."

James grunted and finished off his brandy. He stared at the empty glass in his hand, tapping it with his finger and thinking. Money, that was what this came down to. Lady Goring needed money. If a solution to her financial problems could be found, would she accept Mr Malvon as a son-in-law? Would she release Rebecca from her gossip-mongering clutches? But Rebecca had been compromised, her reputation was in question, and there was only one resolution for that. Marriage.

"I offer my services in whatever way I can," Avers said. "I will no longer be a thorn in your side. For the sake of my cousin, I wish to find another solution to the present coil that does not result in Mr Malvon having to offer for Lady Rebecca."

Hearing it out loud sent a deep ache through James' chest. The idea that she should be lost to him forever, that she would be someone else's—it was enough to press the breath from his body.

"I don't know that there is another way around it. Your aunt has played her cards well."

"That is what I fear," Avers replied, "but the game is not done yet. We still have time to think of something."

CHAPTER NINETEEN

The rest of the ball went off as if nothing untoward had happened. The neighbours ate, drank, danced and went away, secure in the knowledge the new Lord Worth was a good and proper gentleman, and there was value in the name once again. The last of the guests left about two o'clock in the morning, travelling home in their carriages by the light of the moon.

James had not seen Rebecca since he had told her to retire, so gathered she must have obeyed his wishes. He wondered if she felt as awful as he did. Lady Goring and Lady Sophia waited until the last guest bid their goodbyes and then retired. Lady Sophia had appeared a shadow of herself since hearing of what had happened. She had barely spoken, a paleness taking over her countenance, and a look of despair in her eyes. Avers had gone to bed soon after, shaking James warmly by the hand before he did so, in an act of solidifying the truce they had made. The only two who remained were Caro and Felton.

"Is there something wrong?" Caro asked, as they wandered back down the length of the great hall after seeing the others off to bed.

There were glasses scattered over every surface. The garlands were finally wilting after enduring the heat of the ball for so many hours. The chairs around the edges, which had been so carefully arranged, stood in haphazard groups—some even butting out to the edge of the dancefloor—so James and Caro had to skirt around them as they progressed.

"Why do you ask? The ball has been a success, has it not?" James said, wondering if he had missed some other disaster that had taken place this evening. "We have celebrated the arrival of your daughter as the Worth name deserves."

"Oh, indeed we have, brother. I did not mean to imply we have not. I am so thankful to you. It's been a beautiful evening." She squeezed the arm she was on. "You just seemed very distracted."

"There was an issue," James said on a sigh. He passed his hand over his eyes and pressed the bridge of his nose. An ache in his head had been growing steadily worse and now throbbed at his temples.

"Was it with Rebecca? She disappeared."

"Lady Goring found her in my study alone with another gentleman. She also found a note that implies they are amours."

"What?" Caro gasped.

They had reached the music room now. James had already sent the servants to bed, telling them that they may clean up in the morning.

"You'll have to forgive me, for I wish to hear this tale," said Felton, "but I must sit. The soles of my feet have not ached like this in some time."

Each of them took a chair, Felton stretching out his legs and resting his head on the chair back, half closing his eyes in relief. Caro sat on the edge of hers, looking with concern at James, who slumped in his chair, feeling all energy, all fight, all determination had gone out of him.

He sighed and then explained what had happened to both of them. When he had finished, Caro's brow was puckered and her blue eyes staring at the piano in thought. Felton, whose eyes had opened a little at the most shocking parts of the story, had half closed them once again, but said, "This is a dashed mess, then."

"I have to say, brother, I am relieved you have no designs on Lady Sophia, for I can't stand that awful woman—Lady Goring, that is—and I thought you half mad when you invited her here."

James smiled weakly in spite of himself. "Not mad—yet." He put a hand back over his brow, shading his eyes to ward off the persistent ache.

"Can Lady Goring not be persuaded to keep what she saw a secret?" Caro asked. "That would preclude the need for Malvon and Rebecca to marry."

"She could not even keep her mouth shut for the five minutes afterwards when I escorted her back to the hall," James replied in disgust. "She took the first opportunity to tell Avers and Lady Sophia. The poor child, I don't know how she bears it."

"She is a grotesque sort of person, Lady Goring. I don't think her discretion can be relied on if she is not gaining something in return," said Felton.

James lifted his hand an inch and stared at his brother-in-law. He barely took in Felton's shabby ensemble and relaxed repose.

Gaining something in return. That's what Felton had said. James' mind picked up speed as he worked on an idea that Felton's words had just sparked in his mind. Could what he had just thought of succeed? He wasn't sure. He dropped the hand back over his eyes and the trio fell silent.

"Rebecca," said Caro softly.

James didn't move, waiting for the rest of what she was

going to say, but when his sister did not carry on, he opened his eyes again. He saw with a jolt that she had not been referring to her friend—she had been announcing her.

Rebecca stood in the doorway of the music room, her hands clasped together in front of her so tightly James could see the white on her knuckles. Her face was free of powder and patch, the skin a mixture of red and pink under her eyes, and her hair was undressed, plaited down her back. She had removed her red ball gown in favour of a plain cotton dress more appropriate for a summer morning than an appearance in the small hours.

"My dear," said Felton, rising and picking up his shoes with one hand, stretching the other out to Caro. "I think everyone has gone to bed." He looked around to James and Rebecca, but acted as if he did not see them. "I think we should also."

Caro followed her husband's lead, rising and taking the offered hand, the two leaving James and Rebecca alone.

Rebecca thought her wretchedness could not be worse until she saw the look on James' face when she entered the music room. He was so tired, and when his gaze rested on her it was full of such sorrow and disappointment.

She had been in no state to sleep when she had left the ball. She had spent several fretful hours pacing her room, listening to the ball going on below, and waiting, hoping for it to finish before time. It had not, and when her legs had finally grown weary, she'd sat down and written to her aunt, pouring out all her upset on the page. The tears had returned as she had written about her feelings. At first it had been a few tears and she had sniffed once or twice, but before long, she was sobbing, great waves of feeling crashing over her mind and body.

She had started crying for the situation she had found herself in—the despair at not being able to think her way out of it. Then she had cried for James and the realisation he had moved out of her reach forever. With that had come an intense feeling of loss as she recognised that her love for James—a love she had only just started coming to terms with—now ran so deep through the core of her being, that the knowledge she would never have a second chance at seeing it returned might crack her in two.

Hearing her mistress was in her room with a supposed headache, Maisy had come in and been horrified to see her crying on the floor. The faithful servant had put a tentative arm around Rebecca, one to which her mistress had immediately clung, and then the maid had begun murmuring over her soothingly like a child.

Eventually the sobs had slowed, transforming into sniffing, intermittent tears, and finally stopping. Maisy had taken down her hair and helped her change into something more comfortable. In that quiet time, Rebecca let the feelings she had kept trapped for so long keep washing over her. It was not her fate she cried over—it was the knowledge that whatever had grown between herself and James over the last few months was now unattainable. She realised that—though she had rejected him all those months ago—the seeds of love she felt for him even then had not died. They had remained beneath the surface, growing as she came to know him, yet trapped by her desire to keep them from her mind and protect herself against emotions she could not control.

She had rejected James because she had expected something else from an amour. Witty repartee, modishness, dashing behaviour—those were the things she had supposed would sweep her off her feet and into a future husband's arms. When

James had not displayed them, in spite of her feelings, she had thought herself sensible in rejecting him. No, she would wait for a more fashionable man. The thought now made her feel sick. How could she have been so shallow, so foolish?

James might not have the flirtatious tongue of the fashionable young men in Society, but he had something of far more worth. Character. He had worked tirelessly to restore his family name. He had offered help to the woman who had rejected him, disregarding whatever discomfort he felt in order to do good. In the moment James had moved so irrevocably out of her reach, she had realised just how much she loved him.

Rebecca had grown restless in her room and though she knew she should try and obey James' command to stay retired for the night, she could not. Her restlessness drew her out to the hall upstairs. She heard the last of the guests leave, and the servants being dismissed. Drawing back when she heard Lady Goring approach, Rebecca only came out again when she was certain the woman had entered her room and closed the door. Quietly Rebecca descended the stairs, her silk mules discarded in favour of soft slippers. Walking through the deserted ballroom, where evidence of the recent party lay scattered about her, she had followed the sound of murmuring voices to the music room. She had stood there in silence. Caro and Felton had left, and now she was alone with James.

He was not looking at her anymore. After staring at her when she had entered, he'd leant forward in his seat, burying his head in his hands, and not looked up since.

She stood gazing down at the crown of his fair head, the broad shoulders, the tips of his fingers appearing through his hair. She stretched out a hand to touch that hair, but stilled midway. Taking a shaky breath, she brought her arm back to her side.

Turning away, she moved over to the window whose

drapes had finally been drawn. She took the edge of one with a cold hand and pulled it aside so she might look out. Through the distortions of the glass she could see a clear night, the heavens laden with stars shining brightly and a three-quarter moon hanging in its place. It let down its celestial gaze on the landscape below, picking out the tops of the ancient trees in the parkland, reflecting in an ornamental pond just the other side of the terrace, touching newly laid dew on the grass in tiny twinkling hints here and there. It was a moment frozen in time, just hers, and she wished more than anything that she might freeze time in her life now. That she might not have to face tomorrow. That she and James might stay like this, close to each other. If there was no future for them, she did not wish for time to pass at all.

"I am so very sorry," she whispered against the pane of glass, mist rising up to blur her vision. She turned, a shaking sigh passing her lips. "So sorry," she said again, her brow crumpled in regret, her eyes searching for James.

The hands he had over his eyes fell away, and the blue of his locked with the brown of hers.

He sighed, his brow dark and furrowed, his mouth an uncompromising line.

"Please, I beg you will not be angry with me. That note that Lady Goring found—it wasn't mine. It was the one Malvon gave to Sophia and I was hiding it for her. She must have found it somehow—you must believe me."

"I do."

Another shaky breath passed through Rebecca's lips. She waited but James said nothing more and so she turned back to the window.

"All I wanted to do was to help them."

"Why didn't you tell me of the proposed elopement?"

She did not answer immediately, guilt squeezing her chest. "I thought... I thought you would not approve, and I thought that if… if that should be their only option, I would help them."

James emitted some kind of sound, but Rebecca couldn't discern what it meant. Was he angry, amused, frustrated?

"I know it was foolish of me. Childish. I just felt that if that was the only way they could be together, even if Society judged them for it… well… Society is not always right in its judgements, is it? It often puts values on things that are quite the opposite of those that matter. I have learned that." She sighed, wanting to say more but baulking. Instead, she turned the subject. "It doesn't really matter now, does it? At every turn Lady Goring has been against me. Now she has finally won."

James was still saying nothing and so Rebecca, almost feeling he wasn't there anymore, felt free to speak her mind.

"She is so set on her daughter marrying you and… I couldn't let that happen. It wasn't just because Lady Sophia loves someone else. It was the idea that you should be rejected a second time, but by the woman you would call wife. I had already hurt you. If it was in my power, I wished to save you from more pain. And I… it hardly matters now. My path is set, my future sealed, and Lady Goring had to ensure I was no obstacle and now… now I am not. We both know what must happen."

She laughed in disbelief. Of course he did. That was why they were here—her speaking to him, him listening silently. They both knew exactly what must happen.

"How could I not have seen it? Mind you, the sly Miss Dent did her rifling well, for that letter was buried deep within my things, along with the bracelet and ring I said the highwayman had taken. I'm usually so astute, a good watcher of people, or so my aunt has said, but with you near me…" She smiled wanly at the glass. "I find I am no longer watching other people, but thinking of you, and of me. You make my mind..."

She drifted off, not having the courage to finish that thought, remembering James was here.

"Mr Malvon will have to offer for me. It's almost funny." Rebecca let out a hollow laugh. "I said no to you all those months ago because I wasn't sure of my love for you then. Now I am to marry someone I do not know at all, and he loves another. How cruel life is."

She was crying again, and she couldn't speak for a moment as her shoulders shuddered with the expression.

"What do you mean?"

Rebecca jumped. James was beside her at the window. When she turned to look at him, his blue eyes searched her face with an intensity that made her stomach quiver. She gazed back uncertain.

"What do you mean, you weren't sure of your love for me *then?*"

Rebecca's lips parted. She teetered on the edge of divulging everything. Should she? She had always spoken so freely, so frankly. Direct speech was something she valued highly and yet with James, over the past weeks and months, she had been careful to keep her uncertain feelings hidden, not wanting to make the situation between them worse, when she was not sure of her heart.

But hadn't it changed now? She was as sure of her heart as she was that the sun would rise in the morning, and she would be sentenced to marry a stranger. The fear she had felt over giving in to those feelings and allowing them to flood her mind and heart had lifted. She felt them now more strongly than ever as she stood so close to James.

Her eyes traced the line of his chin, the turn of his lips, the shadow of his stubble in these small hours, the slight lines at the corners of his eyes, the strong line of his brow, and those eyes—those deep, earnest blue eyes. How she loved this face. How she loved this man.

Would it be wrong to say it aloud? She might never get another chance to speak so openly, so honestly with him.

"I have been a foolish girl, James," she started, looking away to the window again, too nervous to keep facing him. She reached up a hand to grasp the curtain as if it might steady her racing heart. "I... I thought that a suitor for me would be like all the other men of Society. That was what Society had told me to value. So when you came into my life, so wholly different to that, and yet capturing my affection, I was confused. I thought I knew better than my heart, and I turned you down. I was a stupid child, measuring the value of a man on witty words and dashing manners, but I have come to realise you are—"

She broke off, uncertain how to phrase her next words. Her breath caught in her throat. She clutched at the curtain and felt it really was all that was holding her up as her stomach fluttered and her legs felt weak.

"A gentleman whose character is of far more worth," she finished, not sure she had said the right thing or captured her feelings. "I know you thought I turned you down for your father's misdeeds, but I didn't, James." A hint of pleading came into her tone. He must know this. "I didn't care anything for that. I have never held that against you and count you nothing like your father. You have proven yourself a man of far greater character than him."

Though she did not risk looking at him, she could feel James' presence beside her. Her body prickled with him so close, the sensation growing.

"I was foolish back then. Now I know better what loving someone is, not just flirting with them, hearing flattery from them. That the actions of a man are what makes him, not the words. That it is their character one falls in love with."

"And have you?" James asked, his voice deep and husky. "Have you fallen in love?"

She took a breath of courage and turned back to him. Something had changed in his face. What had looked like anger or disappointment had been removed, and in its place was a passion she had never seen before. It was her turn to put her heart on the line as he had done all those months ago.

"Yes," she whispered.

The searching in James' eyes dissolved in a second and was replaced by a look of deep longing. He stepped closer, his hand taking hers from the curtain and drawing it to his chest. He bent his head as she moved nearer, and then she felt the tickle of his other hand at the back of her neck. His fingers threaded their way beneath and through her braid, pulling her closer until her figure was pressed against his and her lips inches from his own.

Rebecca could smell the spice and cloves from his soap. She could feel the beat of his heart through her hand on his chest. She couldn't look away from those deep blue eyes of his. And then he pressed his lips to hers, expressing the longing, the feelings that had built up over all the months they had known each other, through all the turmoil, all the uncertainty. His lips were soft, savouring hers. She could sense just how long he had waited for this moment and realised she felt the same. Warmth spread out from every place their bodies connected, running to her limbs and hands, sending a thrill throughout her frame.

His lips tasted sweet to her and the feelings she had finally become sure of strengthened and grew as his kiss became more passionate. She pulled a hand from his chest and reached up. How she had wanted to touch that fair hair of his. She pushed her fingers into it, moving up the nape of his neck, and he responded by pressing her closer—so close that they might never be parted. Perhaps this kiss might go on forever. Perhaps all the fears of tomorrow might just bleed away, and they could stay like this, entwined in each other's arms, finally where they were meant to be.

Perhaps.

His kiss slowed, and gently he pulled back, his lips leaving hers as his body moved away. Forever was moving closer, and reality was settling back into its rightful place, destroying the future they might have had and leaving Rebecca where she had been before. Trapped. Ruined. Heartbroken.

CHAPTER TWENTY

As James stared down into Rebecca's beautiful face, he felt all the yearning and hope fulfilled until he remembered what had happened that evening. How he wanted to lean down and kiss her again. To kiss away all the space that had been between them and to finally tell her that he loved her. That he had loved her from the moment he had first met her in Astley's Amphitheatre nearly two years ago. That he had yearned and watched from afar, knowing he was not worthy of such a woman of nobility and character. And now she had said he was. It was everything he had not dared to hope for, to wait for.

He had taken his moment and kissed her, but as he had done so, fears crowded in. Fears that he could not trust this. It was too perfect, too like those desires that resided in the secret places of his mind and heart. Were her words those of a woman who had been compromised? Did they come from her own fears? From a sudden need to feel free when she had been trapped?

"I wanted to do that, just once, before..." He trailed off. How could he be sure?

He saw fresh tears pooling in her brown eyes as she looked at him. He wanted to pull her closer again, but she moved further away, and he released her instinctively.

"Just once?" she said, a mixture of confusion and questioning on her face.

No. He wanted to do it again, and again, and over again. He didn't want to stop kissing her. He didn't want her to ever leave his presence. But there was more to this than just them.

"I know there is no way out for me after what's happened. Not with Lady Goring as a witness and with me so much her nemesis. It is too perfect that I remove the distraction of Mr Malvon from her daughter as well. But if that were not the case..." She was looking at the carpet, too shy to look at him, and she was biting her lip. He felt a yearning deep in his stomach, and wished he could grab her waist and pull her back to him. "Would you only kiss me that once?" She looked back at him and there in the depths of her brown eyes was the courage of the woman he loved.

"Is that what you want—for me to kiss you again?" he asked tentatively, eyes searching her face. He had to be sure. He needed her to be certain.

"I've told you," she said, a look of hurt now forming on her face, then her voice dropped to barely above a whisper. "I love you, James."

He did not want to hurt her.

"Yes, you have." He stepped forward, his hand coming up to cup her cheek. He rubbed his thumb across her soft skin, moving so close that his lips hovered just apart from her own. He could have kissed her again then. He wanted to, but now was not the time.

A look of relief passed over her face as she turned her cheek in his hand, brushing her lips against his palm. The yearning in his stomach crept up to his chest and he knew if he stayed much longer, he would not be able to act the gentleman.

He held her face in his hand a moment longer, gazing into her eyes.

"Go to bed," he said, dropping his hand. "You must try and rest."

She looked confused at the dismissal, but after a moment she did as she was bade and left him. He watched her go, the cotton dress swaying with her figure, the braid mirroring the movement. Turning back to the window he saw the first signs of the new day in the lightening of the night sky. It would still be several hours until full dawn, time enough for him to work out the rest of his plan.

The following morning dawned cold. Clouds had come in overnight and the whole of the sky was blanketed in grey. It cast the Jacobean manor house in a cool light and the interior, which had been so warm and glowing the previous evening, felt chill and draughty this morning.

Rebecca had slept fitfully and not in her bed. She had dragged the blanket from it, sitting in a chair before the fire, watching it burn low and allowing the cold to slowly creep into her limbs, hoping it would numb all the emotions that raged within her.

The moments of sleep she had caught had been filled with anxious dreams of misunderstandings and fear. Nothing had made sense in them, and when she had come fully to, there was no memory left, only the feelings they had engendered. She had risen stiff with the cold and even now, dressed and walking through the hall where servants were at work clearing away the previous night's mess, she was shivering. She pressed her hands together, looking neither left nor right at the servants. Miss Dent had been present when Rebecca had been caught alone with Mr Malvon and Rebecca had no doubt the tale had made its way around the servants' hall already.

When she reached the breakfast parlour and saw it contained only Lady Sophia and Lord Avers, Rebecca paused in the doorway. They had not seen her. She stepped back, deciding to skip breakfast rather than face them, but to her discomfort Avers saw her.

"Good morning, Lady Rebecca. It seems we are the only ones up."

She considered walking away, ignoring the man, but she realised she had been the cause of enough talk already. Coming into the room, she took a seat at the far end of the table. Lady Sophia looked across at her, eyes clearly swollen from crying, but with no reproach in them. So she knew then.

"Actually, that's not strictly true," Avers said. "The Lord of the house is about, I believe. One of the servants, the man from the Indies, is attending him in the study."

Rebecca didn't say anything. She wasn't sure what to say. Avers' tone and conversation seemed to be in complete ignorance of what had happened last night, and yet Lady Sophia's tear-marked face implied the opposite.

"Fetch some fresh coffee will you?" Avers asked the servant present. They left the room obediently and the moment they did, Avers turned back to Rebecca. "I believe Lord Worth is due to see a visitor soon. One Mr Malvon."

Rebecca looked across at him sharply and there was a sniff from Lady Sophia as she started crying again.

"Yes, a fine mess we find ourselves in," said Avers, not pausing to see that his cousin was all right.

"You know?" asked Rebecca, her concerned gaze on Lady Sophia.

"I'm afraid so—Aunt Goring was most insistent on telling us last night in veiled words, much to the chagrin of Lord Worth."

He was telling it as if it were some fun Societal *on dit* that would amuse them all. It did not amuse, and Rebecca's anger at Avers replaced the sorrow she had been feeling for her friend Lady Sophia.

"If I am to trust my recollections," Lord Avers carried on, "then I believe I heard him tell my aunt to shut up. I never thought anyone would have the gall."

"Perhaps you should shut up," Rebecca snapped at him. "Can't you see this isn't an amusing matter?" She shot a sympathetic look at his cousin.

She wished so badly to go to Sophia and comfort her, but she knew she was the last person from whom that young lady would want comfort. Rebecca had inadvertently stolen the man she loved.

"Yes," Avers said, reaching a hand across the table and taking his cousin's. "I've told dear little Sophia not to worry over it, but she will not listen to me."

Rebecca sighed in exasperation, throwing her hands up in the air. "Not worry over it?" she cried, standing up abruptly and sending her chair clattering to the floor. "What good will not worrying do? We are locked in a coil of your aunt's making and only she holds the key."

"Only my aunt? I would not be so sure."

Rebecca rolled her eyes at his cryptic words. He would be forever the flirter and the amuser. Even in this awful situation, he could not stop himself. Why had she ever found such men attractive?

She left the chair she had knocked over where it was. She needed to get out of here. Walking past Lady Sophia, she paused for a moment, placing a tentative hand on her shoulder, and said quietly, "I am so very sorry, my dear. I never meant for this to happen—please know that." The words were lame and hardly a fitting response to stealing this woman's future happiness, but they were all Rebecca could offer.

Leaving the breakfast room, Rebecca headed towards the back hall in order to escape out into the gardens. She needed fresh air—she couldn't breathe in here. Her chest compressed, her ears ringing, she needed to get out.

Making quick work of the music room with her long legs, she knocked into a table on the way past in her haste. The jolt nearly sent a small oil painting flying. She barely stopped to reset it before getting on her way again. The back hall seemed to know of the house's troubles, the cold morning casting it into a sad light, as though it mourned last night's happenings as much as Rebecca did. She went straight to the French doors and just as her hands fell upon the handles, she heard a door behind her open.

She swung round in time to see Mr Malvon leaving the study, James behind him and Safi bringing up the rear.

"I will see it done, but it will take a few days," James said. "My man Safi will leave as soon as possible."

"My Lord, I will travel with all haste," Safi said in his deep voice, bowing to both gentlemen before walking away.

The men lapsed into silence and watched Safi go, and as the servant neared her position, they spied Rebecca at the garden doors.

Mr Malvon's eyes opened wide, colour appearing in his cheeks. Safi did not show any trace of emotion, only stopping to bow politely to her before continuing on his journey, presumably to the stables.

James had been making arrangements. Numbness stole over her. The only reason Rebecca could think of for sending Safi away would be to obtain a special licence from London so she could marry Mr Malvon as soon as possible. Had their kiss last night meant nothing to James then? Did he not mean to fight for her? Or was she being unfair? Could he do so even if he wished it? And would he want to after she had rejected him before?

Rebecca had known the desperation of her cause last night, but she had hoped, like a fool, that something would change after she admitted she loved him. This scene before her showed her that it would not. Her future and the safety of her reputation were being sealed.

"Lady Rebecca, good morning," James said as he bowed to her, and his civility confirmed her fears. He behaved as if he had not pressed his lips to hers last night.

His greeting jogged Mr Malvon from his trance and he too bowed.

"I will send word to you at Singleton when I hear from Safi," James said, turning back to Mr Malvon.

"I cannot thank you enough for helping me, my Lord."

He was helping Mr Malvon to marry her. Rebecca. Lady Rebecca Fairing. She was to be married to this man. The feelings those fitful dreams had left her with last night came back. The awful apprehension, the dreadful misunderstandings, and the anxiety which had blanketed her cold limbs and now caused her to shiver. That kiss between her and James seemed too far away now, so faint, so unbelievable, she wasn't sure it could have even happened.

Mr Malvon took James' hand and shook it warmly. James nodded in response, his mouth a firm line, not responding to the shy smile Mr Malvon bestowed on him.

Rebecca had thought, last night when they kissed, she could finally see James' feelings for her which had been so hidden behind his quiet tongue and his reserved behaviour. But she must have been wrong. Just as she had been wrong to reject him in the first place. Now she must have been mistaken that his love for her had remained after all these months. She could not trust her instincts anymore. Worse, in this moment and before these men, she could not trust herself not to cry.

Mr Malvon bowed again to Rebecca, and then left the hall, the sound of his boots echoing in the space.

"You will have to excuse me," James said. His gaze softened a fraction. She saw it drift over her face and rest fleetingly on her lips before returning to her eyes. "I have the rest of this issue to settle."

She could not read the look in his eyes. He offered her a brief bow and then retreated into his study, closing the door behind him.

Finally taking a breath, after holding it during most of that awkward encounter, Rebecca fell back against the doors, allowing the handles to press into her back until they hurt, breaking the numbness that was stealing over her.

She tried to calm her breathing, but it was just as constrained as it had been when she left the breakfast room. She needed to leave.

Swinging around, she finally flung the doors open, the cold air hitting her like a glorious slap across her pale cheeks. Taking in a great breath, she strode out. She would get lost in the grounds, she decided, and leave the house and its occupants to themselves. For she could make head nor tail of her feelings, and if anyone spoke to her of what was happening, she felt she might scream.

The next few days passed by agonizingly slowly. Rebecca avoided all of the household using the best of her skills. In the mornings she breakfasted in her room. Around midday she would take a walk through the grounds alone. In the afternoons she would read in her room with Maisy under strict instructions not to allow anyone to enter. There were days when reading was replaced with crying. Then in the evenings she would feign a headache or some other such minor ailment so she might be excused from dining with the rest of the guests.

When this pattern stretched into a fourth day, Rebecca wondered if she would be left in this purgatory indefinitely, awaiting her fate but never seeing it realised. She had it from Maisy that the servants were indeed fully aware of the limbo the house was in. Miss Dent had done an infamous job of spreading the story of Rebecca and Mr Malvon's tryst. According to Maisy, the rest of the guests seemed melancholy, not just Rebecca. Lady Sophia was quiet and often looked sad. Lord Avers went riding on the estate a great deal and despite the loss of an amusing house party, did not seem inclined to quit Worth Manor. Caro and Felton were much preoccupied with baby Anne, though Caro had tried several times to gain entrance to Rebecca's rooms to which she had been denied most fervently by a loyal Maisy. The only one of the party who did not seem affected by the tension in the household was Lady Goring.

Maisy said her Ladyship had been seen speaking with the housekeeper and asking for furniture to be rearranged in several of the reception rooms. She had also asked to be shown over the suite of apartments that had belonged to the late Lady Worth. On being told they were currently in use by Lady Rebecca, she had been put off viewing them. But it was clear to Maisy, and the rest of the servants, that Lady Goring was already settling in as the matriarch of Worth Manor, and it would only be a matter of time before Lord Worth offered for her daughter.

That morning Rebecca was told that James had been called away. According to the below stairs tittle-tattle, a letter from Safi had arrived which had preceded his departure and no one knew when either man was set to return. She wondered what Safi's letter could have said. He was, after all, obtaining the licence that was to sentence Rebecca to marrying Mr Malvon. Could there have been a problem? Had Safi been unable to obtain a special licence? She hoped so, but with that hope came the realisation that Lady Goring would not stop. It would not matter to the Countess whether she could remove Mr Malvon and Rebecca at the same time. If she could only remove one by telling the story of the tryst to Society, then she would and Rebecca's reputation would be ruined. At least, if that happened, Rebecca would be removed from Society when James decided to marry Lady Sophia. She would not have to witness it first-hand.

On the afternoon of the same day, Rebecca had abandoned the book she was reading and was staring absently out of the window when the door to her room opened. She didn't bother looking over.

"That was quick, Maisy. Come and set the tea here."

"It's not Maisy."

Caro's voice came from the doorway causing Rebecca to jerk around in her chair, instinctively pulling her shawl tighter around herself.

"I had not expected you. Where's Maisy?"

"I waited by the servants' staircase until she left your rooms." Caro came into the room and closed the door behind her. "I thought it was quite clever, really—something you would do."

If Rebecca had not wanted so much to be alone in this moment, she might have smiled at that.

Caro came forward, her hands clasped in front of her. She swung them left and right awkwardly as she walked, looking sheepish.

"Your maid is far less timid than I thought, you know." Caro was looking at Rebecca through her lashes, as if a bashful look might allow her to stay in spite of her subterfuge. "She absolutely would not be moved when I asked to see you yesterday. She even burst into tears and said her nerves would stand no more asking when I insisted. I could not bring myself to try her nerves anymore. I know you try them enough for her."

Again, if circumstances had been normal, Rebecca would have laughed. She would have agreed that her lady's maid was the most long-suffering in Society and deserved some kind of medal for her perseverance.

Caro came to sit on the window sill in front of Rebecca, so that without being unimaginably rude, Rebecca could not look away or ignore her.

"These were my mother's rooms, you know," said Caro, looking about her at the furnishings and blue paper on the wall. "I used to come here when father was in a temper. It was always so calm here. James did too, I seem to remember, until he was sent off to school. It's a good place to run away to."

Rebecca looked up from Caro's lap into her friend's face.

"I know you're scared," Caro said gently, a soft smile on her face, "but you must trust James. He is settling everything. You needn't be frightened of everyone."

"I'm not frightened of everyone," Rebecca replied, a flicker of defiance in her tone. "Not of you." She smiled sadly. "I just cannot bear to see Lady Sophia's face, or her mother's."

Or James' face.

"Oh, my dear, I am only sorry I can do no more to help you."

"You help by being here," said Rebecca, reaching out a hand and taking Caro's, pressing it gently in a gesture of peace. "You are a good friend to me, my dear."

At that moment there was a knock at the door and a servant appeared.

"Yes?" Rebecca asked. The fire had already been cleaned from the night before. She was not expecting any other maids in here.

"My Lord Worth has requested both your presences in the music room, my Lady, Mrs Felton."

"He's back?" Rebecca asked, the sick feeling of dread that had abated briefly, returning.

"Yes, my Lady, and he bids you come to the music room."

"Tell him we shall be there directly," Caro said, rising. "You may go."

The servant retreated, closing the door again, and Caro turned to her friend.

"My dear, we must at least dress your hair. It is lovely loose, but I fear you might cause a scandal if you go down with it like that."

There was a little quirk at the corner of Caro's mouth and Rebecca couldn't help but answer with a weak smile.

"We wouldn't want a scandal, would we?" Rebecca replied, no note of humour in her voice. "I can call Maisy."

"Nonsense, let me."

Caro took the horsehair brush from the table and drew it through Rebecca's curling brown locks. She repeated the action until all the hair was smooth and shining, then she loosely braided it down Rebecca's back.

"It is not quite the way Maisy would do it, but it will do very well for now."

Rebecca nodded, rubbing her cheeks to command some colour into them, and stood to follow Caro from the room.

CHAPTER TWENTY-ONE

"You will forgive me, I hope, for keeping you in suspense for the last week," said James to the assembled guests. "I'm sure, since the ball, everyone's thoughts have been on what will happen. This has been a most unpleasant situation for all involved."

"Most unpleasant," agreed Lady Goring.

Rebecca's heart was racing so fast she felt like she might faint. They were all sat in the music room—Lady Sophia and Lord Avers were seated together on a chaise longue; Felton stood behind Caro's chair, one hand on her shoulder; and next to them Lady Goring had taken up residence in a large, winged chair as though she were the reigning monarch of this gathering. Rebecca was sat on a smaller chair against one of the walls of the room. Finally, a few steps away from James stood Mr Malvon.

"It was my resolution," continued James, ignoring Lady Goring's interruption, "after the events of five nights past, that I would untangle this coil."

Rebecca was trying not to look at Mr Malvon, but she couldn't help glancing at him every now and then, thinking she did not even know the face of her future husband. A public announcement of her marriage to Mr Malvon would be what was needed so that Lady Goring would be satisfied, and no more reputation-ruining rumours would be spread. James was doing all that was proper.

"Hear, hear," Lady Goring said, patting the arms of her chair, cheering on from the side-lines.

"So I wish to announce that before long we are to celebrate a wedding at Worth Manor."

They were the words that Rebecca had been waiting for, yet though she was prepared, they still forced the air from her lungs.

"The bride and groom may choose to wed in the parish church which is two miles distant. I can arrange for the wedding breakfast to be held here and any guests the couple wish to attend may be invited."

"Most gracious, Lord Worth. Most gracious," Lady Goring said. "I am sure Mr Malvon will have relatives he wishes to invite from Essex. They will be none the wiser as to the impending marriage, for who could know that an event like the ball would hasten such a match. And Lady Rebecca, I'm sure your parents will wish to return from the continent, not to mention that invalid aunt of yours from Bath."

"You misunderstand me, Lady Goring," said James, his voice strong and firm.

The eyes of everyone in the room moved back to their host, waiting expectantly, except Lady Goring who looked irritated at the rebuke.

"It is not the marriage of Mr Malvon to Lady Rebecca to which I refer."

Rebecca's eyes widened. She was barely breathing.

"I speak of the marriage between Mr Malvon and your daughter, Lady Sophia Goring."

There was a moment of shock as James' word sank in.

Rebecca choked on a sigh of immense relief.

"What's the meaning of this?" demanded Lady Goring, rising from her chair and brandishing a fan at James.

"Bravo, Worth, bravo!" Avers drawled from the chaise longue. "There, there, cousin. All will be well," he said, patting Lady Sophia's shoulder, the young lady having burst into shocked tears.

Rebecca's widened eyes were still on James, but then they darted to Felton and Caro who had remained silent. Caro was looking at her, a gentle smile on her face.

"I forbid it! I absolutely forbid it!" Lady Goring screeched, rising from her chair and brandishing her bony fingers at everyone she could.

"Now, now, aunt," said Avers, a hard edge to his voice, "let us not pretend you have any right to prevent Sophia's marrying. You know very well that Lord Goring made my father Sophia's guardian, not you. I believe my uncle may have had misgivings about whether you would act in the best interests of your daughter, to say nothing of his doubts about whether you could be trusted to manage her substantial dowry. Now, I wonder why he would have done that?"

The revelation suddenly made sense of Avers' relentless interest in his cousin's wellbeing.

"Since my father's latest bout of illness, I have stood as Sophia's guardian on his behalf. He reposes full confidence in me as his proxy to act in such a way as to secure my cousin's happiness. So any right of refusal lies with me, not you." Avers took a breath, allowing those heavy words to settle over the room. "Lord Worth," he continued, "you were saying?"

"This is the outside of enough!" cried Lady Goring. "John, you may be acting for your father as Sophia's guardian, however unfit I believe you to be, but you were not there five nights ago. You did not see what I saw."

James held up a hand for her to stop. "Lady Goring, please."

"And you, Lord Worth—do you have addled senses? Don't you remember when we found Lady Rebecca and Mr Malvon secretly meeting during the ball? *Alone*. She may be a woman of loose morals, but she is a lady of quality, and I expected Mr Malvon to offer for her. Has he been such a scoundrel as to refuse? She may be a woman past her prime—"

"You will be quiet!" James commanded so loudly that Lady Goring stumbled backwards, falling into her seat and looking up at him in a state of stupefaction.

"I, along with everyone here, have had quite enough of your poisonous conversation, Lady Goring," James said in a voice so unyielding it could not be ignored. "I will not have you malign Lady Rebecca's name for one more moment. This woman"—James pointed a finger to Rebecca—"has shown nothing but kindness and compassion to your own flesh and blood, and you have repaid her with vicious treatment and spreading false gossip. I will have no more of it, Lady Goring. I have borne it long enough—so have we all."

Lady Goring sucked in air, her lips wavering as she did so, the powder on her lined face damp with perspiration. She licked her lips, inhaling, about to rally.

"Now, if you will be silent, Lady Goring, you will hear the rest of what I have to say."

If her Ladyship had been thinking of speaking again, she reconsidered at the warning light in James' eyes. The whole room was silent, waiting on the commanding master to speak.

"Lady Rebecca told me of Lady Sophia's unhappiness. She had noted several times that in your efforts to interest me in your daughter, Lady Sophia had unwittingly revealed her affection for another.

"Unwilling, or perhaps unable because of her compassionate heart, to leave a fellow creature in such misery, Lady

Rebecca began to try and help your daughter unite with the man she loves—Mr Malvon. A suitor who you deemed ineligible due to his lack of fortune."

Where was he going with this? Nothing had changed, not really. What if Lady Sophia refused Mr Malvon again for the same reasons she had before? There was still no fortune to be had.

"Lady Rebecca, because of her faith in others, believed that it was you, Lady Goring, preventing your daughter from being with the man she loved. She enlisted my help to bring about their union, not realising that it was in fact Lady Sophia's fear for you, her mother, and your dire financial situation, that prevented her from saying yes to the man she loved.

"But my man, Safi, has spent the past few days in London making enquiries among your household, Lady Goring, and he has found your claims of potential destitution have been highly exaggerated. No doubt it was an attempt to ensure the compliance of your daughter in finding a rich husband to suit your spending needs. After all, your husband only settled a modest amount on you when he died and ensured you couldn't touch the dowry left for Sophia."

"Lies," Lady Goring hissed.

"I do not lie," James bit back. "And I ordered you to be silent." He straightened his jacket and resumed his steady tone. "I spoke to your man of business myself—a most amenable gentleman when I expressed an interest in aiding your situation. He told me the truth, your Ladyship." James' eyes flashed dangerously at her. "That it is your refusal to reduce your lavish lifestyle that is sending you into debt. That the fortune your husband left you would be ample for most if they merely took note of a budget. He assured me debtors' prison is not in your future, though a tightening of your purse strings most certainly is."

"Mama," gasped Lady Sophia. "Is this true?"

Lady Goring would not respond. Her thin lips were tightly shut, and her small eyes glittered angrily at James.

"That is where I went after receiving Safi's missive."

He had gone to London to find out the truth? All the while Rebecca had been fearing for her future, James had been out securing it.

"So I can assure you, Lady Sophia, it is indeed true."

"I never thought you could be so selfish, aunt," Avers said, his voice cold.

"I am aware, however, that this marriage may not satisfy you, Lady Goring, and that you may feel the need to retaliate against Lady Rebecca by spreading the rumour of her meeting with Mr Malvon *alone*, as you said, even if he was in fact at the ball to see your daughter. So I have a deal for you. Your daughter was good enough to show me several paintings from your late husband's collection in your London home. As a wedding gift, I will purchase these from you, for the amount written on this piece of paper." James rang the bell and Safi appeared, holding a silver tray in his hand with two folded pieces of paper on it.

He came forward and offered it to Lady Goring. The woman looked disgustedly at the man, then at the papers, reluctantly taking them.

"And the other paper is a document my solicitors have prepared and which you will sign, swearing that it was not Lady Rebecca who was seen with Mr Malvon at my ball, but rather your daughter. I will take it into safekeeping, and should you feel the desire at any point to spread such a wicked rumour abroad, I shall have that declaration published in every reputable newspaper I can find."

Lady Goring's eyes were hard upon James, and when he finally finished speaking, she looked down at the pieces of paper in her hands. She looked slowly at one, then the other.

During this time, Safi had left the room and then re-entered. This time the tray had on it an ink pot and quill. He set them on a small side table which he placed at Lady Goring's elbow.

"For you to sign, my Lady," Safi said.

"Yes, I know that!" she snapped back.

Rebecca could have sworn the usually inscrutable expression of Safi showed the faintest shadow of a smile.

Lady Goring looked again at the pieces of paper. She stared at them for what seemed like an eternity. Then finally, she placed one on the table next to her, took up the quill, dipped it in the ink pot, and signed her name.

James felt a high degree of satisfaction watching Lady Goring sign the document. Safi took it away on the tray, but James noticed her Ladyship still clutched the paper with the figure James would pay for the paintings in her hand. It was an extremely generous wedding gift—the size of a reasonable dowry—though it would never reach Mr Malvon's hands, of that James was sure. The woman could not complain, and if it meant her silence on the score of Rebecca, then James was happy to pay the price.

"Good, then the matter is settled," James said when Safi had left the room. "May I be the first to congratulate you on your engagement, Lady Sophia."

The lady in question looked surprised during the latter part of this episode, but upon James' words, she broke out into the sweetest smile. Her whole face lit up, and there were tears in her eyes to accompany the expression, but this time tears of joy.

"Oh, is it true, George?" Lady Sophia rose from the chaise, turning to face Mr Malvon.

"It is, indeed, my love." He came forward, hands

outstretched, and took hers in his own. "Though I had thought I would be the one to propose to you the second time, not Lord Worth. But I am forever grateful for what you have done for us." Mr Malvon turned back to James, a smile on his face.

"Can we really be married from here?" Lady Sophia asked. "I do not need to go back to London with my mother?"

"If you are happy to be resident here for another two weeks, you may then apply for a licence and be married from Worth Manor."

"And you're sure you are happy to host our breakfast? You have already done so much for us, Lord Worth."

"Not at all. We should be delighted to host your breakfast, and to Society it will appear as though it were all planned before we left London."

"Congratulations." Caro had come over, extending her hands to Lady Sophia who had now taken up residence beside her betrothed. "To you both."

"Yes, I echo my wife's sentiments," Felton said, coming alongside her. "I can vouch for married life. I have yet to regret my own decision."

Caro pushed him with her elbow playfully and the foursome began chuckling together.

Avers was next to join in the felicitations. "Dear little cousin, Sophia. So, you are to be married at last. I hope you appreciated my getting in the way of your and Lord Worth's attempted tendre? Not even aunt realised what I was doing."

It was as if they had all forgotten Lady Goring was still in the room. The older woman, who was usually the cloud over every gathering, had been blown away by James' words and there was now a lightness to the party. He glanced over to the Countess and James saw that under the hard look on her face was something akin to smugness, in spite of what Avers had just said.

"And Lady Rebecca"—Lady Sophia broke through the circle that had formed around her and came to Rebecca's chair, kneeling before her and taking up the hem of her gown as if she were a saint—"we shall be forever grateful to you also. You have been such a friend to me, I hardly know what I would have done without you."

Rebecca looked overwrought. James noted the paleness of her face, the shadows beneath her eyes.

"Shall we adjourn to the drawing room for champagne?" James called, drawing everyone's attention from Rebecca.

There was a universal cry of agreement, and the party began filing from the room. James held back, ensuring Lady Goring was not left alone with Rebecca, and he glanced over to her before he left.

"You will join us?"

"Yes," she said in a quiet voice. "In a moment."

James nodded, wishing he could think of some reason to stay, but he could not. He thought it best in that moment to get the rest of them away from Rebecca so that she might have room to breathe.

CHAPTER TWENTY-TWO

When Lady Sophia and Mr Malvon's happiness had been toasted many times over, Lady Goring left them to announce to family members far and wide her daughter's forthcoming wedding, and begin inviting any family or acquaintance who she deemed high rank enough to attend in three weeks' time.

"You are a brave man, to take on such a mother-in-law," Felton said, raising his half empty glass to Malvon.

"I count myself the most blessed of men," Mr Malvon said, giving a loving look to his bride-to-be.

"I say with the utmost sincerity, that little Sophy is well worth it," Avers said, a sleepy smile on his face.

"You have been very good to me, John. Now I only wish we might find you a wife."

"Alas, I do not think it is to be." Avers' tone turned dramatic, as though he were performing Shakespeare. "I am a confirmed bachelor. I have a penchant for admiring women whose hearts already belong to another." Avers glanced at James meaningfully.

Caro noted her brother chose to ignore the implication. James remained silent.

"Have I missed something?" Mr Malvon said, looking innocently from Avers to James.

"Nothing," James said, voice firm, not a flicker of emotion on his face. "Lord Avers dedicates himself to provoking me without respite."

Caro knew that look. James had his guard up. Surely though, now that he had saved Rebecca, knowing he had done his duty, he might feel able to let it down a little.

"Ah! You have me pegged, Worth, though you must know I only behave so to my closest friends. Is that not right, Felton?"

"Intolerably so," Felton replied.

Caro's eyes remained on her brother and, following his gaze, she realised he was looking at the door. Rebecca had not joined them.

She turned back to the betrothed couple who were exchanging secret whispers and meaningful glances. She saw Mr Malvon's hand on the small of Lady Sophia's back. She remembered the moment Tobias had proposed to her and how all she had wanted was to be alone with him.

"Perhaps, Mr Malvon, you would like to take a turn about the gardens with Lady Sophia?" Caro asked. "You've not seen them yet, and there are some lovely flowers blooming now."

The subtle suggestion was taken up enthusiastically by Mr Malvon, who expressed a deep desire to look at flowers while never taking his eyes from his love's face.

The couple left the room, arm in arm, looking as though they could not be happier if they were walking into heaven together.

"That was incredibly well played," Avers said as soon as they had gone. "My hat, should I have been wearing one, would be doffed to you, Lord Worth." He put one leg forward and bowed.

"Yes," Felton agreed, winking at his brother-in-law. "I particularly enjoyed the set-down you gave Lady Goring. The nerve that took."

"Far more than I have," Avers agreed. "I consider myself in your debt for aiding my favourite cousin. She is probably the only woman in the world I truly care for."

James waited for some barbed comment directed at him but was mildly surprised when it did not come. From a brief study of Avers' face he saw a sincerity there that was often non-existent.

"You truly did well, brother. I am so proud of you."

"Thank you, Caroline," he replied.

Avers and Felton were busy talking about the relatives of Lord Avers and the Gorings who may descend on Worth Manor. There was the roistering set of twins currently at Oxford, an ancient uncle, Avers' parents, should his father be well enough, and his siblings—enough of his family to make him think of crying off from attending, or so Avers said.

"And now," Caro asked quietly so only James could hear, "What will you do?"

James took in a deep breath, letting it out on a sigh.

"She's free now. Free to make her own decisions over her future. That is what matters."

"You will leave her to do so?"

"Yes," James replied. "I would not wish her to feel a debt to me that should force her to act from obligation and not..."

He trailed off and Caro chose not to press him. Looking around the room she noted Rebecca still had not joined them.

"If you gentlemen will excuse me, I will go to Lady Rebecca."

They each bowed, Felton bestowing a kiss upon her forehead as she passed, and she left them behind, going in search of her friend.

On finding the music room empty, Caro went in search of Rebecca, but she was waylaid by a feverish Lady Goring who demanded to be told about the parish chapel her daughter was to be married in and wished to go over possible menus for the wedding breakfast.

Rebecca was therefore left alone. The rest of the day passed away and at dinner the guests gathered, all talk of the forthcoming wedding buzzing around the dining table. James had looked at Rebecca several times, but she could not read the expression in his eyes, and he had made no attempt to engage her in private conversation.

The following morning Rebecca returned to her room after breakfast, a letter from her aunt in hand. Maisy found her mistress half an hour later, staring out of the window, the open letter in one hand, fingers from the other tracing the line of her lips, lost in thought.

"My Lady?"

Rebecca turned, barely seeing her faithful maid, her eyes slowly coming to focus.

"Maisy... "—she trailed off, fingers still tracing her lips, then she looked down at the letter—"Maisy, I think we ought to pack."

Her maid's eyes widened a little. Rebecca explained the sudden plans to leave, and Maisy bobbed her head, telling her mistress 'as she wished'. The next quarter of an hour was filled with carrying clothes and objects to the bed and laying them out. Maisy called one of the footmen to bring my Lady's trunk up to the room and it arrived a short while later.

What neither Maisy nor her distracted mistress realised was that on the heels of the trunk came someone else.

"There, you see," Rebecca said, stepping back from the dress she had just folded on the bed. "It will crease less."

"Rebecca, what are you doing?"

Both Rebecca and her maid turned to see Caro standing where the footman had been a moment ago. The door of the room clicked shut as the manservant retreated.

"Caro—" Rebecca broke off, looking down at the half-folded gowns and back up at her friend.

Caro gestured to the dresses and the trunk.

"Are you leaving?"

"Do as I showed you, Maisy," Rebecca commanded, turning back to Caro but failing to meet her eye. "Maisy is struggling to fold in the manner I like. It is a little tricky, but it saves the lace from excessive wrinkling. Lady Sophia was sweet enough to tell me how." She was speaking quickly. Far too quickly.

"Rebecca," Caro said firmly, placing a hand on her hip and raising a fair brow.

Rebecca felt her chest tighten. She had not looked forward to this, but she had hoped she might break the news on her own terms instead of being caught in the act of escape.

"My aunt has written to me." She held up the letter for Caro to see. "She wrote several days ago in response to my telling her that I would likely have to marry Mr Malvon after what happened at the ball. She comes here and will arrive later today most likely."

That was explanation enough. Caro must understand that Rebecca would wish to leave.

"So?"

Apparently it was not enough. Her friend's hand was still on her hip and the challenge in her eye made Rebecca's heart speed up.

"Your aunt will be welcome to stay once she arrives to find you are no longer in a scrape. It'll be lovely to see her again." Caro did not seem as though she thought it was lovely. "But that doesn't explain why you're packing."

"I... " Rebecca trailed off, frustrated she sounded so lame.

"Are you running away?"

Rebecca sighed. Maisy shouldn't be here for this, and besides, if she knew her maid, Maisy would be wracked with nerves by now. Tapping her servant on the shoulder, she nodded to the door. A grateful look enveloped Maisy's face and she silently withdrew. Rebecca was left alone with her friend.

"Caro—"

"There's nothing to run from."

"You don't understand, Caro—" How could she explain it?

"I understand very well. Don't you think I see the way you look at James?"

Rebecca coloured deeply. She pressed cold hands to her flaming cheeks trying to stay the unconscious reaction.

"Why would you go now, after all he has done for you? Now that you are free again?"

The accusation in her friend's voice increased the wretched feeling in Rebecca's heart. Wasn't it obvious to Caro why she must leave?

"You know he did it for you, don't you? He has compassion for Lady Sophia and her betrothed, I will not deny that," said Caro, "but he moved heaven and earth so that you would not be trapped in a marriage you did not want. I know that I said I should not have passed judgement on what lay between you and James before, but I cannot remain silent while you do something as foolish as running away!"

Tears came to Rebecca's already red eyes.

"I can see as plain as day that you care for him in return. Why can you not finally tell him, my dear?"

"Oh Caro, don't you see?" Rebecca fisted her hands, shaking them in despair, the tears now streaking her face. "I did! I did tell him. He has not come to me since saving me from a marriage I did not want. He has said nothing to me. He is a good man, I know that, but if he loved me... don't you think he would have said something by now?" Rebecca turned back to the bed, resuming the folding her maid had left. "I cannot be here, not like this. I am sorry to leave, but I have celebrated my goddaughter's birth, I have done what I came to do where Lady Sophia is concerned—or at least your brother has—and now I can't bear to be here anymore."

Caro's tone softened. "Oh, my dear." She came and put a hand around her friend's shaking shoulders. "Don't *you* see? He freed you, but he would not put you in a position of obligation to him now. He wants you to come to him freely, because you want to, not because he saved you."

The shaking grew stronger and soon Rebecca was sobbing. Caro turned her firmly and drew her friend into her arms, allowing her to cry into her chest as she rubbed Rebecca's back with a motherly hand.

"I know you love him, and I would urge you to be brave, as you always are, and not run away now."

When her crying finally ceased, Rebecca drew back, wiping away the tears from her face.

"What a ghastly sight I must present," she said, a smile breaking through the despair that had clouded her face.

"It is actually refreshing, my dear, to see you so very human," Caro said, smiling gently at her. "Now, I believe James escaped the wedding planning going on downstairs in favour of inspecting some repairs to the stables."

Rebecca's smile turned nervous. She pressed her hands to her cheeks again.

"Take courage, my friend. Love takes a great deal of courage."

Rebecca nodded. She took Caro's hand and squeezed it, a look of deep gratitude in her eyes. Then she left her there, and went in search of James.

Rebecca's legs felt like they weren't her own as she walked through the house and outside. The further she walked, the faster her heart beat and the less steady her legs felt. By the time she found James in the stable courtyard, staring up at a roof undergoing repairs and listening to Safi explain the next phase of the work, she felt light-headed. James was so engaged in what Safi was saying that, though the steward noted Rebecca's approach, his master did not.

She came from behind, staring at James' broad shoulders. He had discarded his woollen jacket in the warm autumn sunshine, his linen shirt sleeves were rolled up, waistcoat still on. She blinked. How had she ever overlooked him? She could see the muscles in his forearms, the strong profile of his face, and that was just on the outside. Within was a character of far more worth than she had realised.

"And when could we get matching slate shipped in?"

"Not until after the wedding, my Lord, and we are bound to have more horses to stable for that. We only have two boxes left vacant as it stands." Safi took another breath, looking at Rebecca and no doubt making ready to announce her, but James started talking about a temporary fix to enable them to house the guests' horses for Lady Sophia and Mr Malvon's wedding. He was rubbing his chin as he thought aloud, his hand eventually slipping round to the back of his neck where it massaged the muscles as he leant back to take in the full roofline.

"Perhaps we should continue this later, my Lord?"

James must have thought Safi was implying he was tired, and was quick to reassure him.

"No. I'd rather get it done. Besides, avoiding my guests while they talk of the wedding is not the worst thing."

"Surely not all the guests, my Lord?" Safi said, his face a mask of innocence. Before James could reply he called, as if seeing her for the first time, "Lady Rebecca."

She saw James' head jerk round, taking her in with surprise.

"Like I said, my Lord, we can pick this up again later."

Bowing to both Rebecca and James, he collected his papers and notebook from the edge of the water trough they had been balancing on.

"Lady Rebecca tells me we are expecting another guest— her aunt," Safi said, as Rebecca and James stood there in silence. "I have yet to relay the news to the housekeeper so I regret that I must leave you both. Perhaps, my Lord," Safi said, in the same innocent tone he had used a moment before, "you might show Lady Rebecca the flowers the gardeners have suggested using for the wedding decorations."

Whether Safi knew what he was doing or not, he gave nothing away, his face an impassive mask. Having collected all his things, he bowed again, and left James and Rebecca staring at each other across the stableyard.

They were frozen like that for a time, the bustle of the yard happening around them, the whickering of horses, stamping of hooves, the head groom calling out to his underling to bring him a brush. It all happened around them and they were paused there, staring at each other silently.

Finally James, not saying anything, came and offered Rebecca his arm and they began walking out from the stable-yard towards the formal gardens.

"Your aunt is coming?" he asked, once they had been walking for several minutes.

"Yes," Rebecca explained. "She started off as soon as she received my letter about what happened at the ball."

"So, she thinks you are still trapped into marrying Mr Malvon?"

"Indeed." Rebecca's heart was beating so fast it felt as though she couldn't catch her breath. The way James had looked at her when she had arrived at the stableyard—his blue eyes looking so deeply into hers—had made her heart melt.

"No doubt she will come to your rescue."

Rebecca looked across to see a wry smile on James' face. It lit up his blue eyes and curved those well-formed lips of his and he suddenly looked boyish.

"Yes"—she felt a shy answering smile on her own lips—"but you have already done that. I believe she will be quite put out when she's told. You know how she loves a drama."

They had reached the formal gardens now, and whether James meant to or not, he had led them to the far end of it, where a hedge, increasing in height, led them to a little hidden semi-circle, home to a private bench. When someone sat on it, they had a fine view of the parkland stretching out before them, while being perfectly hidden from the house. But neither of them sat down.

"I believe it is a family trait." He smiled ruefully at her and all she wanted to do in that moment was to reach forward and kiss him.

Instead she smiled and agreed.

"I would never have left you in that coil," said James.

Because he was a good man, thought Rebecca. Because in spite of her rejecting him he had cared for her and helped her.

"I believe you are compassionate, sometimes to a fault."

"How do you always see the best in me, even when I get into scrapes that cost you a small fortune?"

"Small?"

"Oh!" Her hand shot up to cover her mouth. "It was not a great deal was it? Oh, I am so sorry. You would never have had to pay Lady Goring such a sum if I had not—" She broke off.

He was... laughing.

She snatched her hand out of his arm and placed it on her hip.

"If I had my fan, I should bat you with it."

"Then I am glad you do not have it."

He touched her arm, his fingers ran down its length, slowing at her palm, tracing the line of her hand, lacing through her fingers. She felt a fluttering running up her chest.

"Tell me, do you still feel the same as you did the night of the ball? Or was it a temporary madness?" His words were tentative, and his gaze had dropped to her chin.

Her lips curved. "I am not sure there was anything temporary about those feelings."

"You are... you are under no obligation to me," he said in no more than a husky whisper.

They had moved closer again.

"Yes, I am," she whispered, her lips almost grazing his.

He pulled back, his brow furrowing.

"Love makes me obliged to kiss you."

He reached up, his hand on her face, his thumb running over her lips.

"And I you," he murmured, dropping his lips onto hers without hesitation.

He kissed softly at first, then with increasing fervour as the passion of the weeks and months poured out. She responded in kind, her heart beating impossibly faster, but now from excitement, not fear. His arms slid around her waist and pulled her closer. She felt as though she had come home, standing here, his strong arms around her.

"Rebecca," James whispered between kisses. "I have

wanted this for so long. I must stop before I... do something ungentlemanly."

She felt a shiver of anticipation run through her. He must have felt it too, for he kissed her again, but this time slowly and gently before stopping and holding her tight against him. She buried her head against his chest, sighing with contentment.

"Will you marry me, James?" she asked.

She felt a deep chuckle rumble up through his chest.

"I know it is unladylike to ask, but I thought it only fair, for you have already proposed to me once and I wish for this to be a marriage of equals."

"Will you stop your wittering, child, and lead me to where your mistress is!" The cry caused both James and Rebecca to turn in each other's arms and look in the direction from which it came.

"Aunt Etheridge," Rebecca said, knowing those imperious tones anywhere.

Just as she uttered the name, her aunt came around the bend in the shrubbery, Maisy hurrying before her. The elderly Dowager had an ebony cane that ground into the gravel. She wore a travelling gown of deep purple and a hat perched carefully on her lace cap. The shrewd eyes of her aunt took in the sight of James and Rebecca before Maisy looked up from her quick steps.

"Well," Lady Etheridge said, halting and leaning her cane to the side, surveying James and her niece.

Rebecca felt heat in her cheeks and pulled a little away from James, a sheepish expression overtaking her face. But James would not let go of her entirely. He kept an arm firmly around her waist as he turned to face Rebecca's aunt.

"Lady Etheridge." He bowed. "It is a pleasure to see you again."

"I couldn't agree more," the Dowager replied, a smile overtaking her lips and a twinkle in her blue eyes. "You may go,

Maisy, but not a word of this in the servants' hall, I thank you. You'll order me some tea when you get back and I'll be in shortly."

The maid, who had been staring open-mouthed at her mistress and the master of Worth Manor, snapped her mouth shut. She shot Rebecca an uncharacteristically secret smile and then hurried away.

"Am I to think then, dear niece of mine, that there is no longer a forced engagement between you and Mr Malvon? Have I rushed across half the country for no reason?"

"Oh, aunt." Rebecca came forward, James finally releasing her, and she flung her arms around her relative, almost toppling her over. "I am so glad you are here."

"Apparently I am not needed though," Lady Etheridge said into her niece's curls, her sharp blue eyes still on James over Rebecca's shoulder.

"You are," James replied, "though not for saving your niece from any scrape. I have dealt with that matter. Rather, it is fortuitous you are here, because now you may attend our wedding."

Rebecca released her aunt from her embrace and came back to stand beside James. His arm found her waist again and she couldn't stop the smile that took over her face.

"We have just become engaged," James said, affirming his answer to Rebecca after their interruption.

"You're happy with this arrangement?" Lady Etheridge asked her niece, eyes penetrating.

"I am," Rebecca replied, the smile broadening.

"At last," the Dowager said on a contented sigh. "I have been waiting for this moment for many weeks, but I had thought I would have to intervene to help you both get here. However, I see that my days of intervening in my niece's affairs are soon to be over, Lord Worth. I have no doubt you will wear that mantle well."

James inclined his head and Rebecca looked up to see a grin on his countenance.

"I thank you, my Lady."

"Are we to plan for a London wedding?" Lady Etheridge asked. "I have had quite enough of the Bath waters and had thought to take a holiday in Cornwall, but I'm quite willing to delay it for you both."

"Actually," James said, "I had thought Saturday, in my family's chapel."

"Saturday?" Rebecca echoed in surprise. "But we can't, the banns have not been read."

"I have a licence."

"How very well organised of you," said Lady Etheridge, amusement in her voice as her eyes moved between the couple.

"What do you mean you have a licence?" asked Rebecca. "We have only just decided to be wed."

"You told me, the night that you were caught alone with Mr Malvon and knew he would be forced to offer for you, that you loved me, did you not?"

Rebecca nodded.

"You told me you were sure, and I have been sure I wished to marry you for a long time. While I was in London I visited Doctors' Commons and obtained a special licence for us to be wed."

"Then it is settled!" Lady Etheridge said triumphantly. "I look forward to you becoming my nephew-in-law, Lord Worth. Now, I'm sure you wish to be left alone, and I wish to have some very particular words with Lady Goring."

She did not wait for them to bid her adieu but turned on her heel with a surprising amount of poise and left the couple where she had found them.

James wasted no time in drawing Rebecca towards him when they were alone again, but before he could kiss her, Rebecca said with asperity, "You mean to tell me you have had a licence for us to wed for two days and have not deigned to tell me?" She pulled away from him and batted his chest with her hands.

He took them both in his and stilled her with a kiss to her lips.

"I had to be sure you did not say those things out of desperation for the situation you were in."

She sighed, rolling her eyes. "If you were not so good a man, I should slap you."

He laughed again, the sound deep and pleasing, and his serious face transformed.

"But I am, am I not?" he asked, a teasing light in his eyes. "Is that not how I won your love for me?"

"You're quite confident now, aren't you, my Lord?" she asked, not being able to help the threatening smile from breaking out on her face and erasing all traces of mock anger.

"With your aunt's approval, how can I not be?" He grinned down at her. "Tell me I am wrong."

She looked at him through her lashes. "I cannot." She pressed against him again, letting her mouth hover teasingly just inches from his own. "For you have most definitely proven yourself a Lord of worth."

In the next moment, James closed the gap, pressing his lips to hers again with no intention of letting her get away a second time.

The End

REVIEW THIS BOOK

Thank you for reading *Lord of Worth*.

If you enjoyed it, please share your review on Amazon, BookBub or Goodreads to help other readers find my book.

GLOSSARY

Bergère hat – a woman's hat in a shepherdess style. Usually made of straw with a shallow crown and a wide brim.

Bosom beaus – best of friends.

Chaise longue – a sofa designed for reclining with an arm only on one end.

Chemise /shift – a plain gown with or without sleeves and often made from linen. It was worn against the skin as the first layer of clothing beneath the stays, hip pads, petticoats, and dress.

Coffered ceiling – coffers are an architectural feature meaning a series of sunken panels often in the shape of squares or rectangles decorating a ceiling.

Confinement – when a pregnant woman would withdraw from society near the time of her birth. She would stay in her residence until she gave birth, after which time she may 'lie in' where she remains in bed for up to one month to recover from childbirth.

Cravat – usually a strip of linen that was tied around a gentleman's neck, the equivalent of a tie for the 18th century gentleman.

Fichu – a triangular piece of material worn around a woman's neck and over her bosom, usually tucked into the neckline of her dress.

Hip pads – exactly as they sound, these were pads worn on the hips beneath the dress but over the stays and chemise, in order to gain the desired silhouette.

Mantua maker – a term for a dressmaker in the 18th century. Mantua, either derived from the place in Italy or from the French word for coat, was the name of a gown which originated in the last quarter of the 17th century. Originally a loose-fitting over-gown all in one piece of fabric (unlike the skirts and bodices of the previous decades), it was worn with petticoats and a stomacher.

Mullioned Windows – windows which contain vertical separators in the form of stone or wood.

On Dit – a piece of gossip.

Patch – patches, or mouches (French for flies), were false beauty spots usually made from black taffeta or velvet and cut into shapes like hearts or crescents. They were worn on the face, neck or chest to hide imperfections and highlight the whiteness of the skin. They became fashionable in the late 18th century, particularly as a way to hide scars caused by smallpox.

Robe à *l'anglaise* – a closed fronted gown. This type of garment fastened in the front over structured undergarments.

Robe à la française – an open-fronted gown. This type of gown did not meet in the front. It would be worn over a matching petticoat and stomacher.

Stays – a predecessor to the corset, stays were usually made of a heavy-weight material and had boning for structure. They were laced either front, back, or both and had adjustable straps to get the desired fit. They would be worn over a chemise.

Stomacher – a stomacher was a 'v' shaped piece of material worn at the front of the bodice to fill in the front of a *robe à la française*. It was generally boned or pad-stitched and the gown was either pinned either side or sewn closed when worn.

WANT TO BE IN THE KNOW?

Be the first to know about freebies, sales and when Philippa's next book releases by signing up to her newsletter.

Sign up below:

philippajanekeyworth.com/newsletter

FREE CHAPTER
DUKE OF DISGUISE

Ladies of Worth, book 4

Chapter 1

Paris, France 1776

Avers moved through the candlelight of Madame Pertuis' salon, the warm glow catching on the silver of his suit's embroidery and the diamonds at his throat. Ostentatious rococo mouldings and gilt furniture, designed to awe visitors, did not attract a second glance from him. Conversation hummed throughout the rooms—snippets of French, Italian and English catching his ear.

The Hôtel du Champions and its famous hostess attracted everyone of consequence in Parisian Society. Avers had secured his invitation after barely a week in the French capital thanks to his friend Wakeford. Now he was here, mingling with those who wished to discuss the latest writings of Marie-Emilie Maryon de Montanclos, and of course those who did not come for philosophy at all, but rather to discover the latest *on dit.* For those who held a penchant for neither of these activities, several gaming tables were set up in an adjacent room, many already in use.

"Bonsoir, Your Grace. How fortunate we are to have you with us this evening."

Avers paused before his hostess. She had used his assumed

title. Good. His fake identity was working. Leaning back on one leg and allowing the other, with its beautifully clocked stocking, to be displayed to full advantage, he met the gaze of his salonnière.

"Madame Pertuis, I am the fortunate one. I can only beg forgiveness for missing the meal. I was at a game that could not be stopped."

"Ah, the cards," replied the handsome woman, chiding him as she would a child. "All men are the same."

"Alas, so we are, and I thank you for your gracious mercy in allowing me to attend all the later. I had not expected such a warm reception here in Paris." Avers examined the beautifully embroidered cuffs of his sapphire-blue suit. "Clearly news of my exploits in Italy have yet to reach your fine ears."

They had an audience.

A coterie of ladies on a nearby collection of brocade sofas had ceased their discourse in favour of watching the new arrival speaking to their host. Avers could not have hoped for a better opportunity to lay out the part he was to play.

He bowed low over Madame Pertuis' hand and, rather than kissing the air above, dared to lay a brief kiss upon the back of her glove, before rising and allowing the most provoking smile to curve his lips.

"I heard you were a lover, Your Grace," Madame Pertuis said, an answering smile playing about her mouth.

Avers surveyed his hostess, her blue eyes making him realise the talk of Madame Pertuis' beauty was not exaggerated. She had been the rage of Paris in her time.

But he was not here to admire beauty. Nor was he here to be a lover as his hostess termed it. His recent foray into that domain had left its mark and those wounds ran deep. When Wakeford had asked for his help urgently in France, it had been a blessing. Avers had left London and *her* behind.

"But I should warn you," she carried on, the smile still present, "I have a jealous husband."

The women behind them, who had been shamelessly listening in, began to titter at their hostess' words. Avers inclined his head in submission.

"I should not, for a moment, wish to come between you."

"You will join us? Or a drink perhaps?" Madame Pertuis asked, raising a hand to beckon a waiting footman. The golden thread in her dress sparkled as she moved, the brilliance of her dress adding to the radiant candlelight glowing from every surface and fixture in the room.

"A burgundy, please," he answered, directing his gaze towards the footman who bowed and disappeared to procure the drink.

Avers' hostess led him over to a vacant chair within the cluster of women who had been observing them. The few gentlemen present, standing behind the ladies, looked somewhat peeved by his being given primary position.

"May I present His Grace, the Duke of Tremaine—"

"Good evening," Avers said, bowing to each lady in turn as Madame Pertuis spoke their names.

Introductions completed, his hostess inclined her head and told the gathering she must go and check on her other guests. Avers felt all eyes on him as he took his seat. There was a brief pause, and feeling some expectation upon him to lead a conversation, he was just taking a breath to begin when one of the ladies spoke.

"And what brings you to Paris?" The woman had been introduced as the wife of a much older gentleman standing behind them. She was fair, pretty, and the heart-shaped patch at the corner of her mouth quirked upwards as she smiled coquettishly at Avers.

He readied his well-rehearsed answer and engaged his audience with a sweeping look. And so the falsehoods began.

Emilie Cadeaux feigned interest in the Marquis de Dartois' conversation. The gentleman—in his early thirties and a close friend of her main admirer—had been telling her about the latest salon at the Académie Royale.

In truth, she would rather be at home right now, not at Madame Pertuis' fashionable gathering. The Comte de Vergelles had requested her presence here tonight, and a woman who relied on the admiration and gifts of others did not disobey their wishes. Even if the Comte had yet to appear this evening.

Vergelles had sent his friend on ahead to entertain Emilie, but the poor man did no such thing. Not that she would ever tell the Marquis that. He was always so attentive.

"It was very tall," Dartois said, describing the sculpture he had seen earlier that day, "and wide." He stretched out his arms and one limb came a little too close to the bundle of white wispy hair curled up on Emilie's lap.

The creature unfurled, emitting a growl, and snapped so quickly at Dartois that it nearly got one of his fingers.

"Sacré bleu!" the Marquis exclaimed, snatching his hand away.

"Lutin, no!" Emilie scolded, stifling a laugh.

"Evil little imp!" Dartois nursed his slender fingers as if the small dog really had bitten them. "Why you are wont to keep such a cur as your companion, I shall never understand."

Emilie bristled. Lutin was indeed a cur—a little stray she had found outside the Théâtre des Tuileries begging for scraps as an abandoned puppy. The memory only incensed her further as she considered the person who had dumped the unwanted animal—defenceless—in the centre of Paris.

But she swallowed the feelings down. She had learned to do so many years ago. Men did not like outbursts of emotion from women. They did not know what to do with them and considered them a nuisance, an irritating by-product of an otherwise entertaining object.

She feigned a laugh, tickling Lutin under the chin, causing the little terrier-like dog to gaze up adoringly at his mistress. "Not you, nor Lucien," she said, referring to the Comte de Vergelles. "But this petit monsieur—he is my sweetest comfort and safest confidant, are you not mon petit hérisson?"

"I have yet to meet a hedgehog that bites," Dartois replied waspishly. "Now, where was I?" He launched back into his description of the sculpture and was just regaining his flow when Emilie caught sight of Lucien.

The noble, clad in silver silk, had an effusion of lace at his throat and diamonds twinkling from both there and the buckles on his gleaming shoes. Gliding through the rooms, he gave off some feeling of otherness, moving like a phantom among the living. That's what had so captured Emilie initially. He had seemed to exude some power over others. A power she could not account for, nor understand.

Many female eyes followed Vergelles' progress. Eyes that vied to be those of his future wife. Emilie was not in the running.

The title of wife would not be dangled before her. No. The Comte had offered her a different one, befitting her status as a commoner—that of mistress.

She had not realised what the Comte expected in return for his lavish gifts at the beginning of their acquaintance. He'd spelled it out for her soon enough and she had been on the verge of letting him down gently when her living at the theatre had gone up in smoke. Now, her position was precarious and unless some other security appeared, Emilie would be forced to consider accepting his offer.

But not yet.

"Bonsoir, ma cherie," the Comte murmured as he reached her side.

The French nobleman bowed over her hand, kissing the air above an emerald ring he had gifted her, hoping to speed her choice. Upon rising, his pale eyes ran over her appearance, and one dark brow arched.

"No matching earrings?"

Emilie's fingers tightened involuntarily around Lutin's collar.

"I have a fondness for my pearls." She raised a hand and traced a fingertip over the perfect white gem dangling from her right ear.

They were not the earrings that Lucien had gifted her to match the emerald ring.

"And I think they suit this gown better than the emeralds," she said it lightly, as if it were a little thing, and turned away from his unyielding gaze. Readjusting the little red neckerchief on Lutin's neck, she focused on breathing, in and out, in and out. He would give in soon. She had to wait for his initial anger to subside, and then she would throw him one of her disarming smiles and hope that he would not hold it against her.

When she finally looked up at him and smiled, he said nothing. Nor did he return the happy action.

She was fast learning that the Comte had particular requirements when it came to the women he courted for the position of his paramour. Number one among them was obedience.

"Sebastien," Dartois began. "You found him well?"

Emilie thanked the Marquis for distracting the Comte's ire from her. She needed to keep the Comte on her side while she made her decision. If she said yes, she would be given financial security beyond what she ever could have imagined. If she said no... well, he could destroy her in Society.

The Comte had turned from the duo to observe the room. His eyes did not stop scanning as he withdrew a solid silver snuffbox from his pocket and flicked the lid open with his index finger. He proceeded to take a pinch in each nostril before deigning to answer his friend.

"Bien," Vergelles replied, eyes drifting from one female to another around the room. "He has been very busy, our Sebastien. I understand his latest employee has proven a good return on investment already."

Emilie noticed several of the young women blush under the Comte's gaze before hiding their whispers and giggles behind painted fans.

"Positive news," said Dartois, not in the least put off by the Comte's impolite lack of attention. "I expect that return on investment to be passed on to us when the time comes."

Emilie knew better than to join in with this conversation. She half-listened, fingers twiddling Lutin's wispy hair into spikes along his back—her little hedgehog.

"You will tell him I am visiting him soon?"

"I already did," the Comte replied, snapping the snuffbox shut. "Mademoiselle Cadeaux, are you of a mind to game or converse this evening?"

She was of a mind to do neither, but she knew better than to say so.

"Whatever my Lord desires."

A smile crept slowly across the Comte's face, not meeting the pale eyes that contrasted so shockingly with his coal-black brows. Others said he was handsome, but the sharp jaw and aquiline features were ones that Emilie tolerated, not admired. She accepted the Comte's attentions because she understood her place in the world and its inherent precariousness. She did so because she wished to survive.

Keep reading *Duke of Disguise* by picking up your copy now:

philippajanekeyworth.com/DOD

philippajanekeyworth.com/ADD

philippajanekeyworth.com/LOW

philippajanekeyworth.com/DOD

REGENCY ROMANCES

philippajanekeyworth.com/TWR

philippajanekeyworth.com/TUE

FANTASY

philippajanekeyworth.com/TE

ABOUT THE AUTHOR

Philippa Jane Keyworth, also known as P. J. Keyworth, writes historical romance and fantasy novels you'll want to escape into.

She loves strong heroines, challenging heroes and backdrops that read like you're watching a movie. She creates complex, believable characters you want to get to know and worlds that are as dramatic as they are beautiful.

Keyworth's historical romance novels include Regency and Georgian romances that trace the steps of indomitable heroes and heroines through historic British streets. From London's glittering ballrooms to its dark gaming hells, characters experience the hopes and joys of love while avoiding a coil or two! Travel with them through London, Bath, Cornwall and beyond and you'll find yourself falling in love.

Keyworth's fantasy series The Emrilion Trilogy follows strong love stories and epic adventure. Unveiling a world of nomadic warrior tribes and peaceful forest-dwelling folk, you can explore the hills, deserts and cities of Emrilion and the history that is woven through them. With so many different races in the same kingdom it's become a melting pot of drama and intrigue where the ultimate struggle between good and evil will bring it all to the brink of destruction.

facebook.com/philippajane.keyworth

twitter.com/PJKeyworth

instagram.com/pjkeyworth

amazon.com/author/philippakeyworth

bookbub.com/authors/philippa-jane-keyworth

goodreads.com/philippajanekeyworth